MW00460736

THE DEAD OF NIGHT

THE DEAD OF NIGHT

Elaine Viets

With Best Wishes,

Elaine Viets

**SEVERN
HOUSE**

First world edition published in Great Britain and the USA in 2023
by Severn House, an imprint of Canongate Books Ltd,
14 High Street, Edinburgh EH1 1TE.

Trade paperback edition first published in Great Britain and the USA in 2023
by Severn House, an imprint of Canongate Books Ltd.

severnhouse.com

British Library Cataloguing-in-Publication Data
A CIP catalogue record for this title is available from the British Library.

ISBN-13: 978-1-4483-1035-7 (cased)
ISBN-13: 978-1-4483-1148-4 (trade paper)
ISBN-13: 978-1-4483-1038-8 (e-book)

All Severn House titles are printed on acid-free paper.

Typeset by Palimpsest Book Production Ltd.,
Falkirk, Stirlingshire, Scotland.
Printed and bound in Great Britain by
TJ Books, Padstow, Cornwall.

To the Portmans – Alan, Molly and L. – with thanks for a terrific idea

ACKNOWLEDGEMENTS

While writing *The Dead of Night*, I enjoyed introducing readers to some of my favorite treats in my hometown, St. Louis. All the places I mentioned are real, from Gooey Louie Gooey Butter Cakes, to the Schlafly brewery, to Kakao Chocolate. And yes, Strange Donuts has those wonderfully weird flavor combinations. When you visit my hometown, be sure to check out the food.

I could not have written this book without the help of so many people. Here are a few:

Detective R.C. White, Fort Lauderdale Police Department (retired) and licensed private eye, and Synae White gave me many hours of advice and help. Thank you to death investigator Krysten Addison and Harold R. Messler, retired manager-criminalistics, St. Louis Police Laboratory, as well as Dr Sharon Plotkin, Faculty/Crime Scene Investigator, Miami Dade College School of Justice. Gregg E. Brickman, author of *Imperfect Friends* helped me kill off my characters. So did Luci 'the Poison Lady' Zahray. These experts did their best to make this novel accurate, but all mistakes are mine.

Many other people helped with *The Dead of Night*. My husband, Don Crinklaw, first reader and critiquer, was the most important.

Thanks also to my agent, Joshua Bilmes, president of JABberwocky Literary Agency, and the entire JABberwocky team. Joshua reads my novels and gives detailed suggestions to improve them.

Thanks to the Severn House staff, especially editor Sara Porter for her deft handling of my manuscript and the skillful touch of copyeditor Penelope Isaac. Piers Tilbury, the talented head of design, once again perfectly captured my book. Martin Brown, senior brand manager, works hard to promote my mysteries.

Some of the names in here belong to real people. Sarah E.C. Byrne made a generous donation to charity to have her name in this novel. She's a lawyer from Canberra, Australia, and a crime fiction aficionada. Valerie Cannata is a friend and racehorse lover.

Jinny Gender, Alison McMahan, and Marcia Talley, author of *Disco Dead*, were helpful, too.

Special thanks to the many librarians, including those at the Broward County, St. Louis, and St. Louis County libraries, who answered my questions, no matter how strange they seemed. I could not survive without the help and encouragement of librarians, the most reliable search engines.

Three books were especially helpful. *The Broken Heart of America: St. Louis and the Violent History of the United States* by Walter Johnson, had information about enslaved people before and after the Civil War. Vernon J. Geberth's *Practical Homicide Investigation: Tactics, Procedures, and Forensic Techniques* was useful. I also relied on *Crime Scene Investigation & Reconstruction* by Robert R. Ogle and Dr Sharon Plotkin. Readers will enjoy the history in *The Broken Heart*, but might find the other two textbooks a bit graphic.

I hope I haven't missed anyone. I also hope you'll enjoy Angela Richman's latest adventure. Email me at eviets@aol.com

ONE

L ike everyone who grew up in Chouteau Forest, Missouri, I knew the legend of the Cursed Crypt. The crypt was at Chouteau Forest University, one of the oldest academies in Missouri. The stories claimed that the restless spirit of a professor nicknamed Mean Gene Cortini had been causing death and destruction in the Forest for two centuries.

I'm Angela Richman, and I learned the legend of Mean Gene and the Cursed Crypt the same way many local teens did: around a campfire in the woods that gave the town of Chouteau Forest its name. When I first heard the tale, I was a gawky fifteen-year-old, the daughter of servants who worked on the Du Pres estate. I didn't get many invitations to mingle with the cool kids, so when I was asked to join them, I sneaked out of the house one Saturday night to drink beer in a secluded part of the Forest. It was a chilly March night, and the bare tree branches scraped together like old bones. I hated the bitter taste of the beer, but I wanted to adore my crush, high-school linebacker Danny Jacobs. The firelight turned Danny's blond hair molten gold and highlighted his six-pack – the one under his tight T-shirt.

Alas, the only sparks that flew that night were from the crackling fire. Danny was devoted to the glamorous head cheerleader. He told us an ancient tale of adultery and betrayal, and we shivered in fear. All except the cheerleader, who was snuggled in Danny's strong arms.

Here's the tale, distilled from a thousand nights around local campfires.

The Cursed Crypt was a story of love gone wrong. What started as ordinary adultery unleashed two hundred years of plague, fire, floods and, finally, murder at Chouteau Forest University. The school was founded in 1820. The first president, Hiram Thaddeus Davis, was a grim, grave man with a grizzled beard and unforgiving eyes. He promised a well-rounded education in Latin, Greek, history, the Classics, mathematics and 'moral philosophy.' Nobody knew what that was, but it didn't seem to matter. The school was immediately successful. By 1822, the fledgling university was housed in a fine red-brick building and needed another professor.

Davis hired a brilliant scholar with a European pedigree, Eugene Franco Cortini, to teach Latin, Greek and biology. Cortini was devastatingly handsome, with thick black hair and sculpted features. He spoke five languages. He discovered two new species of American wild flowers – and named both after himself.

Cortini championed the theory of evolution long before Darwin. He wrote that Native Americans were really the lost tribes of Israel. And he preached that monogamy was 'not a natural or healthy state for the animal kingdom.'

Cortini demonstrated his theory by having a passionate affair with Dolly, President Davis's eighteen-year-old wife. Poor, balding Davis caught his curvy blonde wife in flagrante with Cortini, running her fingers through the professor's thick black curls. Never mind where his hands were.

Cortini was fired on the spot, and banished from the campus. Before he left, he cursed the school on a dark windy night. Cortini stood in a circle of stones in front of the school, his hair wild and his black coat flaring, and shouted over the wind, 'My Italian grandmother was a *strega* – a witch – and I inherited her powers. I am a *streghone*, a warlock. As long as I am banished from this school, death and disaster will fall upon it. As long as I am on the school grounds, it shall be safe.'

President Hiram Davis laughed while the pregnant Dolly Davis, imprisoned in her room, wept bitter tears. After cursing the school, the romantically handsome Cortini left for St. Louis, some forty miles east.

Two days after Cortini left, yellow fever struck the campus, carrying off six of its twenty students. Each month, another disaster hit the campus: lightning destroyed the huge oak in front of the school building. Disease killed the school's milk cows. Chouteau Forest Creek flooded the fields where the school grew its crops.

Each time, President Davis dismissed these occurrences as

unfortunate events and proudly declared that he 'refused to give in to superstition.' He was a man of reason – until a fire broke out in the stables and killed his favorite black stallion.

That's when President Davis invited Eugene Cortini to return to the campus. Cortini could no longer teach, but he was given a brick house to live in and conduct his research. The school flourished for seven years, and expanded to two buildings and a new dormitory.

Then Cortini died suddenly at age thirty-seven in 1845.

President Hiram Davis was taking no chances. He decreed that Cortini must be buried on campus, but he didn't want the man's grave on display. Cortini was buried in a crypt under the steps of the Main Building. His final resting place was hidden by a heavy iron door, but Cortini wasn't forgotten. Students and staff whispered about the late Eugene Cortini, and noticed that Hiram Davis's oldest son had thick black hair. Both his parents were blond.

Shortly after Cortini was in his crypt, President Davis died. But his school lived on, and so did the legend of Mean Gene Cortini. Every seven years, a disaster struck the school. The school tried to placate Cortini's restless spirit by lining his crypt with marble. In 1857, a Victorian administration added a marble divan with a tasseled marble pillow, guarded by two weeping angels. A marble slab on the wall proclaimed the tomb was 'Sacred to the memory of Eugene Franco Cortini, scholar, teacher, and researcher.'

These improvements didn't work. The seven-year disaster cycle continued. While the school prospered, the legend lingered like a cloud over the campus.

More than a hundred years later, Chouteau Forest's crafty one percent figured out how to make money out of the ancient tragedy. In the 1980s, the University Benefactors' Club started auctioning off 'A Night in Mean Gene's Cursed Crypt.'

The money went to benefit Chouteau Forest University, which soon had a fat endowment.

The prize was a big one: if any auction winner could stay the full night in the Cursed Crypt, they would be granted membership in the elite Chouteau Founders Club, which ran the Forest. The winners' future in the Forest would be guaranteed.

So far, only one person had stayed the night in the gloomy crypt.

I was forty-one now, long past drinking beer while listening to ghost stories. I worked for the Chouteau County Medical Examiner's office as a death investigator. That meant I was in charge of the body at the scene of a murder, an accident or an unexplained death. It had been more than a quarter of a century since I'd first heard the legend of Cursed Crypt in the night-struck woods, and I didn't believe a word of it.

Until I saw the bodies.

TWO

I slipped on my sparkly chandelier earrings – the blasted things felt as heavy as real chandeliers – and checked my outfit in my bedroom mirror.

Not bad, I thought. I was wearing black tonight, but not the drab black pantsuits I wore as a death investigator. This was a long black silk evening gown, and strappy black velvet heels.

I was ready for the social event of the local season: the annual Howl-o-ween Benefit Auction for Chouteau Forest University. My date, police officer Christopher Ferretti, had scored two tickets.

My doorbell rang. Chris was here. I picked my way carefully down the stairs in my long dress. These really were killer heels.

I opened the door, and there was Chris, resplendent in a black tuxedo. The well-tailored lines of his tux emphasized his broad shoulders. He was freshly shaven, and smelled of citrus and coffee. Chris was six feet two, a perfect match for my six feet.

He whistled when he saw me. 'You look amazing.'

'You look pretty good yourself, Mr Bond,' I said.

He kissed me hard and whispered, 'Do we really have to go to this shindig? I'd rather be alone with you.'

'Later.' My voice was husky and my pulse was racing. I reined in my excitement at his touch. 'We're at Chief Butkus's table and we at least have to make an appearance.'

'Right,' he said. 'The chief shelled out ten thousand dollars for our table of eight, and he'll never let me forget it if we don't show.'

We stepped out into the clear night, and the crisp air helped both of us cool down. I locked my door and adjusted my black gown.

'Love that dress. It shows off your legs,' Chris said.

Slit to mid-thigh, the black gown was rather daring for staid Chouteau Forest. I didn't mind raising a few eyebrows at the benefit.

'We'll pass your condo on the way,' I said. 'I'll leave my car there. I'm on duty at midnight.'

'So you're on call for Halloween,' he said.

'Yep. I hope the only problems we have are kids egging houses and other minor mischief, and I won't be needed.'

My arrangement as a death investigator was unusual. Most DIs hung out at the office in the medical examiner's building, but my space was taken when Evarts Evans, the ME, wanted a Swedish shower for his office. He expanded into my space. We had an unspoken agreement that as long as I could be quickly reached when I was on call, I wouldn't have to come into the office.

Fine with me. I stayed at Chris's condo about five nights a week, and kept my DI case and a change of clothes in my car. My work cell phone was crammed into my black satin evening purse. Tonight, I was definitely going home with Chris after the benefit. I wanted to unwrap him like a present, starting with his hand-tied bow tie.

Ten minutes later, I was settled back in Chris's car and we were on the way to the Chouteau Forest Inn. As we drove past the Forest mansions, carved pumpkins leered on doorsteps and gateposts. Lawns were decorated with phosphorous-coated skeletons, ghosts, and tombstones, glowing eerily in the dark. Tomorrow the streets would be packed with trick-or-treaters, mostly older teens. The younger kids went to supervised parties at churches or in private homes.

We rounded the curving drive to the old inn, ablaze with lights tonight, and joined the long line of limos and luxury cars waiting for the valet. The 'old money' denizens of the Forest were dressed in their elegant best. Jewels were hauled out of vaults, shops were scoured for designer dresses, and legions of hair stylists spent the day dyeing.

The Chouteau Forest Inn, a sprawling white structure with dark green awnings, was built in the roaring Twenties. Chris and I walked arm-in-arm up the stairs, through the lobby and into the ballroom, shimmering with soft chandelier light. Silver skeletons and real lace cobwebs spangled with rhinestones were the decorations.

'The decorations aren't very spooky,' Chris said, as we studied the seating chart to find our table.

'No. The Forest is terrified of creating anything that might seem tacky, and black and orange fall in that category.'

I was glad that no one else heard me, because we'd spotted our table near the stage, and standing near it was a young woman in bright orange and black. As we got closer, I saw she wore an orange stretch-lace maxi-dress with a deep V-neck and high slits on both sides – high enough to reveal most of her well-toned buttocks. Spike-heeled black leather boots completed the outfit. Thick black curls tumbled down her exposed back.

'What kind of dress is that?' Chris asked.

'I think it's a gownless evening strap,' I said.

Chris struggled to hide his snicker as we approached, and recovered enough to whisper, 'Chief Buttkiss looks like he's been sapped, and he won't let go of the woman's hand.'

'He better snap out of it soon,' I said, 'before Mrs Butkus explodes.'

Daphne, the chief's plump, pretty wife, upholstered in black lace, pried the dazzled chief's hand from the young woman's grasp and said, 'I'm Daphne, *Mrs* Butkus.' Accent on that Mrs. 'A delight to meet you, Trixie. I already know your date, Ray Greiman.'

Figures. Ray Greiman, the worst cop on the force, would bring one of his badge bunnies to this event. I had to admit, Greiman did look good in his tux. Heck, even the balding, tubby chief looked like a distinguished penguin in formal dress.

'Come sit by me, Trixie dear.' Daphne patted the empty seat next to her, proving she was way smarter than her spouse. 'I want to get to know you.' She turned her honeyed smile to the rest of us. 'You'll forgive me if we don't follow the traditional dinner seating, won't you? Ray, why don't you sit next to my husband? Angela, I'm sure you and Christopher would like to sit together. Please take the seat next to Trixie, won't you?'

I did. By that time, the last couple at our table had arrived, Henry and Connie Baker, the Butkus's neighbors. The attractive forty-something couple, impeccable in formal black, appeared overawed by the evening, and rarely spoke.

Meanwhile, Trixie was talking about her job. 'I'm a pole dancer at a gentlemen's club,' she said, 'and when I'm not working, I teach pole dancing at the Forest Gym. Pole dancing is excellent exercise and a good way to stay in shape.'

'I can see,' the chief said, and his wife glared him back into silence. He took a long drink of his wine.

The waiters began serving our salads, and the conversation was interrupted by a screech of feedback and an enthusiastic male voice. 'Good evening, ladies and gentlemen. I'm your host for tonight, Danny Jacobs.'

I turned to see my former schoolgirl crush behind the podium. After graduation, Danny had gone on to a pro football career for two seasons, until he blew out his knee. Then he married his high-school sweetheart and bought a car dealership. At forty-four, his six-pack abs had morphed into a modest beer belly, and his golden hair had thinned, but he was still handsome.

'Welcome to tonight's Howl-o-ween Benefit for my alma mater, Chouteau Forest University,' he said. 'I want to remind you that the silent auction will be open for another forty-five minutes, so don't forget to bid. We have some terrific items, including a month at a chateau in France, a ski vacation in Switzerland, a week on a yacht, a gourmet wine club subscription, and more. So take a look, and bid generously. Our university needs you.

'Then enjoy your dinner. After dessert, we'll begin the bidding for a night in the Cursed Crypt. And if you stay till eleven thirty-nine tonight, you can go with us to watch the lucky winners sealed in the tomb. Stay tuned.'

'Are you going to bid on anything?' Chris asked me.

'Yes, I'd like to try to win the gourmet wine club subscription and one of the trips.' I picked at my uninspired salad – limp iceberg lettuce with a paper-thin cucumber slice and two rock-hard cherry tomatoes – and was glad when the server finally removed it.

The dinners weren't bad. My dinner of crabmeat-stuffed chicken breast was a cut above banquet rubber chicken, and Chris wolfed down his filet.

The servers removed our empty plates and poured hot coffee. Then the lights dimmed, and a phalanx of servers marched out, trays brimming with blue flames held high.

'Enjoy your baked Alaska, everyone!' cried our host, Danny. 'Let's give the chef a big hand.'

The chef appeared and took a bow to enthusiastic applause, and then we dug into the lightly browned igloo of meringue. Inside was sponge cake with passion-fruit ice cream and strawberry sauce.

Yum.

Mrs Butkus addressed the table. 'Did you know that the chef at Delmonico's restaurant in New York supposedly put this new dessert on the menu to celebrate the purchase of Alaska from Russia in 1867?'

I dredged up a long-forgotten historical tidbit. 'And people laughed at the Secretary of State, William Seward, for buying the land. Alaska was called "Seward's Ice Box."'

Mrs Butkus smiled at me. 'Exactly. Imagine what our life would be like if we had Russia sitting on our border today?'

The table went silent. None of us wanted to think about that. Fortunately, Danny the host was back, heralded by another screech of feedback. 'Five minutes left for the silent auction, folks. Last chance to bid and bid generously, before we get to the main event of the evening, the auction for a night with Mean Gene Cortini.'

I excused myself to go bid and Daphne Butkus said, 'I'll go with you, Angela.' The two of us wandered over to the far side of the room, where the silent auction prizes were displayed on long tables. We joined the line to enter the auction area, passing a dinner table where camping gear, pillows, blankets, snacks, a bottle of tequila and six-packs of beer were piled awkwardly in the aisle.

'What's going on with that?' I asked Daphne. The chief's wife knew the juiciest local gossip.

'That's probably Trey Lawson's table,' she said. 'He's determined to win this year and join the Chouteau Founders Club.'

'Trey Lawson the frat-house rapist?' I said.

'Alleged rapist,' she said. 'His girlfriend, Lydia Fynch, testi-fied on his behalf. Trey's lawyer begged the judge "please don't let rumors and innuendo ruin the career of a promising young man" and Trey was acquitted.'

'What a slimewad,' I said.

'Probably,' she said, 'but what really upsets the old guard is that he's the son of a hedge funder, a nobody.'

'A fabulously rich nobody,' I said.

We'd finally reached the silent auction tables. Daphne and I stopped first to check out the wine-club subscription. It had a long list of bidders – it was now up to $1,700. The yacht cruise and the Swiss ski vacation had both been bid up to more than $5,000.

'I'm bidding on the French chateau vacation,' Daphne said. 'Our twenty-fifth wedding anniversary is coming up.'

I wanted to bid on an all-expense paid week for two in a beachfront condo in Fort Lauderdale, Florida. The trip included airfare. That item only had a stingy $250 bid. I bumped it up to $350. If I won, I'd still have a bargain.

The less popular items were near the open bar, and I saw old Reggie Du Pres, unspoken ruler of the Forest, drinking an amber liquid – probably Scotch – with two cronies, his nephew, Vincent, and Jefferson R. Morgan. Vincent's son, Bradford, sat next to his father. Vincent had just downed his drink and asked for a double. The men must have had several. Daphne joined me and raised an eyebrow at the group, laughing and talking loud enough for us to hear their conversation.

Jefferson said, 'Did you see how that Trey Lawson brought his gear so he could go straight to the crypt? He's planning on winning. If he stays the night, he could join the Founders Club. We can't have someone like him joining.'

'Let's not get ahead of ourselves,' old Reggie said. 'Since the Eighties, only one person has managed to stay in that crypt until dawn – my nephew, Vincent.' He patted the younger man's shoulder. 'Most can't make it past midnight.'

'Tonight, my son Bradford is going to follow in my foot-steps,' Vincent said. 'I'm bankrolling his bid up to a million one.'

'Hear, hear.' Jefferson waved his drink defiantly. 'Trey Lawson will join the Founders Club over my dead body.'

'Why not make it *his* dead body?' Vincent said. Their drunken laughter followed us back to our table.

THREE

An energized Danny Jacobs was back at the podium, announcing with a flourish, 'Now, ladies and gentlemen, it's time for the evening's main event – the Cursed Crypt auction.'

He paused for the expected applause and cheers.

'You know the rules: the winner plus one companion will be locked in the crypt at precisely eleven thirty-nine p.m. tonight. That's the exact time when Mean Gene Cortini died. Feeling any shivers yet? You should. That crypt is cold. It's nine forty-five now, so let's get going. Our winner can't miss a date with destiny.

'Last year, the record bid at this auction was eight hundred thousand dollars for a night with Mean Gene. Tonight, let's see if we can beat that record and make it a cool million!'

The audience burst into applause again. Trey Lawson jumped up on his chair, holding a beer bottle. He pumped his fist and shouted, 'Whoo! I'm ready to win! I'll rattle Gene's bones!'

The old guard at the Du Pres table glared Trey back into his seat. Trey didn't bother to look abashed, but he did sit down.

Danny chuckled and said, 'That's the kind of enthusiasm we're looking for, ladies and gentlemen. Now let's open our hearts and our wallets for good old Chouteau Forest U. At each table, you'll see paddles. Your bidding number for the auction is on that paddle.'

I picked up mine. The paddle had a picture of Professor Eugene Cortini on one side, and a large number on the other.

'The prof was quite the hottie, wasn't he?' Trixie said. 'I bet he was a big tipper, too.'

Detective Greiman looked mortified by his date. But Trixie was right: even the stiff, formal style of the nineteenth-century portrait didn't disguise the professor's good looks.

'Definitely a hottie, Trixie,' I said. 'And he had gorgeous dark hair.'

Greiman glared at me. He didn't like me encouraging Trixie.

Danny said, 'Raise your paddle when you want to bid, ladies and gentlemen. And be careful about scratching your head when the bidding is going on, or you could be spending the night with Mean Gene.'

There was polite laughter, and then Danny said, 'Let's start at two hundred fifty thousand dollars.'

'Wow,' Trixie said. 'Can you imagine having that kind of loose change? Those bucks would buy you a very nice double-wide.'

Greiman coughed loudly, but Trixie ignored him and kept talking. 'Don't you agree, Angela?'

'Absolutely,' I said. 'You could buy a nice-sized lot for that money, too. Or a small house.'

Greiman coughed like he was dying of pneumonia. 'Ray,' I said. 'Would you like a cough drop?'

'Perhaps a sip of water?' Daphne added. That was a command, not a suggestion.

Ray took a sip.

'Why are these people bidding at this auction?' Trixie said. 'Spending all this money to sleep in an old tomb. Everyone knows CFU has a great computer department. But the rest of the school is for rich flunk-outs.'

Chris laughed. Trixie turned to my date and asked seriously, 'Chris, do you know why?'

'They want to help the university, of course,' Chris said. 'Private schools are expensive to run, even if the students are rich. But I think the top bidders also do it for the prestige.'

'I guess I understand.' Trixie gave a shrug that nearly made the top of her dress slide off. The chief's eyes bulged at the view of her creamy breasts.

'But you can't eat prestige,' Trixie said. 'Or wear it. Or love it.'

'So true.' Daphne smiled at Trixie. 'But some people have so much money they want to give back to the community. This auction is going to become a battle between the old money Du Pres family, and the new money, the Lawsons.'

A woman in a sparkly pink dress sitting near the Du Pres table gave a genteel shout. 'I bid four hundred thousand dollars.'

'Five hundred thousand,' said a man at a table near the front. I'd seen his photo in the *Chouteau Forest Gazette*. He was on the university's board. Tonight, he was probably acting as a shill to bid up the price. The bids went back and forth between the two – Pink Dress and Board Member – like a polite ping-pong match.

While the bidding slowly climbed, the men at the Du Pres table – old Reggie, white-haired and distinguished, along with his nephew Vincent, who was slowly turning into a copy of Reggie, and finally, Reggie's great-nephew Bradford, lit up their cigars. Jefferson fired up his own stogie and began puffing like a smokestack. Everyone knew this was a no-smoking building, but no one dared complain.

A few tables away, the supposed challenger, Trey Lawson, lit a cigarette, and a waiter discreetly appeared at his side and whispered in his ear. Trey stubbed out his cigarette in a butter plate.

'Why can't Trey light up a cigarette?' Trixie asked. 'And that other table full of old rich guys is smoking those nasty-smelling cigars?'

'Because the rules don't apply to the Du Pres family,' I said, keeping my voice low. 'Welcome to the Forest.'

'I don't understand this place.' Trixie sighed.

'Join the club, Trixie,' Chris said, and she smiled at him.

Finally, after a decorous back and forth between the two shills, the bidding reached $750,000. The shills put down their paddles. Their work was done. Now the real fight was about to start, between Bradford Du Pres, the cream of Forest society, and the newcomer Trey Lawson, probable rapist and hedge funder's son.

Bradford stubbed out his cigar and sat up straight, ready for battle. The Du Pres heir was at least six feet tall, and wore his blond hair in a fringe. He was almost pretty, the way blond men can be in their youth. Too bad an entitled sneer marred his handsome face.

Trey was not as finely made, but he was strong and muscular,

with a crooked grin that gave him a bad-boy vibe. Except Trey
was more than a bad boy – he was bad news. I thought the
'kind' judge who gave Trey a second chance should have been
kicked off the bench – and Trey should have been behind bars.

Trey's father, James Lawson Junior, and his grandfather, the
senior Lawson, were sitting at the table with Trey. Their ill-
fitting tuxes looked rented, but Trey's was definitely bespoke.
Beside James Senior was a distinguished white-haired woman
in pale lavender. The woman with Lawson Junior wore a red
gown splashed with black splotches. I guessed she was Trey's
mother. Trey seemed crazy in love with his dinner date, CFU
alumna Lydia Fynch, who looked glamorous in a black velvet
gown and antique pearl-drop earrings.

Lydia's good looks were a pretty facade, as far as I was
concerned. Her testimony kept Trey, the accused frat-house
rapist, out of jail. Ever since Lydia had saved Trey's hide in
court, they'd had a hot and heavy romance. A diamond the
size of a gumdrop on her ring finger testified to their engagement. Tonight, while the shills' bids heated up, the pair traded
long kisses between bids.

When the bidding number reached $750,000, Trey suddenly
jumped up like he was hailing a cab, waved his paddle and
cried, 'Eight hundred thousand dollars!'

Then he abandoned Lydia. The next fifteen minutes became
a duel between Bradford and Trey.

'Eight fifty,' Bradford said, as coolly as if he was playing
poker for a penny a point.

'Ladies and gentlemen,' Danny shouted. 'We have officially
beaten last year's record bid. Thanks to Bradford Du Pres,
we've reached *eight hundred and fifty thousand dollars*!'

The crowd erupted into applause, then quieted as Danny
said, 'Do I hear nine hundred thousand? Nine hundred thousand? No? OK, eight fifty going once. Going twice.'

'Nine hundred thousand.' Trey waved his paddle. 'I bid nine
hundred!'

'Nine hundred it is,' Danny said. 'Do I hear nine ten?'

'Nine fifty,' Bradford said.

'One million dollars!' cried Trey. 'I'm bidding one million
dollars!' He was greeted with cheers and whistles.

Danny sounded awed. 'We're now at a cool million, folks. Do we want to go higher?'

'One million, one hundred thousand dollars.' Bradford sounded almost bored as he drawled that number. I knew that was his limit – at least that's what I'd overheard while I was at the silent auction tables.

'One million two!' Trey shouted.

Was Bradford going higher? I watched the Du Pres table carefully. Bradford looked at his father, who shook his head no. Old Reggie puffed on his cigar, then held up three fingers.

'One million three!' Bradford said.

'One million four!' Trey said.

Now the audience was stone-cold silent. I held my breath. Were the Du Pres family going to triumph as usual? Would they keep the Chouteau Founders Club their private preserve?

Bradford looked at his great-uncle. I could almost see a plea on that entitled face. Old Reggie slowly shook his head no. For a moment, Bradford's face was a mask of rage. Then his anger quickly disappeared.

Danny said, 'One million four hundred thousand dollars is our last bid, ladies and gentlemen. Do I hear a million five? A million five, a million five?' No matter how much Danny repeated it, the bidding was dead.

'Then one million four it is! Going once! One million four going twice. One million four hundred thousand! Congratulations, Trey Lawson! You've won a night in Mean Gene's Cursed Crypt!

'A round of applause for our generous bidder, ladies and gentlemen!'

Trey grabbed Lydia and kissed her so hard he pulled her hair out of its chignon and smeared her lipstick. Then he climbed on his chair and did a victory dance, waving his paddle.

Most of the diners laughed, but the Du Pres table sat stone-faced.

The Forest had entered a new era.

FOUR

When the historic bidding finished, Danny the announcer was looking a bit frazzled: his tie was askew and his shirt was creeping out of his cummerbund. He shouted above the noisy, excited – and well-oiled – crowd: 'Attention! Attention, please. This question is for our auction winner.'

The noise subsided a notch, but Danny still couldn't make himself heard. The auction-goers started tapping water glasses and coffee cups with their spoons. Finally, the din subsided.

Danny wiped the sweat off his forehead and said, 'Trey Lawson, who is your guest for your night in the Cursed Crypt?'

Trey took his date's hand and said, 'Lydia Fynch!'

Lydia looked even prettier with her hair partially down. She gave a beauty queen smile and a shy wave.

That wasn't enough for Trey. He held up her arm like she'd won a boxing match. Lydia abandoned her polite restraint. She jumped up and down and squealed like a teenage girl while the audience clapped and whistled.

'Adorable,' I whispered to Chris. 'The rapist and the perjurer make a perfect couple.'

'Alleged,' he whispered back. 'For both.' Chris paused and said, 'Although as far as I'm concerned, they're both guilty. Trey raped that poor woman and Lydia lied to protect him.'

Danny was shouting for attention again. This time, even a microphone didn't help. After more tapping on glasses and cups, he held up a huge silver stopwatch and said, 'Lydia and Trey, you have exactly one half-hour to get ready before the crypt-closing ceremony. We'll meet you at the crypt under the steps at the Main Building in thirty minutes.'

He pressed the button on the stopwatch and said, 'Tick-tock. The clock is ticking, folks.'

Lydia and Trey's parents helped gather up the gear at the table. As the group headed for the exit, Danny said, 'Well, this has been a record-breaking fundraiser. The money will go to develop new programs and buy new equipment. Now, another round of applause for Trey Lawson. He deserves it!'

The applause was loud and sustained, and the Lawson family smiled and gave one-handed waves all the way out the door.

Once they were gone, Danny said, 'Ladies and gentlemen, if you bid on a silent auction item, you can check your cell phones and see if you've won. Winners are being notified by text and they can pay instantly.'

'Gotta see if I've won,' I told Chris, and opened my cell phone. 'Yes!'

'What is it? What did you win?'

'An all-expense paid vacation for two to Fort Lauderdale, Florida. With airfare.'

'I know you'll have fun.' Chris sounded so formal, I almost laughed.

'So will you. You're going with me. Well, you are, aren't you?'

'Yes, of course.' He kissed me hard.

'I hope that's a preview of the rest of tonight.' My face felt flushed and my voice was husky.

'The party's not over, ladies and gentlemen,' Danny said. 'It's a mild night, so let's all meet at the crypt for the closing ceremony. And I do mean closing. In less than thirty minutes, the Cursed Crypt will be locked.

'Chouteau Forest University is only a five-minute walk from here. The path to the campus is straight out the Forest Inn's back exit, and the path is paved for easy walking. Or you can drive. The valets are standing by, ready to retrieve your cars. There's plenty of free parking on campus. If you take the path, just follow the lighted pumpkins to the crypt. The pumpkins were carved by the university students for the pumpkin-carving contest. See you at the crypt!'

Danny left the podium. Most of the auction-goers headed for the front exit and the valet stand. A few younger, more adventurous partygoers went toward the back exit to walk the short distance to the crypt.

'I'll go get the car,' Chris said.

'Let's walk,' I said.

'Can you walk in those shoes?'

That's another reason I loved Chris. He was thoughtful.

'For five minutes, I can.'

I tried to step confidently down the stairs to the back entrance, but I had to hold on to the banister. I wasn't used to high heels. As a death investigator, I wear sensible, flat shoes when I'm working. I wouldn't admit it to Chris, but these sexy shoes were killing me.

Once we were outside on the concrete path, walking was easier for me. Chris gave me his arm, and we strolled along. Other auction-goers pushed past us, but we were in no rush. The night was comfortably cool, the fallen autumn leaves turned the path into an orange-and-yellow tapestry, and the pumpkins cast an orange glow.

We admired the hand-carved pumpkins on either side of the path. 'These are incredible,' I said. 'That one is a work of art. The pumpkin looks like lace. I wouldn't mind it in my living room.'

'There's Darth Vader.' Chris pointed to the one next to the lacework.

'And the pumpkin across from it looks suspiciously like the university's Dean Stiller. Those are certainly his glasses.'

Classic grinning jack-o'-lanterns, laughing ghouls, toothless hags, spiders, as well as several portraits of Mean Gene Cortini lined the path, all cleverly carved by the university students.

'Too bad these artworks are going to rot,' I said.

'The benefit committee should have used the students' pumpkins,' Chris said. 'These are far more imaginative than bedazzled black lace and skeletons.'

Suddenly, I stopped. 'Chris, look at that pumpkin.'

The pumpkin was bigger than most, almost the size of a plump ottoman. Carved on it was a replica of the crypt's wrought-iron doors. One door was open, revealing the inside of the marble tomb, draped in cobwebs.

Under the carving was this message in gothic lettering: *Mean Gene will not sleep alone. Tonight, two will join him – permanently!*

FIVE

I bent down and read the shocking inscription on the giant pumpkin again, just in case I'd been wrong. Nope, I'd read it right: *Mean Gene will not sleep alone. Tonight, two will join him – permanently!*

'Is that a threat, Chris?'

'It could be a joke,' he said. 'Or maybe Bradford Du Pres is a sore loser and he's trying to scare Trey and Lydia into backing out of spending a night in the crypt.'

I photographed the pumpkin with my cell-phone camera as if it was evidence: wide shots, medium and close-ups, including several close-ups of that inscription and the elaborate carving of the tomb on the pumpkin, then noted that it was the fourth pumpkin from the end of the walkway to the campus. It was right next to an ornamental lamppost.

'I think we should report it. We'll have to show this pumpkin to Trey and Lydia before they're locked in that crypt.'

'We should tell Chief Buttkiss first,' he said.

I started giggling. 'It's *Butkus*. This is no time to dredge up the chief's nickname.'

We both started laughing – we'd had a little too much dinner wine. Then I noticed the time on my cell phone.

'We should get a move on, Chris. The door-locking ceremony starts in ten minutes.'

I walked as fast as I could in those hellish heels. We soon saw the tent erected at the entrance to the crypt. Champagne-drinking partygoers were scattered about in noisy groups. Excitement rippled through the crowd. Thanks to Trey's record auction bid, they knew that tonight they were part of Forest history.

Chief Butkus was standing at the far edge, regaling the mayor and Reggie Du Pres with some kind of story. His face was smeared with a sycophant's smile, and his chest was puffed up. Clearly, the chief loved attention from the Forest's rich and powerful. It's how he'd earned his unflattering nickname. The Forest's wealthy regarded him with polite condescension, as they would any useful servant. The chief's long-suffering wife stood next to her husband, studying her shoes. I suspected she was embarrassed. Daphne was smart enough to figure out what the mayor and Reggie Du Pres really thought of her husband, but she seemed to love the man despite his faults.

As we neared the chief, I heard him say, 'And that's how I caught the last Ghost Burglar.'

I knew what had really happened, and the chief had nothing to do with the man's capture, but this was no time for the truth.

'Chief Butkus.' Chris pronounced the man's name slowly and carefully. I bit my lip to keep from laughing. 'May I see you for a moment, please? It's important.'

'Of course, Officer, of course.' He smiled and said, 'Excuse me, gentlemen. Duty calls.'

As soon as the chief was out of earshot, his face changed to hot fury. He blasted Chris. 'Why the hell did you drag me away, Ferretti? This better be important.'

'There may be a threat against the auction winner,' Chris said. 'Something that appeared to be a threat was carved on a pumpkin on the path to the campus.'

'A threat? On a pumpkin?' His scorn was withering.

'Here, Chief Butkus.' I stepped in front of Chris, hoping to deflect the chief's anger. 'Take a look at these photos.'

'I see a pumpkin, Angela.'

'Check out the writing. It says, *Mean Gene will not sleep alone. Tonight, two will join him – permanently!*'

He laughed, then talked to me like I was a slow learner. 'It's a joke, Angela. A mean joke, maybe, but still a joke. You don't think any of these people' – he waved his hands at the wealthy, well-dressed crowd – 'would really hurt anyone, do you? This is the cream of society.'

I'd worked as a death investigator long enough to know that cream could curdle.

The chief metaphorically patted me on the head. 'You work too hard, Angela. Why don't you just forget about this prank and enjoy your evening, OK?'

'But what if something happens?' I said. 'That crypt is two hundred years old. What if a brick comes loose during the night and accidentally injures Trey or Lydia? We weren't the only ones who took the path with that pumpkin. Several people must have seen that threat. If something happens, the police department could get sued.'

Sued. I'd said the magic word.

'Well, um, OK,' the chief said. 'I'll talk with Trey and Lydia as soon as they arrive. But let's keep this information quiet for now. This is a great night for the university! And the Forest!'

He bustled back toward the tent. The mayor and Reggie had disappeared, but Daphne was chatting with Greiman and his date, Trixie. Chris and I joined them.

Suddenly, we heard loud cheers and cries of 'Yay, Trey! You did it, dude!' Voices chanted 'Trey! Trey! Trey!' Drunken college students, waving beer bottles, pushed to the front near the driveway to the Main Building, as a black Land Rover rolled by. Trey and Lydia waved to the crowd as if they were in a parade.

'Oh, that's so nice,' Trixie said. 'Trey's fraternity came out to support him. I know those boys. Hey, boys! Over here! It's Trixie!' She waved enthusiastically.

'Did you date someone in the frat?' Daphne asked.

'Oh, no. I dance at the frat house or they come see me at the club on special occasions. You know, like bachelor parties and twenty-first birthdays. They're so sweet. Good tippers, too.'

'What's the name of the frat?' I asked.

'I don't know Greek, but we girls at the club call it Tappa Kegga Day. When those boys show up, it's par-tay time!' She shimmied her hips and ample bosom.

Greiman tried to distance himself from her, looking mortified. Trixie took his arm and said, 'Ray, don't be such an old grump. This is fun!'

He tugged his arm away from her, and Trixie looked like a kicked puppy.

'Trixie, dear,' Daphne said. 'Come over by me and tell me how you met Ray.'

Trixie trotted over and Ray followed. Chris and I were enjoying this performance.

The podium had been brought out to the tent and a sound system set up. Danny Jacobs was back at the microphone. 'Is this a perfect evening or what, ladies and gentlemen? Now it's almost time for the moment we've been waiting for. We're about to unlock the doors of the Cursed Crypt.

'Chouteau Forest University student Emily Roseman will be doing the honors tonight. Emily is a senior with a major in biology and a minor in chemistry. And in case you didn't know, Emily's family endowed the Roseman Computer Lab.' The crowd applauded, and Emily, a curvy brunette, took a mock bow.

'It's a shame they have to keep the crypt's doors locked all year,' Daphne said. 'But things are different these days.'

Trixie gave a mischievous laugh. 'You know why they're locked, don't you?'

'Vandals?' Daphne said.

'No, silly. The students like to "bone on the bones." Doing it in the crypt has way more prestige than joining the Mile-High Club. Especially since so many of these students' families own their own planes.'

Before anyone could reply, Danny the announcer said, 'Trey and Lydia are unloading their creature comforts for their night in the crypt now.'

The couple, dressed in matching red plaid flannel shirts and Levi's, were hauling items out of the Land Rover, while Emily Roseman checked them to make sure they complied with the auction rules.

'Remember, Trey and Lydia can bring in creature comforts,' Danny said, 'but no cell phones or any other electronic devices.'

'What do they have so far, Emily?'

Emily checked off the items. 'Four heavy quilts. Two pillows. Four battery-operated Coleman lanterns. Two Maglite flashlights and one portable camping toilet. Plus two pizzas – one pepperoni and mushroom and one sausage and hot peppers – and a forty-ounce steel Thermos of hot coffee, a six-pack of Fiji water, two six-packs of Corona and a bottle of tequila.'

'I see why they brought that portable potty,' Danny said. 'You're gonna need it with all that drinking.'

Danny stopped, and peered into the distance. 'Wait, what's that coming up the driveway?' he asked. 'Looks like a special delivery.'

A lime-green Kia with a plastic sign on its door that read 'Tara's Taste of the Forest' stopped right behind the Lawsons' Land Rover. A man in his early twenties with a mop of dark hair tipped blond hopped out of the toylike car. 'I have a delivery from Tara's for the winners.'

The basket he hauled out took up the whole passenger seat. 'This basket has many St. Louis specialties,' he said. 'Beer from the Schlafly Brewery. Plus gooey butter cake from Gooey Louie and sea salt truffles and dark chocolate bark with Missouri pecans from Kakao Chocolate. Oh, and two bottles of Merlot.'

'I'll be happy to take any leftovers you don't want,' Danny said, and the crowd laughed.

'There's more,' said the young delivery man. 'I have a special thermal container stuffed with toasted ravioli and St. Louis baby back ribs.'

'That's quite a gift,' Danny said. 'All the local favorites. Who sent it?'

'Don't know.' The delivery man shrugged. 'There was no name with the order. Whoever sent it delivered some things to the store, along with instructions to add St. Louis favorites. The instructions also said I should say, "Congratulations, Lydia and Trey. Glad you're finally getting what you deserve!" and give you the message on this note.' He handed them the note, waved, and jumped back in the car.

'Awesome,' Trey said, and hugged Lydia.

'Chris, they're going to unlock the crypt any second now,' I said. 'I'd better find the chief so he can warn Trey and Lydia.'

'I'll tell him,' Chris said.

'No, he's not happy with this idea, and if he gets angry, he'll take it out on me instead of you.'

'I can't let you take the heat for me.'

'Yes, you can. Stay here. I'll be right back.'

I gave Chris a quick kiss then, before he could stop me, I

slipped through the crowd and found the chief near the podium. 'Chief! Chief Butkus,' I called. When he turned my way, I said softly, 'Don't forget your promise to tell Lydia and Trey about the warning.'

He gave me a condescending smile. 'Angela, if you weren't so darn pretty, I wouldn't put up with you. OK, I'll do it. But I want you to make me a promise. The crypt opens at six in the morning. I want you to be here at six a.m., so you can see just how silly your idea was. Will you do that?'

'Yes, sir.' I hated the thought of leaving Chris's warm bed so early in the morning, but I was on call anyway. 'You've got yourself a deal, Chief.'

'Text the photos to my phone, Angela, so I can show them to Trey and Lydia.'

Once the chief had the photos, I waited in the shadows until he approached Lydia and Trey. I saw them talking, and then Trey and Lydia looked at the photos, shrugged, shook their heads, and laughed. In fact, they guffawed. They sure didn't seem worried about the threatening pumpkin.

I shivered. 'Are you cold, Angela?' Chris asked.

'No, I'm worried. That threat scared me. I'm afraid this situation could get ugly. A lot of money was in play here tonight. It could turn dangerous.'

'I don't think this crowd would hurt Trey and Lydia,' Chris said. 'They'd try to wipe them out financially, but they wouldn't get their hands dirty.'

'More than a million dollars changed hands here tonight, and Trey challenged the Du Pres family for control of the Forest. The Du Pres family lost and – if Trey and Lydia make it through the night – that powerful family will lose their standing. They tried to save their position by bidding a million three. We've both seen people get killed for pocket change.'

Chris put his arm around me and kissed me on the cheek. 'You worry too much,' he said.

Danny announced, 'It's almost time, ladies and gentlemen. Please gather round while Emily Roseman unlocks the crypt.'

Emily approached the crypt with two huge iron keys. Silver and black ribbons hung from the round loop at the end of the key. Wrought-iron gates in the shape of weeping angels guarded the crypt door. A big padlock held them together.

Emily used one key to unlock the gates, and the wrought-iron angels swung free. The crowd applauded.

The second lock was harder to open, but Emily managed it. The door opened with a soul-tearing shriek, and the crowd gasped. The crypt's dense, black interior seemed to pulse with a malevolent force.

For a few seconds, no more, it seemed that the darkness above the crypt had grown thicker and heavier and come closer. Then it was over. I looked around for signs someone else had experienced this. No. The faces around me displayed the usual glassy-eyed, well-lubricated cheer. Someone shouted, 'Trey and Lydia will share a bier with old Cortini.'

'We brought plenty of beer,' Trey said, high on adrenaline and alcohol. 'There's enough for Gene.'

'Were you asleep during English class?' Lydia playfully punched his shoulder. 'That's "bier" as in coffin.'

'Then Gene can share,' Trey shouted. 'We'll show him how to have a good time.' Someone else tried a wolf – or was it a werewolf? – howl. I looked at Chris. Was he aware of this creepy interlude? If he was, it didn't show.

Danny broke the mood when he said, 'It's black as a bill collector's heart in there.' He spoke with renewed energy. 'Emily, could we have a little light on the subject, please?'

Emily turned on the Coleman lanterns, and now we could see the interior. In the center was the gray marble divan with a tasseled marble pillow, guarded by two sorrowing angels. The deathly tableau was shrouded in cobwebs from ceiling to floor. The dirty-white cobwebs swirled in the air like lost souls.

'Oh, jeez, Chris,' I said. 'I'm glad I'm not sleeping in there.'

'Is that a gray carpet inside?' he asked.

I stood on tiptoes to get a better look. 'No, it's dust. Decades of dust and dirt. No wonder most people didn't last the night in this creepy place.'

The couple were carrying their creature comforts into the dark, dank tomb.

'Trey and Lydia, are you ready for the door-locking ceremony?' Danny asked.

'Yes!' They were holding hands and smiling as they answered.

'Let me recite the rules.' Danny announced them with a flourish. 'First, a student guard will be posted outside the crypt door. Second, a camera will be trained on the entrance as soon as it is locked. That is the only way in or out. Third, if Trey or Lydia wants to leave before six a.m. tomorrow, they must knock three times on the door. If Lydia leaves before Trey, he will forfeit his chance to join the Chouteau Founders Club, even if he stays inside until six a.m.

'The doors will be padlocked at precisely eleven thirty-nine p.m., the time of Professor Eugene Cortini's death. Any last words?'

'Yes,' Trey said. 'Earlier tonight, Chief Butkus showed me something that a few people thought was a threat. Carved on a pumpkin. A pumpkin, can you believe it?'

He laughed. The crowd stayed silent.

'I don't like this, Chris,' I whispered.

He squeezed my hand to reassure me.

Trey finally stopped laughing and continued. 'This so-called threat said, "Mean Gene will not sleep alone. Tonight, two will join him – permanently!"'

He glared into the crowd. 'Well, I want to tell you that I'm not afraid and neither is Lydia. We're going to stay the night and then I will be a member of the Chouteau Founders Club. The members have done everything they can to keep my father and me out of the club. Why? Because we're so-called "new money."

'Here's the thing about new money: we're not afraid to spend it because we know we can make more. That's why we outbid the Du Pres tonight. They've forgotten how to make money.'

'Chris,' I said, 'can't we stop them? He just issued a direct challenge to the Forest powers. He insulted the Du Pres family.'

'Trey knows what he's doing,' Chris said. 'Besides, the Du Pres need to be challenged. They've run this county as their private fiefdom for too long.'

Now the beer-swilling students began chanting, 'Bone on the bones!'

The partygoers tried to shush them, but the students only chanted louder.

Trey shouted over the commotion, 'Like the note on our gift said, "Glad you're finally getting what you deserve."'

'I deserve all the Forest has to offer. And tomorrow morning, I will claim it. See you at six o'clock!'

He and Lydia waved as the crypt doors clanged shut.

SIX

The crypt was sealed and the first student guard was posted – an earnest young woman with a gray hoodie, jeans, and pink hair. She stood at attention by the tomb, but I saw her own creature comforts were stashed in a nook: a folding lawn chair and a Thermos of coffee.

Now that the formalities were finished, the scene swiftly emptied, and the guests began heading home. Champagne flutes were abandoned on any surface, from tables to stones to grinning pumpkins. Cocktail napkins fluttered to the ground like dying birds. The auction guests broke into gossiping groups. A white-haired woman in a sparkly black gown said, 'Did you hear what that young man said about Reggie Du Pres? What was he thinking?'

'The old lions are always challenged, Eugenia. You know that,' her escort said. 'Reggie's up to it.'

'And those disrespectful students, shouting "Bone on the bones!"' she said. 'What's wrong with them?'

'Nothing.' He laughed. 'They're young and their blood runs hot. Like ours used to.'

'Used to?' Eugenia said. 'It still does!' She planted a kiss on his mouth that made me want to applaud. The couple hurried off into the darkness.

The clean-up crew had arrived by the time Chris roared up the drive in his car to pick me up.

On the trip to Chris's condo, I was lost in thought. So lost, Chris had to ask me twice, 'Angela, are you OK? You're so quiet.'

'Just thinking,' I said.

'Are you worried the chief will embarrass you when you show up at six tomorrow morning, and see Lydia and Trey walk out of that crypt?'

'That's the least of my worries. I won't mind a few horse laughs at my expense if they both come out of that crypt alive.'

Chris looked over at me. 'You really think something bad will happen? This event has been a fundraiser for more than forty years – four decades – and there hasn't been a single problem. How can there be? We saw the crypt doors sealed and a guard posted. There's no other way in or out of that tomb.'

'That crypt auction is exactly what's bothering me,' I said. 'Tonight was a seismic shift in the Forest. Trey openly challenged the Du Pres family. He insulted them in public.'

Chris pulled into his condo lot, parked his car and took me into his arms.

'Yes, Trey insulted Reggie Du Pres. But what do you think the old man will do? Shoot the kid when he walks out of the crypt?

'I'll tell you what's happening, Angela. Right now, old Reggie is holed up with his cronies, smoking expensive cigars and drinking single malt. He and his rich pals are looking for every loophole possible to keep Trey out of the Founders Club. If they can't find one, and Trey does join the club, they'll do everything in their power to isolate Trey, so he has no influence. Then they will scheme to ruin Trey and his family financially and drive them out of the Forest. You've lived here all your life, Angela. You know how these old, inbred families work.'

I did. 'You're right, Chris. Tonight unnerved me. Too many skeletons and tombs, I guess. I can't help feeling uneasy.'

He kissed me hard, and I kissed him right back. 'I know a way to make you feel better,' he whispered. 'Let's go inside.'

'Good idea.' I was surprised how fast I could run in those high heels. And up the stairs, too.

I groaned when my phone alarm went off at five a.m. The morning was cold and dark, and my head throbbed from last night's champagne. I yawned, stretched, slid out of bed, then quickly showered and dressed. By the time I was downstairs, Chris had brewed coffee and filled a Thermos for me. He handed me a bacon-and-egg sandwich and a cup of coffee to go.

'You're wonderful,' I said, kissing him.

'So are you. Let me know if Trey and Lydia didn't make it through the night.' I studied him carefully to make sure he wasn't mocking me. Of course he wasn't. I was touchy about that Cursed Crypt.

'I will. Thanks for breakfast. You saved my life.' I raised my coffee in salute. Outside in the clear Halloween morning, I found my car and drove to the crypt while eating breakfast. The coffee helped me wake up.

When I arrived at 5:56, white fingers of morning fog still lingered, giving the scene a ghostly, graveyard feel. A small cluster of people were shivering in the cool air. They included Danny, last night's announcer, plus a university vice president, and the auction chair, all looking considerably less chipper this morning. Surly-looking photographers from the campus newspaper and a local TV station were loaded with gear.

Adam Nesbitt, this morning's pale, bearded student guard, couldn't stop yawning, despite the industrial-sized foam cup of coffee he was holding. Chief Butkus wore his uniform and a smug smile. He was the first to greet me.

'Angela. You're here.' He sounded surprised.

'Of course, Chief. You asked me to be.'

'Yes, but I'm not your supervisor. You didn't have to show up.'

Yeah, right, I thought. You play golf with my boss, Evarts Evans, at least once a week. And you can make Chris's life hell.

I smiled at him.

Adam checked his cell phone. 'It's six a.m. Time to open the crypt.' We all moved in closer. The photographers pushed in front of us to get the best shots when the doors opened.

I listened carefully for signs of life inside the crypt, but heard nothing. Cold fog fingers gripped my heart. You're being ridiculous, I told myself. Those are brick walls covered with stone. Nothing can get through them – or past those locked gates and iron door.

Adam took out the same iron keys Emily had used last night, the ones with the silver and black ribbons. It took at least a minute to wrestle the gate locks open. There was a hellish squeal as he dragged the guardian angels away from

the iron door. That door was even harder to open, and Adam
let loose with a couple of expletives while he struggled with
the lock.

'I expect Trey and Lydia will be waiting at the door,' the
chief said.

Finally. The iron door opened with a ghoulish screech and
revealed the inside of the tomb. The cobwebs hung from the
ceiling like dirty curtains. The Coleman lanterns flickered in
the dark tomb, creating spectral shadows. Even four strong
lights couldn't banish the oppressive gloom. We were dead
quiet, silenced by the scene the lights revealed.

Trey and Lydia were lying in each other's arms on the
marble divan, which was draped in a red blanket.

'Looks like the tomb scene from *Romeo and Juliet*, my
class play,' Adam said, his voice a whisper. 'Without the
empties, of course.'

A small mountain of empty beer bottles, wine bottles, and a
tequila bottle was piled at the foot of the marble divan, and
the remains of the pizza and the half-eaten gift-basket goodies
were scattered about. A limp slice of pepperoni pizza was
draped over an angel's head like a flat hat. The other angel
had the six-pack of water balanced on its wings.

'Well, I'll be darned,' the chief said. 'I expected Trey and
Lydia would be awake and waiting to claim their prize. Instead,
they're asleep. Dead to the world.'

'Dead drunk is more like it,' the surly newspaper photographer
said, giving the nearest empty beer bottle a good hard kick. I
jumped when the bottle hit the crypt wall and shattered.

The couple didn't move. They didn't even twitch. That
wasn't right. Now I was freezing.

'Chief,' I said, 'Trey and Lydia are still out cold, despite
the racket we're making. Should I call nine-one-one for an
ambulance? They could have alcohol poisoning.'

The chief whipped around and hissed at me, 'Are you always
such a whiny old woman, Richman? Shut up. Just shut up,
until the student wakes them.'

Adam approached the marble divan warily, avoiding step-
ping in a slice of gooey butter cake. The photographers
followed him. Then Adam stopped.

'Hurry up,' the newspaper photographer said with a snarl. 'Shake these overprivileged slugs out of their drunken stupor. I can't spend all day here.'

Adam hesitated just before he touched Trey. The color drained from his face and his hand trembled. 'They're not . . . they're not . . . They're not breathing.'

The photographer spoke with a growl. 'They're out cold. Quit screwing around and wake them up. Now!'

Adam gingerly poked Trey's shoulder with two fingers, and the man's head rolled back, revealing a gaping maw of bloody red tissue and white bone. That movement disturbed Lydia's body, and her head rolled back and nearly fell off.

Adam made a high, shrill sound like a tea kettle boiling, which soon turned into a terrified scream.

'They're dead! They're dead! Both of them. Their throats are cut. Their heads almost came off! That's not a red blanket – it's blood!'

SEVEN

'I'm gonna hurl,' Adam said.

I grabbed the tomb guard's arm and hurled him out the crypt door. 'Not in a crime scene,' I said.

Adam staggered across the sidewalk and made it to the grass alongside the tomb before he erupted.

The words 'crime scene' seemed to wake up Chief Butkus. He went into full police mode. 'Ladies and gentlemen, this is a crime scene,' he said. 'I'd like all of you to exit now.'

They did, with the shell-shocked look of passengers filing off a plane after a rough flight.

'And don't go anywhere,' the chief said. 'I'll need your statements and your shoe prints.'

'Shoe prints.' The TV cameraman snorted like a Clydesdale. 'You've got to be kidding me.' He wore a ragged safari jacket, combat boots and a permanently sour expression. 'Take me first. I have important work.'

'We all have work,' the chief said. 'And nothing is more important than the deaths of those two young people. So you can all wait outside.' He shooed the witnesses out like a flock of chickens, then turned to me.

'Angela, you're on call today. You can handle the death investigation.'

I could also be considered a witness, and that might disqualify me in a bigger jurisdiction, but the Forest had a small staff. We made allowances.

'I'll get my DI case out of my car,' I said. 'Are you going to call Detective Jace Budewitz?'

'Nope. I want the best,' the chief said. 'I'm calling Detective Ray Greiman.'

The best . . . right. The chief's best errand boy. Greiman was the best man when Buttkiss needed someone to fudge a report on an accident caused by some drunken Forest bigwig, or excuse some fat cat's kid who'd been caught breaking windows at the high school. He 'lost' items the chief wanted to disappear. When the chief wanted to play poker, Greiman would call the Butkus's home and claim a work emergency. In return, the chief overlooked Greiman's sloppy investigations and lazy ways.

On the long walk to my car, I tried to suppress my dread. I'd be working a politically difficult case with the worst detective on the force. Being trapped in a tomb with Greiman and two dead bodies was a nightmare in so many ways.

Halloween morning was warming up. It was a crisp sixty degrees and a cheerful sun gilded the sweet-smelling grass. I breathed in the fresh air while I could, then took time to call Chris.

After a warm greeting, I told him the bad news. 'When they opened the tomb this morning, they found Trey and Lydia both dead. Not just dead – slaughtered.'

Chris paused to take in this news. 'You were right.'

'I was, but I don't want to be. I'll be at the crypt all day with Greiman, but at least Nitpicker will be working the case.'

'Promise me you'll come to my place to unwind.'

'Chris, I may need to be alone after this.'

'Angela,' Chris said. 'You can do that here. You can go into the guest room and close the door. I'll bring your dinner on a tray. You don't have to talk to me, but you do need to take better care of yourself. Your evaluation said you were a good worker, but you got too emotionally involved in your cases. You're close to burning out. You need to talk over the bad things. Might as well tell them to me.'

'I'm OK. Really, I am. And it's part of my job to care about people.'

'You care too much,' Chris said. 'Let me tell you about a cop I worked with. His heart bled for every murder victim. He used his personal time to comfort the families. He attended the victims' funerals. He visited the families until he thought they were on the road to recovery.'

'That's a little extreme, but what's wrong with caring?' I asked.

'Some dirt bag assaulted and murdered five-year-old twin girls. Their parents were crushed. The cop worked on his own time to solve the girls' murders, hoping to bring the family closure. He caught the guy. It was some twisted teenager, who wanted to see if he could kill and get away with it.'

'Like Leopold and Loeb?' I said.

'Yes, but they went to jail for killing Bobby Franks. This kid was released after his parents promised to get him counseling. It was too much for the cop. He ate his gun.'

'That's horrible,' I said.

'You're missing the point, Angela. You can care too much. That's what happened to the cop.'

I thought for a moment and finally said, 'You're right. I promise I'll call you when I'm finished.'

'And come over here to see me?' he said.

'Yes.'

It was hard for me to slow down during a case, and after it was closed, I tried to forget about it and stuff the bad memories in the back of my mind. Both bad habits were hard to break.

I hauled my DI case out of my trunk and rolled it toward the crypt. My case looked like any ordinary black rolling suitcase, but it contained the tools of my trade. Among the things packed inside were nitrile gloves, a digital thermometer to measure the air temperature, evidence bags, evidence tape, a point-and-shoot camera, sterilized bed sheets sealed in plastic, and plastic containers that looked like guests of honor at a Tupperware party – except nobody wanted to open those 'burpable' bowls.

By the time I approached the crypt, Patrol Officer Mike Hannigan had taped off the crime scene. He lifted the yellow tape to let me through. I loved it when Mike was on duty. He was a cheerful older uniform with a broad, kind face and loads of good gossip.

'The chief is pissed because he can't reach Greiman this morning,' Mike said.

'Greiman's probably hungover,' I said. 'He was sitting at the chief's table at last night's shindig.'

'Heard Greiman brought a sidewalk stewardess as his date.'

'Trixie isn't a hooker, Mike. She dances at a gentlemen's club. She was a bit scantily clad, but I liked her.'

Mike shook his head. 'A half-naked girlfriend won't help Greiman's career.'

'It might. Chief Butkus certainly enjoyed the view.'

Mike laughed. 'I bet he did. Sign the scene logbook, Angela, and put on these booties, though the scene looks like a herd of buffalo stampeded through.'

As I signed the book, I noted that Detective Jace Budewitz had signed in ahead of me.

To the chief, Jace might be second-best, but he was definitely my first choice. This day just got a whole lot better.

Jace met me at the entrance to the crypt, stooping slightly to keep from hitting his head on the sloping ceiling. His short brown hair wasn't much protection from a bump on the stone surface. Jace had a boyish face and shrewd eyes. Cop's eyes.

'This is a mess, Angela,' Jace said, 'and there's so much blood spatter, you should wear a Tyvek suit for protection.'

I opened my DI case and slipped on the disposable coverall I'd stashed in there, then stuffed eight pairs of gloves in my pockets. I'd change gloves several times during the body examination, to keep from cross-contaminating evidence. I powered up my iPad and followed Jake inside the crypt. It was cold and dank.

A brightly colored magenta head popped up over the bodies splayed on the marble divan. My favorite tech, Sarah 'Nitpicker' Byrne, was working the scene, too. 'You'll definitely need that suit, Angela,' she said. 'That's not pizza sauce splashed everywhere.'

Powerful portable lights had been set up, revealing the scene details. I stopped in my tracks, stunned by the horror.

The weeping angel at the head of the divan, the limestone ceiling, and the walls were painted with blood. More blood had soaked the marble divan, along with the blankets and pillows the victims had brought with them.

On the divan, Trey was holding Lydia in his blood-drenched arms. Both heads had fallen back, revealing deep wounds and yellowish-white bone, but they were still attached to the victims' necks.

'Go ahead,' Jace said. 'We've already taken our photos and video. Your turn.'

I took wide shots, medium and close-up photos with my point-and-shoot camera. These photos would go to the medical examiner's office.

I opened the Death Scene Investigation Form. Jace gave me the case number and I approached the bodies on shaky legs. Just last night, this couple had everything – money, beauty, and a bright future. Now they were three hundred pounds of rotting meat.

Stop! I told myself. Pull yourself together, or you'll never find who killed Trey and Lydia.

I took a deep breath, and concentrated on my professional routine, taking the tomb's ambient temperature. Inside the brick and stone crypt it was a chilly forty-eight degrees, even with the powerful lights.

I started with Lydia first. She was lying on her right side on the tomb's marble divan, Lydia's head pointing north toward the weeping angel with the pizza slice and her feet to the south. She faced Trey. His right arm was around her torso.

I began the body inspection, what we called the actualization. I estimated Lydia's weight at about a hundred pounds and measured her height. She was five feet three.

My examination started with her head. Her blonde hair was drenched in dark red blood and plastered to her head. Her blue eyes stared blankly into eternity. Her tongue was pulled out of her open bloody mouth. Why was it bloody?

'Jace, Nitpicker, what happened to the victim's tongue?'

They moved in for a closer look, and Jace shined a powerful flashlight into Lydia's mouth, revealing expensive dentistry and an ugly cut on her tongue.

Nitpicker spoke first. 'Someone's sliced her tongue from the back down to the tip, splitting it in two pieces.'

'Why would someone make a cut down the middle of Lydia's tongue?' I asked.

Jace shrugged. 'Beats me.'

'It has to mean something.' Nitpicker began reciting phrases using the word 'tongue.'

'On the tip of her tongue?' she said. 'Tongue lashing?'

'This is more like a tongue slashing,' I said.

'Hold your tongue?' she said.

'No, they would have cut it out and stuck it in her hand,' I said.

'Silver tongue?' Jace said.

Nitpicker and I both nixed that one.

'Tongue twister?' Nitpicker said. 'Speak in tongues?'

'No, wait, I've got it,' I said. 'Speak with forked tongue! Isn't that what most people think Lydia did? Lied on the witness stand to save Trey from being convicted of rape?'

'She sure did,' Jace said. 'Even the judge was shocked when Lydia called the poor girl Trey raped . . . excuse me for using the phrase, but it's a direct quote . . . Lydia called her "Susie Spreadlegs."'

'That's disgusting,' I said. 'The poor girl testified she was a virgin. What a horrible first time, drugged and raped in a frat house.'

'I guess Lydia did have a silver tongue,' Nitpicker said, 'but so did Trey's lawyer. He told the judge if Trey was convicted "it would ruin that poor boy's promising future."'

'And what about the poor girl's future?' I asked.

'Last I heard, she dropped out of school,' Nitpicker said. 'She was black and didn't come from a big-deal family.'

None of us said anything. Her mistreatment was an old story in the Forest.

'Let's check Trey before you continue, Angela,' Jace said. 'He has a bloody mouth, too.'

Jace shined his flashlight into Trey's mouth. Something was stuck on his tongue – or rather, stuck *in* his tongue, like it was a pincushion. I moved closer for a look. 'It looks like a fraternity pin,' I said. 'It's enamel with Greek letters in gold. And there are three words along the outside of the pin.'

'Can you see them?' Jace asked.

'Not quite. I don't want to remove the pin, but I have a magnifying glass in my DI case.'

'Go get it, Sherlock,' Nitpicker said.

I quickly found it, and peered closer at the frat pin in Trey's tongue. 'The words are "truth," "honor," and "integrity."'

Nitpicker had the last words: ''Nuff said.'

EIGHT

I t was 11:39 Halloween morning. Exactly twelve hours earlier, I'd watched Trey and Lydia being locked inside a crypt. Now their bloody, butchered bodies were displayed in the Cursed Crypt, an evil tribute to an adulterous warlock who'd lived two centuries ago.

There was no such thing as a curse. I knew that. But the powerful generator lights threw ghostly shadows, and the cobwebs swayed in the slightest breeze. And I needed to get back to work. I was a professional. I didn't believe in spook shows.

After that short, horrific detour, I resumed Lydia's body inspection. I noted there were no wounds on her right side. 'Will you help me turn the decedent so she's on her back?' I asked.

Trey was facing Lydia, and his right arm was around her blood-soaked torso. Jace and Nitpicker gently tried to loosen Trey's arm.

'The arm is starting to stiffen, but it's not quite in complete rigor,' Nitpicker said.

'Rigor mortis sets in at about eight to twelve hours,' I said.

'Full rigor will take longer in this cold tomb,' Nitpicker said. 'Let's be glad it's delayed. This is awkward enough.'

I brought out two white sterilized sheets from my case to spread on the divan. Lydia was first, after we managed to pry Trey's arm off her. We gently rolled her into place on the sheet so her head wouldn't disconnect from her body. Trey got the same careful treatment.

'The killer must have really hated him,' Jace said, 'if he urinated on the victim's body. Is there enough to get a sample?'

After we moved Trey's body, the tech shined her flashlight around the Victorian bier, festooned with marble scrolls and roses. 'Yes, there's a small pool of something in a swag right here.'

'It's starting to dry here, and it's a clear liquid. Might be urine,' I said, 'but I think I can use an eyedropper. I may get enough for DNA.'

I took a sterile eye dropper out of my DI case, and a clean pill bottle with an airtight lid, and collected the small puddle, then sealed the bottle with evidence tape.

'My mom was a housekeeper for old Reggie,' I said. 'She hated polishing his Victorian furniture. I remember her grumbling about it. "All that pointless folderol," she'd say, "and I have to clean those little carvings with a blasted Q-tip. That style is so useless." She'd be happy to know some of it wasn't useless.'

'She'd be happier to know it was baptized in urine,' Nitpicker said, and we both started laughing.

Jace coughed slightly to get our attention. He didn't like giggling at a crime scene. 'What about the female victim?' he asked.

'I don't see any urine,' Nitpicker said, 'but let me look at the bodies under ultraviolet light. We might as well do it here, so we don't lose any evidence.'

Nitpicker put on protective goggles and brought out her UV lights, which looked like black flashlights. 'See the way Trey's body fluoresces pale yellow, especially around the chest,' she said, holding the light. 'The killer urinated on him.'

She turned the lights on Lydia. 'She only has a few splashes.'

I resumed my examination on Lydia, beginning with her wounded tongue. After measuring the longitudinal cut, I noted it as a 'cutlike defect,' three and one-sixteenth inches long. I couldn't say 'cut' in my report, in case something else had disfigured her tongue. That judgement could be disputed in court. Then I took close-up photos of her damaged mouth.

Next, I measured the cutlike defect on her neck. It was eight and a half inches wide. Her throat was slashed from ear to ear. The cut was high on her neck, near the esophagus. It missed the tougher parts of the neck, including the hyoid bone and the cartilage in the larynx. Whatever cut her throat was sharp enough to go through her spinal cord between the C-3 and C-4 vertebrae.

The majority of the cuts were on Lydia's chest. She wore

a plaid shirt that was red before the blood spatter. I counted twenty-seven stab wounds, between two and a half and three inches wide. I knew knife wounds were usually longer than the widest part of the stabbing weapon.

'Look at this, Jace,' I said. 'Lydia has two V-shaped stab wounds in the area around her heart. That means the killer stabbed her and then twisted the instrument.'

Nitpicker winced at my words. Her magenta hair was looking a bit wilted after almost six hours in the tomb.

I found three more stab wounds on her abdomen, but none in her genital area. There wasn't a scratch on her legs and feet. She was wearing socks and tennis shoes.

There were also no stab wounds on her arms and hands. Lydia did not try to fight her killer. I checked her ring finger – the third finger of her left hand. The ring with the massive rock was missing.

'Lydia's engagement ring is gone,' I said. 'She was wearing it last night at the auction, and that sparkler must have cost a pretty penny. Was it stolen, or did she leave it at home when she spent the night in the tomb?'

'I hope the killer swiped her ring,' Jace said, 'and the stone was graded by the GIA. It will have an engraved serial number, and we can trace it.'

'I didn't know the CIA graded rings,' Nitpicker said.

'They don't,' I said. 'Jace was talking about the Gee-I-A, the Gemological Institute of America.' My tongue tangled in the word 'Gemological.'

'Let's hope Trey's family hasn't been rich long enough to have heirloom diamonds,' I said. 'Those can be harder to trace.'

'How big was the ring?' Nitpicker asked.

'Huge. Major bling. Like Liz Taylor bling.'

Jace asked another question to make us focus on the decedent. 'Any sign that the killer yanked off the ring?' Jace asked. 'Any scrapes or wounds on her finger?'

I examined her ring finger with the magnifying glass and said, 'Lydia's hand is so blood-drenched, I can't see anything useful.'

I wasn't allowed to clean her hand, or any other part of her body, and I couldn't remove her clothing for a closer look. 'The medical examiner will have to check when Lydia is cleaned up.'

'I had one scumbag who stole a dead woman's wedding ring set,' Jace said. 'He broke her finger to get the diamond.'

'What a creep. I don't think her finger's broken.' I gently placed both of Lydia's hands in paper bags and sealed them with evidence tape.

It took half an hour to measure and photograph the patches of blood on the front of Lydia's clothes. Everything had to be carefully documented. I knew this case would go to court when the killer was caught.

Nitpicker and Jace helped turn Lydia's body, so I could examine the back part. Blood had seeped into the back of her shirt, and some wounds on her front were so deep the knife had gone right through her slender chest – and through the ribs.

'Look at this,' I said, pointing to her back. 'In two wounds the weapon went all the way through her body.'

'Definitely overkill,' Nitpicker said.

'If that's true, the killer must have hated Trey even more,' I said.

I'd finished with Lydia and moved on to Trey, starting at his head. We'd already examined and documented the pin stuck on his tongue. Now I had the gruesome task of counting Trey's knife wounds. It took nearly ten minutes to find them all in that bloodbath. 'He has thirty-six stab wounds in his chest, and ten in his genital area. He's been stabbed right through his jeans.

'Oh, ho,' I said. 'What's this?' I spotted a hair on Trey's chest. 'Looks like a blond pubic hair. And it may have a root.'

'That could be helpful, if it doesn't belong to Lydia,' Nitpicker said.

'There are no defensive wounds on Trey's hands,' I said. 'He didn't put up a fight to save his life, either. How did the killer subdue the victims without a struggle?'

'We think some of their food or drink may have been drugged,' Jace said. 'All the food and the bottles are going to the lab for testing.'

'And there are a lot of those.' Nitpicker's eyes brightened in the harsh generator lights as she detailed the pair's last meal.

'These two didn't die hungry. They ate two pizzas – except for that pepperoni slice flopped on the angel's head. I found the gnawed bones of the baby back ribs tossed in that corner, like this was some Neanderthal cave.

'All that, and they still kept eating. They had a full order of twenty-four toasted ravioli, and only one measly toasted rav was left in the foam container.'

Toasted ravioli, an appetizer beloved by St. Louisans, were deep-fried ravioli. Cooked right, they were tasty little morsels. Cooked wrong, they turned into fried footballs.

'How do you know there were twenty-four ravioli?' I asked.

'I counted the fancy toothpicks,' Nitpicker said.

'And the couple were just getting started on their food binge. They ate half a blueberry gooey butter cake.' A swoon-worthy concoction of butter and sugar, gooey butter cake was a coronary on a plate.

'On top of that, they polished off six sea salt truffles,' Nitpicker said. 'For some reason, Trey or Lydia took one bite out of the dark chocolate bark and left the rest. I guess they were finally full. Left some prints in the warm chocolate, too.'

'Take those prints,' Jace said. 'And check the chocolate for DNA. Just in case the killer was hungry.'

We knew killers sometimes ate at crime scenes. A few even fixed themselves a sandwich. Murder must be hungry work.

'Trey and Lydia definitely laid down a base of food before they guzzled everything in sight,' Nitpicker said. 'The two of them demolished ten bottles of beer, a bottle of tequila, and two and a half bottles of Merlot.'

'Good lord,' I said. 'If I didn't see all the stab wounds, I'd figure they'd died from eating and drinking everything.'

'Not everything,' Nitpicker said. 'They planted the six-pack of water in the other angel's wings, and probably never opened the Thermos of hot coffee.'

'Any signs that they were sick?' Jace asked. 'From over-eating, or poison?'

'Nope. Nothing. Though they did use the camping toilet,

and someone, I'm guessing Trey, had a very shaky aim,' Nitpicker said. 'Can't wait to sort through that. It looks like once those two passed out, the stabbing started.'

'Jace, do you think there was one killer or two?' I asked.

'Looks like one,' Jace said. 'But that's a guess.'

'Judging by the force of the blood spatter,' I said, 'the killer must have hit the victims' arteries. Have you found a weapon?'

'Nothing in here,' Nitpicker said. 'The uniforms are searching the grounds, but they haven't turned up anything yet. I'm guessing the killer took it with him.'

'Do you think Trey and Lydia were attacked because he challenged the Du Pres family?' I asked.

'I heard about that,' Jace said. 'Trey's words are the talk of the Forest. But why kill Lydia?'

'They were engaged,' I said. 'He proposed after he was acquitted of rape. Lydia would join him as they became the new rulers of the Forest, the new blood. When she lied to save Trey, she saved her own future.'

'Or not,' Nitpicker said. 'The only future those two have is six feet under.'

'That scene at the auction means I'll have to talk to Reggie Du Pres.' Jace looked weary.

'Buttkiss won't like that,' Nitpicker said. 'The chief owes his job to old man Du Pres.'

'That's too darn bad,' Jace said. He rarely cursed, which made him a figure of fun at the station.

'We all know this is a politically sensitive case,' I said. 'Even the chief.'

'Right now, we have nothing,' Jace said. 'There's no other way in or out of here. Yet somehow, someone got into a locked and bolted crypt while a guard stood outside the whole time.'

'Guards,' I said. 'There was more than one.'

'Maybe a guard fell asleep,' Nitpicker said.

'Doesn't make any difference. A camera was trained on the crypt door all night until it was officially opened at six o'clock this morning. In front of dozens of witnesses. Worse, the press was there when the crypt was unlocked.'

'And you know what the press is going to call this,' I said.

'A locked tomb mystery.'

NINE

Trey and Lydia left the Cursed Crypt in black body bags. The challengers to Chouteau Forest's power were carted out like rejected packages. I signed the paperwork and handed it to the morgue conveyance, to preserve the chain of custody. The brutalized bodies would be delivered to the medical examiner's office.

Once the bodies were gone, I photographed the white marble divan covering Mean Gene's final resting place. It was stained a deep rust red. I noted that nothing had been under the bodies except more blood, and measured the areas.

'I hope some of this blood belongs to the killer,' I said.

'I doubt it.' Jace was running his fingers through his short hair. He still had a cobweb clinging to his ear. I pulled it off. Ick. The unwanted webs were everywhere.

'The victims didn't fight back,' he said. 'Unless the killer accidentally cut himself while he was stabbing them, there isn't much chance we'll find his blood.'

'What did you think of the pumpkin?' I asked.

Jace smiled at me. 'The ones the students carved? Pretty cool. I wish my boy could have seen them. They must have looked amazing last night when they were lit.'

'No, I mean the pumpkin with the death threat on it.'

'The what?' Jace stared at me.

'Last night, after the auction, Chris and I took the path from the Forest Inn to this campus for the closing ceremony. The fourth pumpkin from the end of the walk was way bigger than the others. It had the crypt's wrought-iron doors carved on it. One door was open, and we could see the tomb's interior, cobwebs and all. The message under the carving said, *Mean Gene will not sleep alone. Tonight, two will join him – permanently!*'

Jace looked gobsmacked. 'That's a death threat.'

'I thought so. I photographed the pumpkin with my cell phone and Chris told the chief about it. We insisted Buttkiss show the photos to Trey and Lydia. The chief treated the whole episode like a joke. He actually said, "Angela, if you weren't so darn pretty, I wouldn't put up with you."'

'What a jerk,' Jace said. 'He should have stopped those two from going into the tomb.'

'And mess up the Forest's biggest fundraiser? In front of all the local fat cats? No way. After the chief quit laughing, he made me promise to show up at six this morning when the crypt was unlocked so I could "see just how silly" – his words – my idea was.'

'Did he show the photos to the victims?' Jace asked.

'Yes. I insisted. Didn't do any good. They all thought it was a big joke.'

'Yeah, well, nobody's laughing now.' Jace looked grim. His face turned darker when I showed the detective the photos I'd taken with my cell phone.

'That's the first I've seen this,' he said. 'Buttkiss didn't mention it, that son of a—' He caught himself and finished, 'that son of a gun.'

'You can blow off steam with a good loud "son of a bitch,"' I said. 'I don't care.'

Jace shook his head. 'I'm trying to set a good example for my eight-year-old son. He's at that stage where he and his friends think cuss words are cool.'

'You're right. I should clean up my language, anyway.'

'I'm not criticizing you, Angela. I know I'm laughed at because I try not to cuss.'

'So what?' I said. 'You don't need to drop F-bombs to be tough. Do you know the story of the most famous four-letter word in history? My dad told me when I went through my cussing phase. It happened in World War II during the Battle of the Bulge. The 101st Airborne Division was trapped in a little town. They were outnumbered, outgunned, and out of almost everything – food, ammunition, medical supplies. The Germans demanded the Americans surrender. The US general answered with one four-letter word, "Nuts!"'

'Is that true?' Jace asked.

'Yes. You can look it up. Brigadier General Anthony McAuliffe used that word.'

'Man, that's class. I'll have to tell my son. Let's get out of this tomb and take a look at that pumpkin.'

As I turned toward the entrance, I walked into a massive cobweb, gray and dirty. It covered my head and shoulders like a filthy cape.

Nitpicker poked her head up and howled while I swatted at the cobweb and stomped it into the dusty tomb floor. 'You look like the Bride of Frankenstein,' she said.

'It's not funny,' I said. 'I could get bitten by a spider.' I sounded snappish. I could deal with dead bodies, but spiders creeped me out.

'Cobwebs don't have spiders,' Nitpicker said. 'Do you know the difference between a cobweb and a spider web?'

Jace and I shook our heads.

'Dust,' she said. 'Cobwebs are *abandoned* spider webs. When the web gets too dusty, it's not sticky enough to attract bugs, so the spider takes off and builds a new, better web somewhere else. The old web hangs around, collecting dust.'

'Just so the spider moves to another neighborhood.' I brushed the grimy web off my white protective suit.

'Huh,' Jace said. 'Let's get out of here and go see that killer pumpkin.'

'Have fun, guys.' Nitpicker sounded wistful. She brushed a thick cobweb off her face and said, 'I'm still working shoe prints. And while I think of it, Angela, let me step outside with you and get your prints.'

The entrance of the crypt was quiet now – almost as quiet as a tomb. (I couldn't resist that.) The three of us moved away from the entrance and patted and brushed the cobwebs off our protective suits. We looked like three dingy snowmen.

Mike, the uniform keeping track of the crime scene log, waved to us and held up a big foam cup of coffee.

'Hot coffee,' he said. 'Come and get it. The university just sent it over, along with oatmeal cookies. There's enough for everybody – and cold water, too.'

We crowded around the big coffee container like cats at feeding time, all craving our caffeine infusion. Once we had downed the coffee, we each took a bottle of cold water and a couple of cookies and sat on a nearby bench. The fresh air and bright sun lifted our spirits.

Nitpicker drank her water in two gulps. 'This is thirsty work.'

Her face was smeared with dirt, like a little kid's. I poured water on a napkin and said, 'You might want to wipe off your face.' The damp napkin was gray when Nitpicker finished cleaning her face.

'Blasted cobwebs,' she said.

'Think of them as blighted housing waiting for demolition,' I said.

When we finished our break, I asked Nitpicker, 'How are you taking my shoe prints?'

'Old school,' she said. 'My scanner is out of commission, and someone ran off with my spare, so I'm inking the bottom of the shoes. Except for that TV cameraman, who thought he was such a big deal. I seized his boots. Said I couldn't ink them.'

'Tick off the police, and they will make your life interesting,' I said.

'He deserved it,' Jace said. 'I asked for a copy of his tape when we opened the tomb, and he said he needed a warrant. That's standard procedure for the media, but he gave me a ten-minute lecture about freedom of the press.'

'He had holes in his socks, too,' Nitpicker said. 'He'll get his boots back when he turns over the tape.

'But you, my good friend, Angela, will get the quick and dirty treatment.'

I slipped off my crime scene booties and untied my shoes. Nitpicker came back with her kit. Now she was gloved up.

'I'm using fingerprint ink on a roller,' she said, her voice – apparently warmed by the spider sermon – was deepening into full lecture mode. 'I'm putting a small blob of what is basically printer's ink on this paper to get an even spread.'

Jace and I ate more cookies while she demonstrated her technique, then held the inky paper up long enough to make sure the boneheads in the back row – that was Jace and me – could take it in.

'Now I have to roll the ink smooth and thin.' Nitpicker's tone in its full 'now class' zone. 'In the old days, before my time, the cops would press or roll fingers in that ink before they were transferred to the standard ten-print card.'

'Oh.' Jace shifted on the bench.

'Um.' I took a long sip of water.

'Now I'm using this inked roller to apply ink to the sole of your shoe, Angela.' Nitpicker was cheerfully oblivious to our fidgeting. 'Then I'll press the shoe to a sheet of paper. When it's finished, I can apply the inked print to a sheet of clear plastic and use it as an overlay on the shoe print.'

At this point Jace and I were silently debating – yes, I could read his mind, or at least his body language – who's going to be the first to say, 'We love you, Nitpicker, but we've got a couple of gruesome murders to solve. Enough forensics one-oh-one!'

Nitpicker, maybe sensing she was losing her audience, put away her symbolic pointer and handed me back my inked shoes. We all dusted the cookie crumbs off our clothes and threw our bottles and cups in the trash. Nitpicker went back inside the tomb.

Jace and I strolled off to find the pumpkin with the death threat. We were in no hurry to get back inside that cobwebby crypt.

'It's on that walkway, Jace.' I pointed out the direction. 'See where the pumpkins begin?'

The pumpkins were starting to shrivel a bit around the eyes and mouth, but they still looked good. Under the cover of tonight's Halloween darkness, they'd be restored to their previous glory.

'OK,' I said. 'It's the row of pumpkins on the east side. It should be the fourth pumpkin from the top here.'

We counted down, until we came to that pumpkin.

And saw an ordinary jack-o'-lantern. It mocked us with its empty-eyed grin.

'What? It's gone!' I opened my phone and showed Jace a wide shot. 'See, there's the first pumpkin, then the second, and the third. The death-threat pumpkin should be right here.'

Except it wasn't.

I pointed to the spot where the orange imposter laughed at me. I wanted to kick it in its teeth.

'Maybe the one you saw last night was vandalized,' Jace said.

We did a quick check of the lawn, the trash bins, and the nearby foliage. Nothing.

'Nope,' I said. 'It's gone.'

Jace looked furious. 'Aw, son of a—'

He stopped and said, 'Nuts!'

TEN

Nitpicker greeted Jace and me at the entrance of the crypt as if she was welcoming us home.

'Did you find the Great Pumpkin?' she asked.

'That's in the Peanuts cartoons,' I said.

Nitpicker looked at me blankly. She was wearing cobwebs like lace trimming.

'You know, Snoopy.' I waved my arms. 'The Great Pumpkin rises from the pumpkin patch on Halloween evening, and flies around bringing toys to children.'

'Like Santa, only orange,' she said.

'Right. This pumpkin was far more sinister. It has a death threat carved on it.'

I showed Nitpicker the photos I'd taken on my cell phone. She whistled. 'Definitely a gruesome gourd. What took you two so long?' Nitpicker gave us a mock frown and demanded, 'Were you trying to breathe air that wasn't filtered through cobwebs? I feel like I'm wearing them.'

'You are.' I brushed a thick clump off her forehead. It left an ugly gray smear. I didn't even attempt to remove the others. We'd be there for an hour.

'We were searching for the threatening pumpkin,' Jace said.

'I don't know how you can say that with a straight face,' Nitpicker said.

'Whatever you want to call it, the pumpkin is gone,' he said. 'Vanished. Now the uniforms are doing a grid search of the grounds, but I don't think they'll find it.'

'I'm about finished here,' Nitpicker said.

'I'm ready to pack it in, too.' I turned for my case and a thick, dirty web dropped from the ceiling and landed on my head. Ugh. I couldn't see. I fought with the creepy veil, and stumbled over Nitpicker's kit. My arms windmilled wildly. I grabbed the nearest angel wing, and hung on. The marble wing stopped me from falling, but I heard a grinding, grating sound, and a surprised screech from Nitpicker.

'The wall! It's moving!' she shouted.

Still blinded by the web, I said, 'Is the crypt falling down?' That's all we needed, to be trapped in this tomb. I struggled to pull the cobweb off my face.

'I've got you.' Jace grabbed my arm, steadied me, and used his pocket handkerchief to clean the mess off my face. Now I could see that I'd grabbed the Pizza Angel, and her wing was pulled sideways. I'd dislocated it.

'Oh, no. Did I break the angel?'

The weeping angel, already humiliated by the greasy pizza slice on her head, gazed sorrowfully at the bloody tomb.

Would the curse follow me now, if I'd offended Mean Gene? I tried to brush that thought away like a cobweb, but it was too sticky. Don't be ridiculous, I told myself.

'No, you didn't break the angel,' Jace said. 'You unlocked a secret passage. Look! The marble slab moved.'

Behind the Pizza Angel, the marble slab on the wall proclaimed the tomb was 'Sacred to the memory of Eugene Franco Cortini, scholar, teacher, and researcher.' Now the heavy slab had slid sideways, revealing a passage, a rectangle maybe three feet square.

'Cool,' Nitpicker said. 'A secret passage. Just like in the movies.'

Nitpicker and I were both on our hands and knees at the tunnel entrance, exploring the dimensions of the passage with our flashlights. 'We can't stand up in it,' she said. 'But it seems to stop about six feet down.'

'Great,' I said. 'Six feet by six feet under.' The thought made me shiver. I was feeling claustrophobic in the cobweb-draped tomb.

My flashlight beam caught the passage's walls and ceiling. They appeared to be shored up with thick timbers. The secret passage looked like photos of nineteenth-century mining tunnels, and cobwebs were draped everywhere except straight down the middle of the tunnel. The floor was dark dirt, and seemed slightly moist.

'Let's take a look,' I said.

'Wait!' Nitpicker said. 'There's a shoe print. Right over the threshold.' She examined it with her flashlight. 'And there's blood on it. This is not your usual Nike or Adidas print. It has lots of tiny little diamonds. There's a brand name in cursive on the arch, but it's smeared. Further on, I see what looks like hand and knee prints from someone crawling.'

'Jeez. How are you going to work in that narrow space?' I asked.

'Carefully.'

Nitpicker saw my face and burst out laughing. 'Sorry. Couldn't resist. I'm going to work the scene a little bit at a time, on my hands and knees, and use oblique lighting to highlight the tiny ridges in that shoe print when I photograph it.'

'What's oblique lighting?' I asked.

'It's side lighting that fills in an area that would normally be shadowed.'

My face must have shown my confusion, because she said, 'Ever have the early morning sunshine through a window and highlight every frigging speck of dust on a table? Each speck casts a shadow. That's oblique lighting.'

I nodded. 'Got it. What are you going to do about the blood in the shoe print?'

'Document the print as we found it, then photograph it and collect a tiny sample for DNA. The soil is dark, so I'll enhance the shoe print with BlueStar and photograph it again.'

I knew in some police departments, including ours, BlueStar had replaced the Luminol that TV shows were so fond of. The police found it easier to use.

'Then I'll cast the shoe print,' Nitpicker said. 'We can use good old Dental Stone.'

Yep, like the stuff your dentist uses to make casts of your teeth from impressions.

'I can help,' I said. 'I'm on call until six this evening, so unless I get called out on a case, I'll stick around.'

She put me to work as her lighting assistant inside the tunnel. Nitpicker used an L-shaped ruler to measure the shoe print in the soil. The ruler was in the photos to give them the right scale. We crawled through the cramped tunnel, stopping every few inches to cast and photograph knee prints and handprints.

After an hour spent mostly on my hands and knees, I said, 'I have to stretch. My back is killing me.'

'Mine, too,' Nitpicker said. 'Let's go outside and get some air. What do you say we get rid of these hot, sweaty suits?'

When we changed out of the suits, we saw Jace at the end of sidewalk talking to Mike, who was still keeping the logbook. Jace waved us over and handed us water bottles from a cooler. Nitpicker and I drank thirstily while Jace talked to us.

'The last of the uniforms reported in. No sign of the threatening pumpkin.'

'Too bad,' I said. 'It only exists in my photos.'

'At least you were smart enough to take photos and tell me about them,' he said. 'That's more than I can say for Chief Buttkiss.'

'Have you seen the note that came with a basket of goodies?' I asked.

'No. What now?' Jace looked annoyed.

'Right before Trey and Lydia were locked in the tomb, there was a surprise delivery from Tara's Taste of the Forest. A huge basket stuffed with local goodies, from gooey butter cake to baby back ribs.'

'And those two tossed the gnawed ribs in a corner, like cavemen,' Nitpicker said. 'No respect.'

Jace frowned. He didn't appreciate the interruption. 'Let's get back to this deliveryman, Angela. Did you see him?'

'Yes. He looked to be in his early twenties, maybe a college student. He had thick, dark curly hair tipped blond.'

'What's his name?' Jace asked.

'Don't know. He didn't say. But he drove a lime-green Kia. How many of those are around here?

'The deliveryman handed the couple an envelope and said the message out loud so we could all hear it: "Congratulations, Lydia and Trey. Glad you're finally getting what you deserve!"'

'In light of what happened, that message sounds ominous.' I realized how stupid that sounded, but Jace didn't snark at me.

'No kidding,' he said. 'Nitpicker, did you find the note in the crypt?'

'Yes,' she said. 'There wasn't much left in the basket except empty wrappers, and I photographed them all. The note was at the bottom. I photographed everything and bagged them. They will all be sent to the lab for processing. Hope the lab finds some prints.'

'That's a start,' Jace said. 'I'm ready for lunch. Let's order. I'll have it delivered.'

Mike wanted a meatball sandwich, but the rest of us couldn't stomach anything with red sauce – or catsup – after working that crime scene.

Soon we were sitting on the sun-warmed concrete benches, crunching our salads, while Mike tried not to slop tomato sauce on his uniform. 'Wish I'd chosen the rabbit food,' he said, taking the last of the napkins.

We tossed the remains of our lunch in the trash, and Nitpicker and I put on fresh protective suits. Soon we were back in the tunnel in the underground tomb, working our way steadily to the end. We worked a little faster now that we were refreshed by the food and water. We were about eighteen inches from the end, when Nitpicker made her first major find since the shoe print at the entrance.

The tunnel seemed barely big enough to contain her excitement. She pointed her flashlight at the beam almost over our heads. 'Look at this! Hair! On this crossbeam! Three of them, all short and brown.'

'Have they been there a while?' I asked.

'Nope, the underside of the beam looks clean and the hair is snagged on a splinter.'

She bagged the hair.

Half an hour later, we finally reached the wooden wall at the end of the tunnel. It had once been painted white.

'Thank goodness, this tunnel is almost over,' she said.

Nitpicker took extra time to photograph the wall. 'The paint is peeling off the wood,' she said. 'I'll try to print the wall, but I don't think we'll have much luck.'

I handed her the print kit. She gently touched the wall, and it swung open.

'It's a door,' she said.

'To a room.'

ELEVEN

Before Nitpicker and I could explore the newly discovered room, I heard Jace yell, 'Angela, your cell phone is ringing.'

I'd left it outside with Mike the cop. No way would I get cellular coverage in a crypt.

'Who is it?' I asked, carefully backing out of the tunnel and away from the tantalizing mystery.

'Detective Ray Greiman,' Jace said.

'Aw, nuts!' I was starting to like that vintage expletive.

Once I was at the crypt entrance, Jace handed me the phone. Greiman gave me his usual friendly greeting. 'Richman, what took you so long? Where the hell are you?'

'Chouteau University,' I said. 'Wish you were here.' In the tomb, I thought. Permanently.

'Well, get your ass over here. We've got a fatal car accident at Weston Place. A hiker called it in.'

'A hiker called in a car accident?'

'Is there an echo? That's what I said.' Greiman gave me detailed directions.

As I stripped out of my sweaty protective suit, I told Jace, 'I have a fatal accident at the entrance to Weston Place, right off Gravois. I'm still on call.'

Nitpicker had crawled out of the tunnel and joined us. 'It's four thirty, Jace, and we're looking at another major job in that new room. I'd like to tackle it fresh tomorrow.'

'Fine,' he said. 'I'll station a uniform outside the tomb.'

'We'll need one inside, too,' Nitpicker said. 'Looks like there may be an opening at the other end of the room. There's probably another entrance to that crypt.'

'I'll get two uniforms,' Jace said. 'One can stay outside and the other can spend the night inside the crypt.'

I was rolling my DI case toward the crypt entrance when I saw Jace with Pete, a recent hire built like a mountain range.

Jace told the uniform, 'Yes, you have to spend the whole night in here.' Pete looked green, and not because he was new.

Jace tried joking. 'The last people who spent the night there paid more than a million dollars for that privilege.'

'And they woke up dead,' Pete said.

I smothered a laugh. Was the muscular newbie's voice quavering? Surely the man mountain couldn't be afraid.

Jace showed no sympathy. 'Then you'd better stay alert, Pete. Drink lots of coffee.'

Personally, I didn't blame Pete for feeling uneasy. I wouldn't stay all night in that creepy crypt if you *paid* me a million dollars.

On the drive to the accident scene, I thanked whoever watched over death investigators that I didn't have to work the crypt homicide with careless, uncooperative Greiman. Soon I was at Weston Place, a private street off Gravois, the main artery through the Forest. The street's entrance was surrounded by cop cars and other official vehicles. I parked my car on the gravel shoulder. Now I could see tire tracks ripping through the well-kept sod and down a steep embankment. The tracks disappeared in a stand of oak.

Detective Greiman walked carefully toward my car, as if the ground might give way underneath him. With his pale, unshaven face and wrinkled shirt, he looked hungover.

'Hi, Ray.' I was annoyingly cheerful. 'I enjoyed meeting your girlfriend, Trixie, last night.'

'She's not my girlfriend.' His voice was somewhere between a snarl and a mumble.

I popped the trunk and hauled out my DI case.

'Well, she made quite an impression,' I said.

Ray glared at me.

OK, I'd tormented him enough. 'Where's the car?'

He pointed down the embankment. 'About fifty feet into the woods. Car wrapped itself around a tree. Driver must have died instantly, sometime last night.'

'Why last night?'

'The driver's watch stopped at twelve minutes past twelve and he's in full rigor.'

Rigor often took eight to twelve hours to set in.

I carefully made my way down the treacherous slope, my feet slipping in the grass until I reached level ground, then followed the tire tracks into the woods. The car had crashed through a clump of poison sumac, a dangerously pretty plant. Now that it was fall, the leaves had turned bright red and yellow. A poison sumac rash was worse than poison ivy, and every part of that plant was poisonous to humans – the leaves, bark and berries.

When I rounded the poison sumac clump, I saw the tiny car, crushed like a used candy wrapper against the oak. The death car was a lime-green Kia. I moved closer. The driver's door was hanging open, and a man had been dragged out on to the damp ground. He was somewhere in his early twenties. He was lying on his side, and his body was contorted into a sitting position. His dark, curly hair was tipped with blond. Was he the deliveryman from last night? The one who brought the big basket of food from Tara's Taste of the Forest to the crypt?

'Hey, Greiman, I think I've seen this dead man before.'

'Well, what's his name? We didn't find any ID on him.'

'I don't know his name. But at the final ceremony last night, before the crypt was sealed, I think this is the same guy who delivered the basket of treats from Tara's. Don't you remember?'

'I'm not in the habit of noticing delivery people.' Greiman's haughty tone made him sound like a Forest dowager.

'How about if I call Jace?' I said. 'He already caught the double murder in the crypt. This death may be related.'

'So you're going to hand over my case to your boyfriend, Jace?'

I shrugged, pretending I didn't care about getting Jace here. 'Hey, no skin off my nose. If you want to do the paperwork, help yourself.'

I kept my head down, studying the Vehicle Related Death form on my iPad, while Greiman stayed silent, possibly holding a lengthy internal debate. Finally, he said, 'Go ahead and call him. I'm leaving.'

I had to fight to keep from cheering. I kept my voice flat. 'If that's what you want. Let me make sure Jace hasn't gone home yet.'

Jace had been finishing up at the crypt scene. When I said the accident death might be connected with the crypt homicide, Jace said he was on his way.

'Jace is ten minutes out,' I said.

'Fine. You interview the witness, then.' Greiman sounded like a petulant child. 'She's over there. Name's Roberta Hixson.'

He pointed toward a tall, spindly woman in a khaki sunhat and pants and sturdy hiking boots. She was leaning against a police car at the top of the embankment, drinking from a reusable water bottle.

As I hiked back up the hill, I saw that Roberta was in her vigorous early sixties. Her gray hair was pulled into a bun, which emphasized her long, patrician face.

'Call me Bobbie,' she said, after I introduced myself. 'I live on Weston Place. I was hiking in the woods this afternoon, when I found that unfortunate man in the green car.'

'What time did you find him?'

'About three forty-five,' she said.

'Did you move the body?' I asked.

'Yes. I thought I heard a noise inside the car and hoped he might still be alive. I dragged him out, but he was dead. Poor fellow. He looks so young.'

'Do you know him?'

Bobbie shook her head. 'I've never seen him before. After I called nine-one-one, I checked for a wallet, but didn't find one. His back pocket, where most men keep their wallets, was pulled inside-out. Do you think his wallet was stolen?'

'It's certainly worth noting,' I said. 'I'm glad you're so observant. Did you notice anything else?'

'Yes. Although the car was wrapped around the tree, the driver's side door was open. The car was badly damaged, and I wondered if someone had pried the door open before I got there. Otherwise, I would have had a difficult time opening the car. I thought there might be pry marks in the paint, but I guess you'll need an expert to determine that.'

'Did you hear any unusual sounds last night or this morning?'

'No. These houses are so big, I can't hear my husband when he's on the first floor.'

Bobbie wasn't bragging. That was a Forest fact. The older mansions were large and well insulated.

Bobbie agreed to write a statement, and I left her working on it inside a police car. By that time, Jace arrived, looking weary and rumpled, but he greeted me with a smile, then wiped the sweat off his forehead with his tie. He'd used his pocket handkerchief to clean the spider webs off my face.

As we carefully made our way back down that hill, I filled Jace in on what I knew. 'So you're thinking we may be looking at a third murder tied to the Cursed Crypt,' he said.

'From some of the details the witness Bobbie gave us, we might.'

I carefully steered Jace around the clump of poison sumac. He was a city boy who barely recognized poison ivy. Finally, we reached the crumpled car.

Jace whistled. 'That car is smashed.'

'I'm pretty sure this is the car and driver who delivered the goodies to the crypt closing ceremony,' I said. 'But I don't see any sign for "Tara's Taste of the Forest."'

'It could have been one of those magnetic signs,' Jace said, 'but it should be around here somewhere.'

'Along with the victim's missing wallet,' I said.

While Jace examined the car and the area around it, I started the death investigation, noting the time, weather conditions, ambient temperature (eighty-eight degrees), and location. Insects, nature's clean-up squad, had begun their work, and I had to fight buzzing flies and a parade of ants. I gloved up, photographed the decedent, and then began the investigation.

I noted that the decedent had been removed from the wrecked vehicle, and was lying on his right side on the ground, his head pointing east and his feet west. The body was in full rigor and in the sitting position.

His demographic information, from his name to his age and address, were unknown. I estimated his age in his early to mid-twenties and his weight at about one hundred forty pounds. He was five feet seven inches tall. In other words, about average. He wore a blue plaid cotton shirt, khaki pants, loafers and no socks. There was no jewelry on his body. I did not smell any alcohol on the body. The medical examiner would test the victim's blood.

Purple and red marks ringed his neck, signs of strangulation. So were his puffy, swollen face and open, bulging eyes. I could see tiny red spots in the white part of his eyes, known as petechial hemorrhages. Strangulation had left a groove around his neck 1.8 inches wide, about the width of a seatbelt.

I measured the long, deep cuts on his face and hands, and the areas of blood. Three fingers on his right hand were broken. He had no blood on his feet, and no mud or grass on the bottom of his shoes.

I spread out a clean, sterile sheet and Jace helped me turn the body. There was blood in the decedent's hair from the head wounds. I noticed another scrape and contusion on the left side of his neck. I lifted his shirt and saw the contusion crossed his chest and stopped at his right hip. Classic signs of a seatbelt injury.

I walked over to Jace, who was examining the car's inside. 'I think our victim may have been strangled with his seatbelt.'

Jace pulled his head out of the car and said, 'That could explain why the seatbelt on the passenger side was cut out.' He pointed toward the missing seatbelt with a gloved finger.

'The cut seatbelt wasn't near the decedent,' I said.

'I'll have the uniforms do a grid search for the seatbelt and the door sign,' Jace said.

'The decedent could have survived the accident and then someone strangled him,' I said. 'Did the airbags deploy in this car?'

'No. They were either disabled or stolen. I've been looking for a VIN.' The VIN, or vehicle identification number, was in several spots in cars.

He pointed to the broken windshield. 'Looks like someone pried the VIN plate off the top of the dashboard, where it meets the windshield.'

Next, he showed me the driver's side doorjamb. 'They did a good job of ruining the certification label here. That also has the VIN. But they weren't quite smart enough. The VIN is also under the hood, punched on the front sidewall of the engine bay. I'll have the wreck towed and taken apart when we're finished.'

'Find any of the usual trash you find in cars – fast-food wrappers, gas or grocery receipts, soda bottles?' I asked.

'Not a thing,' Jace said. 'Someone jimmied open the glove box and cleaned it out.'

'So are we looking at a thief?'

'Either that, or the driver was murdered,' Jace said.

TWELVE

At six o'clock, I handed over the mysterious body from the green car to the morgue van, along with the paperwork. My job was finished – twelve hours after I entered the Cursed Crypt, I'd processed three gruesome murders. What the hell was happening in the Forest?

I called Chris, and said I was near my house, but my lover insisted that I stay at his place. 'I know you're tired, Angela, but you shouldn't be alone. Not after the day you've had.'

'I'm not much company. I want to crawl into bed and pull the covers over my head.'

'You can do that here. You don't have to be good company. But you know damn well you'll burn out if you don't take care of yourself. You get too involved in your cases.'

'But—' I started to protest.

His voice turned firm. 'Angela, this is no time to be stubborn. You promised. Get over here. Please.'

'Well . . .'

He used the ultimate threat. 'If you don't stay here tonight, I'll tell Katie.'

'I'm on my way.'

Dr Katie Kelly Stern was my best friend and the Forest's assistant medical examiner. Katie was constantly after me to take better care of myself. The last thing I wanted was for Katie to unleash that razor wit on me.

Fifteen minutes later I was at Chris's condo. He met me at his door with a kiss and a glass of wine. 'Sit and relax in the living room,' he said. 'Have a snack and then tell me about your day.'

Chris's living room was done in basic bachelor: a cushy black leather sofa, a sleek leather recliner, stadium-sized TV screen and state-of-the-art sound system. And books. Lots of books, from fiction to criminology.

On his coffee table, he had a cheese board and small plates.

I put a generous chunk of white Cheddar on a water cracker and took a cluster of green grapes. The cheese and crackers were just what I needed.

Chris fixed himself a plate, sat next to me and sipped his wine while I ate. When I felt revived enough to talk, I told him about my day.

'Sounds horrible,' he said.

'It was. I didn't like the two victims, Trey and Lydia, but no one deserves to die like that.'

'Do you think the delivery guy in the green car was part of the plot?'

'Haven't the foggiest. But someone definitely wanted him dead. The killer took that man's life and his identity. And inside the tomb, there was blood everywhere. It was a nightmare.'

Tears welled up in my eyes, and I fought them. To my horror, I burst out crying. Chris wrapped me in his arms. 'It's OK to cry, Angela.'

'I hate crying. Hate it. It's weak.'

He sighed. 'Where did you get that idea? Why do you think it's weak?'

'It's what girls do.'

'You're a woman. You're human. And humans have feelings. What makes you think you're better than the rest of us?'

'I don't. I just expect better from myself.'

He rocked me and soothed me, and I must have fallen asleep in his arms, because the next thing I knew, he was carrying me upstairs.

'Where are we going?' I asked.

'To bed. Do you want to sleep in the guest bedroom where you'll be alone?'

I was grateful for his question, but I didn't want to leave the warm comfort of his arms. 'No, I want to sleep with you.'

He carried me to his bed. I dropped my clothes in a pile, and snuggled into the cool, fresh sheets. Chris joined me, and I put my arms around him and he kissed me, a sweet, honeyed kiss with a touch of fire, and soon we weren't sleeping at all. My sad, deadly day ended with us celebrating life.

*   *   *

I woke up in a panic, remembering I was on call last night. Chris had left my work cell phone on the nightstand. I quickly checked it, and felt a wave of relief. No calls. Everyone in the Forest had stayed alive while I'd slept. It was seven o'clock, and Chris was already downstairs. I showered, dressed in jeans and a comfortable T-shirt that I kept at his place, and followed the fragrance of hot coffee downstairs to the kitchen. Chris met me with a lingering kiss.

'You look much better this morning,' he said.

I smiled, stretched and said, 'I am better, thanks to you.'

He handed me a cup of hot coffee. 'What would you like for breakfast: scrambled eggs with cheese, or French toast or waffles?'

'Eggs with cheese,' I said.

I set the table on his balcony. It was a fine autumn day, and the trees around Chris's condo looked like they were on fire: the leaves were flame-red, orange and yellow. I made toast and brought out a big bowl of fresh strawberries. Soon Chris arrived with two plates of eggs, and we sat at the table. The eggs were creamy with melted cheese and I demolished my breakfast in short order.

'Delicious,' I said. 'Thank you so much.'

'More? You didn't eat dinner last night.'

'No, thanks. I'd better check in with Jace.' I put my cell phone on speaker so Chris could hear the conversation.

Jace answered right away. 'Angela, we've been working since six this morning. Would you mind helping Nitpicker work the rest of the tunnel?'

'No, I'm curious about it, too. But I'm on call today.'

'I checked with your boss, Evarts Evans, and he says you can help me unless there's another DI case.' We were a small department, and often had to make informal lending arrangements.

'Wear something cool,' he said. 'You'll be in a protective suit all day. Oh, and Mike will escort you in.'

'Why?'

'Where have you been? The media has gone crazy. They're calling it "The Locked Tomb Mystery."'

'So predictable.'

'It's not funny, Angela. You'll have to dodge reporters from the *New York Times*, the *Washington Post* and *USA Today*. Along with Fox News, CNN, CBS and the locals. I'm texting you Mike's cell number. Let him know when you arrive and he'll bring you in.'

'See you shortly at the Cursed Crypt.' I wasn't looking forward to the media scrum.

On the way out the door, Chris handed me a foam cooler bristling with bottles of ice water, a pack of wet naps and a big bag of chocolate chip cookies. 'That should get you through till lunch,' he said. 'What else do you need?'

'I need another rolling suitcase,' I said. 'The media is crawling all over the place. I can't be photographed with a bag of cookies.'

He quickly repacked the treats in a small suitcase and rolled it to my car. I slipped on my white protective suit.

'Call me if you need anything,' he said.

'Just you.' I kissed him again and left Chris's condo feeling a heck of a lot better than I had last night. Damn, I was a lucky woman. My lover was one in a million.

My good mood vanished when I got to the Cursed Crypt. Fewer official vehicles were at the scene, but it was still a cop car convention. Yellow tape flapped in the light breeze, and a horde of media were on the other side of it. I parked and texted Mike the uniform, who waved and ran to my car.

Mike helped me unload the suitcases and we rolled them toward the sidewalk. 'I guess Pete, the newbie who had to spend the night inside the crypt, is still alive,' I said.

'I've never seen anyone look so relieved when he was off-duty this morning. OK, Angela, you know the drill. Let's run the gauntlet. Keep your head down.'

I pulled up the hood on my Tyvek suit, and Mike and I rolled the suitcases toward the entrance, ignoring the shouted questions and the mics thrust at us.

We ducked under the yellow crime scene tape. Mike logged me in and handed me a pair of booties. He took a handful of cookies but nixed the water. 'Got my own, thanks.' He held up a bottle.

At the entrance, Jace's warm smile cheered me. He was

pleased with the goodies I'd brought. We couldn't go outside
in the sun, but we took a break at a command center he'd set
up in a tent, just outside the tomb's entrance. He wiped the
cobwebs off his face with the wet naps, then helped himself
to water and cookies. Nitpicker joined us for a break. They
both looked tired today, and Nitpicker's magenta hair was
wilted. We sat on a bench, munching cookies. My descent into
Hades was temporarily delayed.

All too soon, it was time to go to work. I felt like a miner
going into the center of the earth. Inside, the stink slapped me
in the face – the coppery scent of blood, voided bowels and
urine, and the sweet, sickly odor of decaying meat, all cooking
under the glare of the portable crime-scene lights. Add that to
the tomb's damp, dismal atmosphere, and I hoped my nose
would short out soon.

The stink diminished as Nitpicker and I crawled through
the cobweb-laced tunnel to the room at the end. 'I've already
processed this room. It's OK to come in.'

The room was maybe four feet wide and five feet high,
paneled in peeling once-white wood. Inside, we both moved
with an awkward, hunched stoop.

Nitpicker pointed to the floor, the thick dust crisscrossed
by footprints and shoe prints.

'I found a million fingerprints and a lot of footprints. Many
of the prints were made by bare feet. Some were child-sized'
– she pointed to a slender print smaller than my hand – 'and
others definitely belonged to adults. Like that one. I'd say
that's a man's foot, probably a size fifteen.

'Some shoe prints seemed to be from thick, old-fashioned
shoes with nailed-on soles. I'm not even sure those shoes were
made in the twentieth century. I did find modern shoe prints
from some kind of sports shoe. Those were on top of the old
prints. The only blood was in that shoe print by the entrance
that we found yesterday.'

'So this tunnel has been here a while,' I said.

'At least a hundred years, maybe more. You can tell by the
furniture.' A wooden table, missing its paint along with one
leg, leaned against the wall. Next to it was an old-fashioned
kerosene lamp with a broken chimney. Beside the lamp was

a fat china pot decorated with pink roses. The pot had a cracked lid and a handle on one side, like a huge mug.

'What's that?' I asked.

Nitpicker laughed. 'That's a chamber pot, or "thunder mug," as my granny used to call it. Before indoor plumbing, everyone used them.

'The tunnel continues past this room,' Nitpicker said. 'I think there's an entrance at the far end, but I didn't want to tackle it alone.' She pointed to a section of the wall that seemed to be pushed out into the tunnel, like a gate.

'I'll go.' I was eager to finish working the scene. I'd brought a miner's lamp I could wear on my forehead, so I could crawl with my hands free. I gingerly picked my way through the gate and down another cobwebbed passage, Nitpicker following in my wake. About ten feet down the passage was another door with a rusted handle, on the right side of the tunnel. I pulled on the handle and the door slid open on a well-oiled track.

The interior was dazzling.

'Nitpicker.' My voice was an awed whisper. 'You won't believe this.'

THIRTEEN

I nside the long, narrow room were two stone crypts of nearly translucent white marble, flanked by a pair of alabaster vases. A sculpture of a woman reclined on the crypt closest to the sliding door. She appeared to be asleep. I was fascinated by the delicate details. The bow at her waist seemed freshly tied and she had lace – actual marble lace – around her graceful neck. The sleeping woman had high cheekbones and full lips. Her hair fell to her shoulders in loose waves. Her long, slender fingers clasped a carefully wrought marble bouquet of roses, each petal visible. I'd put her age in her late thirties. Her beauty was obvious, but I could also feel the sculptor's profound grief.

On the side of the crypt was this inscription: 'Sacred to the memory of Elizabeth McKee, beloved wife of Jonathan McKee. Born in slavery, died free. November second 1857.'

Next to Elizabeth's crypt was another one, a simple white slab that said, 'Jonathan McKee. Sculptor. Died 1888.'

Nitpicker and I stayed at the entrance, and examined the room with our lights.

'What gorgeous work,' Nitpicker said. 'This sculpture belongs in a museum.'

'Elizabeth's face looks familiar.' I stared at the lovely features, wondering where I'd seen them before. An old photo? A painting? A history book? Her ethereal face made her look like an . . .

'Angel!' I shouted. 'Nitpicker! This woman is the model for the angels guarding the Cursed Crypt.'

Nitpicker stared at Elizabeth's face. 'You're right. Put wings on her and it's the same person. You know what else is odd? There are no cobwebs in this room, and both crypts are dust-free.'

'The flowers in the vases are fresh, too. Bronze chrysan-themums.' The vases were close enough I could smell the slightly bitter odor of the 'mums. 'There's fresh water in these vases, too. Someone visited here recently.'

Nitpicker and I both photographed the double crypt, then we turned around to get Jace, brushing aside the clinging cobwebs and crawling back as fast as we could toward the entrance. Nitpicker quickly showed him the photos, though we knew they didn't do the scene justice. When Jace joined us at the entrance to the hidden crypt, he was as awed as we were. 'Dust this crypt for prints, Nitpicker. The killer could be the person taking care of it. Angela, let's see where the rest of this tunnel goes.'

I was grateful Jace wanted to come with me. It wasn't safe to explore that eerie, cobwebbed tunnel alone. On the other side of the double crypt, the tunnel was slightly wider. The floor and walls were still dirt, shored up with thick wooden beams.

Jace went first and I followed behind him, hoping he didn't send any startled rats, mice or spiders my way.

'Jace, do you think the killer maintains that beautiful crypt?'

'Haven't a clue, Angela. You know these people better than I do.'

'I know the Forest loves ancestor worship, Jace, but why hide that tomb? It should be proudly displayed in a cemetery. In some St. Louis cemeteries, like Bellefontaine, people take tours to see the funerary art. The Du Pres family have their own section in Chouteau Forest Cemetery, with two mausoleums. One is a small chapel and the other is a miniature white granite castle with Tiffany glass windows. It reminds me of Ambrose Bierce's line about mausoleums: "the final and funniest folly of the rich."'

But there was nothing funny about Elizabeth's crypt. It was a monument to Jonathan's heartrending grief. Was the sculptor her husband? Or did she have a son by the same name? And what forced him to hide his sorrow?

Finally, Jace said, 'Angela, I see a light at the end of the tunnel.'

I groaned. 'You've been waiting all day to say that.'

'Yep. And here it is.'

I shined my light at the exit. I could see only the faintest glimmer of light through the dense cobwebs. 'Some super-spider has been at work here,' I said. 'These cobwebs must be a foot thick. How do we get through them?' I shuddered at the thought of pushing through that dense, sticky substance.

'Easy.' Jace sat back on his haunches and pulled on a fresh set of gloves from his pocket, then pushed an iron rod at the top of the tunnel out of the way. The cobwebs swung with the rod toward the side of the tunnel. They'd been hanging there like a curtain. 'Those are fake cobwebs,' he said. 'Made out of the same stuff I use to decorate my house for Halloween.'

'And Dad cracks the case.' I laughed.

The cobweb curtain revealed a square opening, about four feet by four feet, covered with a thick wooden panel. Light was bleeding around the edges. Jace used his flashlight and his fingers to examine the panel. 'I'm looking for a lock or a latch, Angela. This door – or whatever it is – doesn't have hinges. Here goes.'

He kicked the door hard with both feet. Nothing. He tried three more times, and the panel didn't budge. Next, he rammed it with his shoulder. The panel gave way, and Jace fell forward. I heard a loud rustle-crunch, then a clatter of metal and rattle of sticks.

'Jace! Are you OK?'

I poked my head through the opening and saw Jace was in what looked like a large janitor's closet. He'd landed on two huge dust-covered cardboard boxes with 'Crestview Quality Bathroom Tissue' in faded blue letters. The boxes had hit a collection of mops and push brooms, and those had fallen against two rolling metal mop buckets.

Jace rubbed his neck, then stood up and straightened his protective suit. 'No harm done,' he said. 'The toilet paper boxes are dented, but we can turn those parts against the opening, so they won't show. I have an idea how to catch this killer. We need to see someone in administration.'

He gave me a hand to help me climb out of the tunnel. It felt good to stand up straight. I stretched, then helped Jace put the closet back to rights. We restored the cobweb curtain and the panel, then put on gloves when we put the dented boxes, mops, brooms, and mop buckets back in place. 'There are dirty prints on these boxes,' Jace said. 'We may get something useful.'

'Jace, I don't think anyone has used this equipment in a long time. The bucket is rusty and mops and brooms are too worn to be any good.'

'It does look abandoned. But why was the light on?'

'So the killer can come back?' I said. 'What's your plan?'

'You'll see.' He refused to tell me more.

We gingerly opened the closet door and found ourselves behind a huge, dusty coal-burning furnace with gray octopus arms. We were in a basement with white limestone walls and a cracked concrete floor.

'Looks like that furnace hasn't been used in decades,' Jace said. 'There are shoe prints in the dust. Be careful not to step on them.' The shoe prints seemed like they'd been made with modern sports shoes.

'I'll have Nitpicker photograph them,' he said.

We followed the shoe prints through the old basement, which was used as a storage area for broken chairs, lamps and tables, all draped with decades of cobwebs. Finally, we reached a flight of wooden steps that had once been painted gray. Again, Jace and I carefully skirted the footprints as we climbed to a wooden door. It opened into a cleaner, more modern basement with concrete walls and floors. The shoe print trail stopped at the doorway.

'I wonder if the killer took off his shoes here,' Jace said.

We passed a newish heating and air-conditioning system that made loud chugging sounds, a room marked 'Electrical,' and storage areas with labels like 'folding chairs and tables' and 'holiday decorations.' We found a freight elevator, but didn't have the code to access it. Next to it was a door that opened on to a set of concrete stairs. We followed the stairs up, and learned we'd been in sub-basement two. Three more flights and we were on the first floor in the old Main Building of Chouteau Forest University. Several packs of roaming students stared at us.

'Jace, before we see anyone in administration, we'd better get out of these filthy suits.'

A bell rang, and the students scattered, probably heading for classrooms.

Jace and I followed the signs to a pair of restrooms. Inside the women's restroom, I tore off the protective suit and booties, washed my face and hands, and tried to make myself presentable. Jace must have done the same thing. At least, when we emerged, we didn't look like we'd come from another planet.

The university had an impressive bureaucracy. Jace and I were referred from one administration office to another, until we wound up in a meeting room with Dr Madison, the university's assistant vice president, and a public relations officer, both twenty-something women, and the head of security. The assistant veep and the PR person were dressed in nearly identical navy suits and white blouses. The head of security wore a suit that was as gray as he was.

Jace revealed some – but not all – of what we'd found. 'There's a tunnel that runs from the Cursed Crypt to an old sub-basement – it still has an old coal furnace.'

The head of security looked surprised. 'You're kidding. That area was closed off twenty years ago when we installed the new heating and cooling system.'

'How did the person get into the tunnel?' the assistant veep asked. 'We checked that crypt thoroughly.'

'There's a secret entrance. If you move one of the angel wings, the tablet dedicated to Professor Cortini slides back and there's a tunnel.'

'I had no idea,' security said.

'None of us did,' Dr Madison said.

Jace didn't mention the double crypt we'd discovered. Instead, he said, 'We're keeping the tunnel off-limits for now. I believe the killer may come back, and I'd like permission to put a camera in the closed sub-basement.'

'By all means,' security said.

'We'll do everything to cooperate,' said the PR person, and Dr Madison nodded agreement.

'I also need you to keep this plan secret for now.'

'Absolutely,' security said. 'The sooner this nightmare is over, the better.'

Jace slapped the table and stood up.

'Then it's all settled,' he said. 'I'll handle the arrangements and install the camera. I want our killer to look real pretty for his close-up.'

'Anything else we can do to help?' Dr Madison asked.

'Yes,' Jace said. 'We'd like to talk to the student guards.'

'There were two,' Madison said. 'Bella Hamilton and Adam Nesbitt. Bella works part-time in my office. She helps with the filing. She's there now if you want to talk to her.'

We followed Dr Madison to his office, a two-room suite. On the walk there, Jace said he wanted to work with a tech on setting up cameras in the sub-basement. I said I'd talk to the student guards. We agreed to meet back at the crypt.

Bella was organizing a tall gray file cabinet in the veep's office. She was the pink-haired student who had the first shift, from 11:40, when the tomb-closing ceremony ended, until 3:40 in the morning. 'I never left the crypt entrance.' She set a big stack of folders on top the cabinet and sat in a side chair.

'Did you have the keys to the crypt?' I asked.

'No, Emily gave those to Dr Madison. I had his phone number in case of an emergency, as well as the number for the campus police and Chief Butkus. Dr Madison made sure Adam and I put those numbers in our cell phones.'

'Did anything unusual happen during your shift? Were you alone the whole time?'

'At first, the cleanup crew was there, picking up trash and glasses from the party. They left about one o'clock.

'About ten after one, I heard some noise near the walkway from the inn, where the carved pumpkins were. I couldn't see anything there and I didn't want to leave my post. I called the campus police. A cop came over, but he said nothing was out of place.'

'Did the cop check all the pumpkins?' I asked.

'I don't think so. He told me he didn't see any that were smashed. He figured I heard some drunken students making noise.'

Drunken students, I thought. The all-purpose excuse for any campus disturbance. Was that when the killer removed the death-threat pumpkin? Were Trey and Lydia dead by then?

Bella was still talking. 'After that – after the campus cop left – nothing happened, except I got really cold.'

'Did you hear anything from the tomb?'

'No way. Those walls are really thick. It was so quiet, it kinda creeped me out.'

'Did you fall asleep?'

'No! I was too cold. Even the coffee in my Thermos didn't keep me warm. I really wished I'd brought a blanket. I set an alarm on my phone to call Adam at three o'clock. My teeth were chattering by then. Adam oversleeps a lot, and I didn't want to stay out there one minute longer. I told him to dress extra warm. Adam said he was already awake and he'd be at the tomb by three forty when his shift started. He got there at three thirty and said I could leave.'

'What did you do next?'

'Ran to my car, turned up the heater full blast and raced back to my dorm. I was freezing. I was asleep by four thirty.'

I remembered that big Thermos. 'You drank a lot of coffee that night, Bella. What did you do when you needed a bathroom?'

Bella's face turned pinker than her hair. She hung her head and said, 'Uh . . . I'm a hiker. I have a pee funnel. A portable device so women can . . . you know . . . so we don't have to . . .' The next words came out in a rush. 'So I can pee standing up. I used the bushes nearby.'

'Thank you,' I said. 'Do you know where Adam is now?'

She looked at the wall clock. 'At this hour he's usually in the campus library. On the third floor. He and his friends hang out in the blue chairs, near the Psychology books section. It's just to the left of the elevators.'

As Bella predicted, Adam was exactly where she said he'd be. He looked a lot better today than he did when he found the bodies. The bearded student was sprawled in a blue club chair, regaling a brunette with long, curly hair how he found Trey. 'It was like a horror movie.' His voice was low. 'The crypt was dark and cobwebby. I just touched the guy's head and it nearly fell off.'

The girl shivered and her eyes widened. 'I don't know how you did it,' she said. 'I'd have nightmares forever!'

'Didn't bother me at all.' Adam left out the part where he threw up.

'Excuse me, Adam,' I said. 'But I have to ask you some questions about your shift at the Cursed Crypt.'

I smiled at the girl. 'I'm Angela Richman, a death investigator with the Chouteau Forest Medical Examiner's office.' Might as well give my full title to impress her.

'Sara,' she said. 'I'm Sara Ripley. I have to go to class.' She grabbed her backpack and stood up to leave. 'See you tomorrow, Adam.' She gave him a warm smile.

After Sara was on the elevator he said, 'Thank you for not mentioning that I barfed when I found the bodies.'

'Happens to everyone, even homicide detectives.'

'What do you need?' he asked.

'Can you tell me what happened during your shift guarding the tomb? When did you get there?'

'My friend Bella called about three o'clock that morning and said she was freezing. I got at the tomb a little early, at three thirty, and told her to go home. And then, nothing happened. Not a thing.'

'No noises?'

'I heard something rustling in the bushes about four o'clock. A little while later, a raccoon came waddling out, so no big deal. After that, nothing. Not a single person until just before six a.m. when everybody arrived for the opening, and well, you know what happened then.'

Adam had nothing else to add except, 'I do have nightmares, Angela. Will they go away?'

He looked terribly young. 'Yes. But you may want to talk to a counselor.'

He shrugged. 'I'll tough it out.'

FOURTEEN

Nitpicker and I spent the rest of the afternoon processing the secret crypt and the tunnel. Actually, I helped while she did the real work.

'We have a zillion prints and shoe prints,' she said. 'Let's hope they lead us to the killer.'

About five o'clock, Jace showed up inside the Cursed Crypt. 'I'm beat,' he said, and he did look tired. 'Let's call it a day.'

Nitpicker and I didn't waste any time packing up. Jace walked us to our cars. After Nitpicker drove away, Jace said, 'Tomorrow I want to interview old Reggie Du Pres, his nephew, Vincent Du Pres, and Vincent's son, Bradford, along with Reggie's smoking buddy, Jefferson Morgan.'

I stared at the rumpled detective. 'Jace, do you have a death wish? Reggie and Jefferson can have you fired for even daring to question them.'

'I have to talk to them,' Jace said. 'I heard about the conversation they had before the bidding started. Jefferson was worried Trey would win and join the Founders Club if he stayed the night. Reggie said only his nephew Vincent had ever made it through the night in the crypt since the Eighties.'

I chimed in with, 'That's when Jefferson said, "Trey Lawson will join the Founders Club over my dead body." And Vincent added, "Why not make it *his* dead body?" Then they all had a big laugh.'

Jace looked at me in surprise. 'How did you know that?'

'Because I heard them,' I said.

'Well, so did the chief's wife.'

'And she told you? Doesn't she care about her husband's job?'

'I'm sure she does, but I think she's brave,' Jace said. 'She told the truth. Maybe if other people stood up to the Du Pres family, the Forest would be a better place.'

'I keep forgetting that you're not from here. You view the

Forest with a different perspective. The Du Pres have that power because we gave it to them. It's time to take it back.'

My high-minded words suddenly slammed into an ugly reality: if Jace was fired or forced out, I'd have to work with Greiman, the Forest's fair-haired boy.

'What can I do to help?'

'I'd like you to go with me when I interview Reggie, Vincent and Jefferson Morgan tomorrow.'

I gulped. 'At Reggie's house?'

This was hitting close to home. My home. I inherited my parents' house, a former guesthouse on the Du Pres estate. Mom and Dad had both worked for the Du Pres family. My parents bought the house for $25,000, when that was a fair price. But crafty Reggie owned the land it was on, and he could turn me out at any time – and pay me exactly what my parents had paid for that house, which wouldn't buy much these days.

So be it. I could work somewhere else. I should woman up.

'Reggie and his friends won't be at his house tomorrow morning,' Jace said. 'They'll be at the Chouteau Forest Founders Club for some kind of meeting. The meeting is at nine and it will probably be over about ten o'clock. I thought we could show up then.'

I was impressed. 'How do you know this?'

'Friends in low places.' Jace grinned. 'I live next door to the Founders Club bartender. Henry likes to come over for beer and burgers. The old guard are lousy tippers, and Henry loves to tell me what goes on at the club. He says Reggie and his cronies have been in a lather since the killings at the Cursed Crypt. The story is all over the media. They want those murders solved quick.'

'I've never been inside the Founders Club,' I said. 'It's men only, except for wives and girlfriends at social events. I'm curious what it looks like inside.'

'See you there at nine forty-five tomorrow,' Jace said.

I spent that night at my home – did some laundry and cleaning, shopped for food – all the domestic chores I'd ignored when I stayed with Chris. I checked in with him. As I whipped around my house with a dustcloth and vacuum, I realized how lonely I felt without him.

What started as a cautious romance was turning serious. I wasn't quite ready to admit that, especially to myself. We'd both said the L-word – love – but I wasn't ready for the next one – live with. Would I move in with him, or would Chris move into my place? Chris had never stayed the night in my home. It was too crowded, filled with happy memories of my husband, Donegan. He'd died young of a heart attack, and I'd resigned myself to the loveless twilight of widowhood.

I spent that night tossing and turning, trying to reconcile my love for Chris with my love for Donegan. The gray light of dawn was just visible when I finally fell asleep. When my alarm went off at nine that morning, I awoke tired and groggy. A cold shower and three cups of coffee later, I was awake enough to scramble myself a breakfast egg. I arrived at the Founders Club on time, right behind Jace's car.

The club was in a grandiose white stone building with three pairs of Corinthian columns and massive black double doors. A valet came out to take our cars.

Jace and I marched up the white stairs to a portico guarded by spiral boxwood topiary trees in ebony pots. 'Even the trees are twisted,' I said.

Jace rolled his eyes, then held the door open for me. We were greeted by a white-haired man in his sixties. His long nose, thin face and beautifully cut suit gave him a look of distinction.

'Good morning.' He eyed us as if we were there to steal the silver. 'Do you have an appointment?'

'Don't need one.' Jace held up his badge. 'We're here to see Reggie Du Pres, Vincent Du Pres and Jefferson Morgan. Please tell them it's about the deaths on the Chouteau Forest University campus.'

The man reacted as if Jace had said something embarrassing. 'Of course, sir. I'll tell the gentlemen you're here. Please have a seat.'

Jace and I sat in two thronelike chairs in the entrance hall, next to an umbrella stand. 'Remember,' Jace told me, 'I'm going to pretend I don't know Henry the bartender.'

The white-haired man glided back in and said, 'Mr Du Pres will see you in the bar.'

At ten in the morning? Sure enough, that's where we were going. The bar was dark wood and red leather. A tall, dark-haired bartender in a white coat was polishing glasses. Henry, I suspected.

Reggie was sitting at a round table in the center of the room, along with Vincent and Jefferson. All three men were smoking cigars and drinking what I guessed was Scotch.

'Please join us, Detective. Angela.' Reggie gave me a regal nod. 'I thought you were a death investigator.'

'She is,' Jace said. 'But I have her on loan to help with the case.'

That was stretching the truth, but Reggie bought it.

'Good,' he said. 'Would either of you like a drink?'

'Black coffee,' we both said.

'Henry!' Vincent called. 'Two coffees.'

The bartender put down the glass and began filling two cups.

'I'm glad to see you're not drinking on duty, Detective.' Reggie sounded condescending. 'What are you doing about that heinous crime?'

'Terrible, just terrible,' Jefferson said.

'These things don't happen here,' Vincent said.

I was glad Henry arrived with the coffee to distract us. If I had a nickel for every time I heard the phrase 'these things don't happen here' I could retire. I took a sip of the coffee. Hot and strong, it tasted freshly brewed.

'We've discovered a number of shoe prints and fingerprints that are being processed,' Jace said. 'We hope to have some solid information soon.'

'Well, then why are you here?' Reggie asked. 'Why aren't you working?'

'We're waiting on the lab,' Jace said. 'I have a couple of questions for you.'

'Of course, as long as they help solve this.'

Jace turned to Vincent Du Pres. 'We'd also like to speak to your son, Bradford. Where does he work?'

'In the family law firm,' Vincent said. 'Du Pres, Dunworthy and Damon.'

Reggie looked thunderous. 'You could have called a secretary for that information, Detective Budewitz, instead of disturbing us at our club.'

Jace shrugged. 'Where did you four go after the auction?'

'Really,' Reggie said. 'I see no reason why we have to answer that.'

'You can answer it here, or down at the station,' Jace said. 'And I'm sure you want to cooperate.'

'If you must know,' Reggie enunciated every word carefully, 'my nephew Vincent and my friend Mr Morgan went back to my home for cigars and brandy.'

'And Bradford?'

'You can ask him yourself.' Reggie was seething.

I held my breath, sensing that Reggie could erupt at any moment, but Jace kept going.

'I have one more question that I wanted to ask you three,' Jace said. 'The night of the auction, you gentlemen were overheard discussing the idea that Trey Lawson might win the bidding, and join the Founders Club. Mr Morgan said that Trey Lawson would join the Founders Club over his dead body, and you, Mr Vincent Du Pres, said, "Why not make it *his* dead body?"'

The silence that followed was arctic. I could feel the room turn to ice, and wrapped my hands around my coffee cup for warmth.

'And that's what you came to see us about?' Jefferson's voice was dangerously low. 'A comment that someone may have overheard – or made up?'

'It wasn't made up,' Jace said. 'Two witnesses heard that conversation.'

'So?' Jefferson said. 'It's a figure of speech. I also said I'd kill for another dessert, but the waiter is still alive.'

'That's my point,' Jace said. 'The waiter is alive, but Trey Lawson is dead.'

Vincent stayed silent. Reggie did the talking for the family. 'And you're implying that my nephew Vincent killed that man.' Reggie's voice was low and deadly. 'Be careful what you say and where you ask your questions, Detective.'

He turned his stony glare on me. 'Oh, and Ms Richman,

I suggest you should be careful, too. You have a very nice house.'

'I do, but it's not the only house in the Forest, Reggie. Are you threatening me?'

'I don't make threats. I take action. And I will. Keep that in mind.' Reggie stood up. 'Now. We have business to conduct. Good day to you both.'

FIFTEEN

I left the Founders Club feeling slightly shell-shocked. As we waited for the valet to bring our cars, Jace said, 'Let's talk. Supreme Bean is about ten minutes down the road. Care for a cup of coffee?'

Supreme Bean was an indie coffee shop: one room with a worn oriental rug, lots of bookshelves, and homemade pastries. Students camped out on the floor or in the battered leather chairs. Less flexible coffee lovers sat at repurposed dining sets.

Jace and I ordered coffee and I bought a chocolate chip cookie the size of a saucer. I needed some sweetness that morning. At least, that was my excuse.

Jace and I sat at a chrome-and-Formica table. The first sip of coffee was hot and strong. I broke my cookie in two and said, 'Would you like half?'

'No, thanks.' Jace patted his stomach. 'I'm getting a bit of a belly.' He quickly steered the conversation back to our meeting at the Founders Club. 'Why did old man Du Pres mention your house, Angela?'

I told him the deal he'd made with my parents and how I could lose my home.

'He can't threaten you like that.'

'This is the Forest, Jace. He can try, but I'll put up a fight. He pulls anything, and he'll have to go up against Montgomery Bryant, the best lawyer in the Forest. Monty's not afraid of Reggie and neither am I. So, where are we going next?' I bit into my cookie. Just the right amount of sweetness.

'Nowhere,' he said. 'You can't risk your home to help me.'

'Yes, I can. You're risking far more than I am. You could lose your job.'

He shrugged. 'Then I'll get another one.'

'But what about your son?'

'I've heard that excuse too often: "The boss made me do something terrible, but I can't quit my job because of my children." I promised myself I would never use my kid as an excuse to stay in a bad job. My son will respect me more if he has a father who does the right thing, than someone who can buy him anything he wants. Got it?'

'Deal. What's our next move?'

'Let's visit young Bradford Du Pres,' Jace said.

I nodded. 'Bradford laughed along with the older men before the bidding war with Trey, but when his family was putting up the money and refused to top Trey's last bid, he was furious.'

'He's a spoiled kid who didn't get his way, Angela. Of course he was angry.'

'You're right. And just like a kid, the rage quickly disappeared.' I paused. 'Maybe I misinterpreted his anger; it could have been disappointment. The light wasn't very good in the ballroom that night and the Du Pres family say things like that all the time. I doubt that Trey could seriously challenge their power?'

'It's unlikely,' Jace said. 'But since Bradford is on my radar, I should at least talk to him. That family wanted to spend more than a million dollars to keep Trey from winning that auction.'

'Look, I don't like the Du Pres, but they're not cold-blooded killers.'

'So now you're standing up for that family when Reggie just threatened to take your home, Angela?'

'Threatened,' I said. 'Reggie *threatened* me. Whether he'll spend the money for a lawsuit is another question. I don't think Bradford is the killer, but I'll go to the law firm with you.'

Jace took a last sip of his coffee. 'I don't either. But I may learn something. It's just an interview. Must be nice to have a job in a big-deal law firm waiting for you when you graduate, like Bradford did.'

'You'd think so,' I said. 'But the rich kids I went to high school with complained they didn't have any career choices: they had to take jobs in the family firm.'

'Was that true?'

'Not really. If they told Mummy and Daddy to keep their

money, those kids could have had any career they wanted – even risky careers in the arts. They had an education and contacts. But they're too afraid to risk failure. They lock themselves in careers they hate with golden handcuffs, and then regret their decision for the rest of their lives.'

'Maybe they would have been better off without that money.'

'It's possible. But security is hard to give up. Especially when you have kids of your own.'

We were back to the sacrifices people made for their children. Our conversation had come full circle. We'd finished our coffee, and I'd polished off the last crumb of cookie. Jace and I left. He said he'd meet me at Bradford's law office in downtown Chouteau Forest.

Du Pres, Dunworthy and Damon was in a Georgian-style building. We were greeted by a receptionist, Hayley, a pale, prim young woman in a gray suit and tight bun. Jace showed his credentials and she didn't raise an eyebrow.

Odd, I thought. Most people showed some reaction when they saw a homicide detective's badge. Hayley must have been warned. I melted into the background and let Jace do the talking.

'He's not here. I mean, Bradford, uh, young Mr Du Pres isn't here.' Hayley's face was bright red and she stumbled over her words. She was a bad liar.

'Where is he?' asked Jace.

'Uh, out of the, um, office.'

'And when will Bradford be back?'

Jace repeated his question and Hayley grew more flustered. 'I don't know. He's on a business trip. I'm not sure where.'

Now Jace sounded angry and impatient. 'So a member of your firm took a business trip and left no way to contact him?'

'Yes, yes. Young Mr Du Pres is very forgetful.' Hayley looked around frantically, as if hoping for rescue.

'I bet,' Jace said. 'Well, if he calls in, give him my number.' Jace handed Hayley his card.

'Yes, sir. I certainly will, sir.' She looked ready to cry.

Out in the parking lot, Jace said, 'She's lying.'

'Definitely. What are you going to do?'

'Wait a couple of days and then track Bradford down,' Jace said. 'He's not my main suspect, just someone I want to question. And he's not going to skip town. A spoiled kid like that enjoys his creature comforts too much to go on the run. His father has the money. Bradford will be back soon.

'Meanwhile, let's go to Tara's Taste of the Forest. It's two blocks away. Tara called and left a message she wanted to talk to the detective in charge about the delivery to the Cursed Crypt.'

The fall air was cool and crisp and the short walk felt good. Downtown Chouteau Forest was bustling with shoppers, and many of them waved to me.

'Do you know Tara?' Jace assumed I knew everyone in the Forest because I grew up here. This time, he was right.

'I went to high school with Tara Fordham. We weren't in the same crowd. Tara's family is second-tier Forest society – they're invited to the Du Pres's B-list parties. I met her mother a few times. Mrs Fordham was a terrible snob. She looked down on people she considered inferior, saying they had to buy their own furniture.'

'What's wrong with that?' Jace said. 'I don't want my mom's flowered sofa.'

'Beats me.' I shrugged. 'Tara's mother was thrilled when her daughter married Stu Lavigne, a distant cousin of the Du Pres. Mrs Fordham considered the marriage a step up the social ladder, and Stu and Tara had a fancy wedding. Too bad the marriage wasn't a success. Stu was a hound, and cheated on Tara. She put up with his tom-catting until he had a child by his secretary. Then she divorced him.

'I give Tara credit. Stu didn't give her much in the divorce, but she started her own business and made a success of it.'

'Do you like her?' Jace asked.

'Not much,' I said. 'She was a typical high-school mean girl.'

Tara's shop was easy to spot, with its cheerful, blue-striped awning and delivery van parked in front. The car was 'wrapped,' covered in shiny vinyl printed with photos celebrating local food: a giant Gooey Louie gooey butter cake was on the hood, a thin-crust pizza on the van's back doors, and the sides were covered with pictures of toasted ravioli, chocolates from Kakao, and baby back ribs smothered in St. Louis barbecue sauce. The van was a rolling tribute to local delicacies.

A bell announced our arrival in the shop. Tara herself was behind the counter, wrapping a big basket of goodies with a giant bow. She looked like a lot of Forest divorcees: blonde and thin, with good teeth. She wore a blue jumper embroidered with 'Tara Fordham, CEO, Tara's Taste of the Forest.'

She greeted me with a smile. 'Hey, Angela. Good to see you.'

When Jace showed his credentials, Tara said, 'I called about that delivery to the Cursed Crypt. Terrible what happened to that poor young couple.'

'Yes,' Jace said. 'What do you remember about the order?'

'The afternoon of the auction, I guess that was October thirtieth, I got a call from someone who wanted a deluxe basket. That's five hundred dollars. The caller told me to leave room for two bottles of Merlot.'

'What time was the call?' Jace asked.

'Just after lunch, about one o'clock.'

'Did the caller leave a name?'

'No, but it was definitely a man. I couldn't tell his age, but he wasn't an old man or a kid. He was well-spoken and sounded educated. He said he'd pay cash, and give me another five hundred dollars if I'd stay open until eleven o'clock that night.'

'What time do you close?' Jace asked.

'Six o'clock,' Tara said. 'It was an unusual request, but we're a small business and an extra five hundred dollars was hard to pass up.

'I asked the caller where he wanted the basket delivered, and he said he'd send someone to pick it up at eleven that night. I got the basket ready, except for the food in the fridge, and sent the staff home at our regular closing time. Then I stayed here, working on the books. At ten forty-five, I got the cold items out of the fridge and prepped the pizza and baby back ribs. Then I waited for the delivery person. He was late, and I was getting worried. Finally, he showed up at eleven ten, holding two bottles of wine. I put the Merlot in the basket, tied the ribbon, and he was ready to go. I helped him carry it out to his car. The basket took up the whole backseat. He was driving a Kia.'

'What color?' Jace asked.

'Squashed bug green.' I smiled at the apt description.

'What did the delivery man look like?' Jace said.

'Youngish, somewhere in his twenties. Thick, dark hair tipped with blond. About five six or seven – a little taller than me, but not as tall as you.'

'Did he tell you his name?'

'No, and he didn't mention who sent him. He handed me a thousand dollars in cash and said he was here to pick up the deluxe basket. I've never seen the man before.'

'How did you know where he delivered the basket?' Jace asked.

'I saw the crypt closing ceremony on TV after the murders, and recognized that car. Also, the young man's face. That hair is hard to forget.'

She looked at Jace with pained eyes. 'I killed those two people, didn't I?'

Jace didn't answer her question. Instead, he said, 'Who packed the basket?'

'I did. I always pack the big orders.'

'Did you open any of the items before you put them in the gift basket?'

She pointed to the shelves in the shop stacked with local chocolates and other delicacies, and the glass-fronted coolers with gooey butter cakes, beer and other cold items. 'No. Everything was in the original containers. Just like you see here. But I feel terrible. I should have reported this odd order to the police.'

Jace seemed to take pity on her. 'And tell us what? That someone ordered a deluxe basket and paid extra to pick it up late at night? We wouldn't have paid any attention to that.'

'Please. Can you tell me? Did my food kill those people?'

'I don't know, ma'am. We'll know after the autopsy.'

'Let me know as soon as possible,' she said.

I was starting to revise my harsh opinion of her when she said, 'That murder is costing me business. People think my food killed them.'

SIXTEEN

Jace's cell phone rang as we walked to our cars. He listened, said 'uh-huh' a few times, and then added, 'Thanks, Katie. Angela's here with me. We'll be there at eight tomorrow. I'll bring the coffee.'

He hung up. 'Katie caught the autopsy on Trey and Lydia.'

'Of course she did,' I said. 'My boss, Evarts, is too smart to wander in to that political minefield. I'll bring doughnuts to the meeting.'

I spent a lovely night with Chris at his condo. That man was becoming a major part of my life. We had poached salmon with dill sauce for dinner and avoided talking about work.

After dinner, Chris and I watched the TV news. That's when it finally dawned on me that the Cursed Crypt murders had burst like a bomb on Chouteau County. The frightened Forest dwellers were convinced a crazed killer was running loose, slashing innocent citizens. All the major television stations carried versions of what the press called the 'Locked Tomb Mystery.' Jace had succeeded in keeping a tight lid on the news that the crypt had a secret entrance. The university wasn't going to say anything. Their spokespersons were working overtime claiming that there had never been a problem with the crypt before, and the strictest safety standards were followed.

Everyone who had even the faintest connection to the murders was interviewed. Remember Adam, the tomb guard who'd 'discovered' the bodies? He was now on a first-name basis with the dead couple. 'I knew Trey and Lydia were dead the moment I saw them,' he told a CNN reporter. 'They looked like Romeo and Juliet in the tomb scene.'

Adam told MSNBC he didn't hear any sounds coming from the crypt, 'but the air around it felt extra cold. There was definitely a cold spot, like you find in haunted houses, around that tomb.'

Every student who had a class with one of the victims

seemed to be interviewed. Many of the young women wept. 'Lydia was so talented,' said a sorority sister. 'She was a fashion icon. We all admired her.'

No one mentioned the rape trial, or Lydia's perjured testimony that saved Trent from prison. The pair were transformed in death, their lives prettified and darkest deeds whitewashed.

As Chris watched this news, he said, 'Angela, I'm worried about you. I'd feel better if you have something for self-defense.'

'You want me to take a class and learn how to poke people in the eyes with my car keys?'

'I was thinking more along the lines of a Taser. Civilians can use them in Missouri.'

'I already have pepper spray, Chris.'

'And the last time you used it, you sprayed yourself in the face.'

'I did, but I still got the killer on the second try.'

'With this dirtbag running around with a butcher's knife, you may not get a second try. I'd feel better if you had a Taser.'

'Chris, it's sweet that you're worried about me—'

He interrupted me. 'Damn right I'm worried, Angela. Where's your purse?'

'On the table by the door.'

'Go get it.'

I stared at him. I didn't take orders from any man.

Chris softened his voice. 'Please. Humor me.'

I dutifully trotted over and picked up my purse. When I was halfway back, he said, 'Now! Get out your pepper spray.'

He caught me off-guard. I rummaged in my purse, rejecting my make-up bag, tampons, sunglasses, until I finally grabbed the canister of pepper spray.

'Forty-two seconds,' Chris said. 'If I was the crypt killer, you'd be bleeding out on the floor.' He had a stopwatch.

'You were timing me?'

'Damn right. Time is crucial when you're under attack.' Chris reached behind a couch pillow and pulled out a yellow plastic gun.

'I got you a Taser 7 CQ.'

'Where? At Toys R Us?' The blocky yellow plastic gun looked ridiculous.

'Pay attention, Angela. This is the best Taser I can get for you. It has two cartridges. You can hit someone close up, but it has a twelve-foot range. When you hit him, the shock will last about five seconds – and those will be the longest, most miserable seconds of his life.'

'Don't I need training to use a Taser?'

'Yes, and I'm a certified trainer. So I'll train you. Please, Angela.'

He was begging me.

'When do we start?'

'Right now.' He showed me a black plastic briefcase that was beside the couch. 'Your Taser 7 CQ comes in this case. Oh, and CQ stands for close quarters.'

I sat next to him on the couch. He found the battery, which was about the size of a cigarette pack, and stuck it in the handle. He turned on the Taser. The effect was blinding. I scrunched up my eyes and shielded them with my hand.

'That's the LED light,' he said. 'It also has a red laser light.'

He pointed the Taser at the TV set, and a red dot appeared on the anchor's face.

'Just like in the movies,' I said. 'When the guy knows the sniper is going to shoot him.'

'Well, yes, but it's supposed to help you aim.'

Chris was as excited as a kid with a new toy. It was catching. I found myself interested in this new weapon.

'See this black button here? The square one, right by my index finger.'

I nodded.

'You can also use the Taser as a stun gun. Here. Fire it.'

He put the gun in my hand. It wasn't heavy, but it felt awkward. 'Now, point it away from me and fire it.'

I pressed the button and nearly dropped the gun. The clacking noise was loud and frightening. Electricity arced from the top to the bottom of the muzzle, or whatever it was.

'See, you can use it as a stun gun if you don't have the cartridges in,' he said. 'All you have to do is touch someone with it.'

'Right now, I'm the one who's stunned,' I said.

'You fire it for five seconds. Check the LED here and you'll see the numbers.' He pointed to that display on the Taser, then said, 'Try it again. You have to get used to it. Now turn it off. That's right. That button.'

I turned it off with shaking hands. The Taser unnerved me.

Chris brought out a small yellow plastic holder and said, 'The cartridges come in this sleeve and you load them like this.' He stuck them in the front of the gun.

'Now you try it.'

I did, though it took a while.

'Good,' he said. 'Do it again.'

I did, faster this time.

After the third time, he was satisfied with my performance.

Chris found a target – a human shape – in the carrying case and stuck it on a tall cardboard stand.

'Now, we fire,' he said. 'First turn off the power switch. Now, aim at the center mass of the target – that's the torso. Avoid the face, neck, and genitals. The Taser will fire two barbed darts, penetrating the bad guy's clothes, and deliver the electrical current. Once the darts hit the target, hold the trigger for five seconds, so the guy gets the full effect.'

Now he had some red plastic doohickeys in his hand.

'Taser cartridges can only be used once, so I'll load this with training cartridges.'

He did, then said, 'OK, hold the Taser with a firm grip. No, use both hands, Angela. And don't lock your elbows. Keep them slightly bent. Press the trigger. That's right. Keep it smooth. That's it. You've got it.'

My first shot, I got three probes in the target – two in the gut and one in the leg. One went wild and bounced off the wall.

'That's good,' Chris said. 'Again.'

I shot.

'Again.'

All four probes made it in the target.

'One more time.'

Four probes hit again.

'Can we quit?'

'Not yet. You should be Tased.'

'I'm definitely finished.' I grabbed my purse and started for the door.

Chris stood up. 'Come on, Angela.'

'No way. I've read about people getting killed by Tasers.'

'That's rare, Angela.'

'Rare! Police-issued Tasers have killed more than two-thousand Americans in the last two decades. Two thousand people! I'm not going to be one of them.'

'OK, Tase me.'

'No way. What if I kill you?'

'You won't. The newer Tasers are supposed to be safer.'

'Famous last words. Look, Chris. I'll make a deal with you. I'm grateful for this Taser and I'll practice as often as you want, but I'm not shooting you and you're not shooting me.'

'OK. Put your Taser in your purse.'

I hesitated.

'Please.'

As I zipped my purse he took down the target and packed it, along with the training cartridges, into the carrying case. 'Practice with these, promise?'

'I promise, but I have a question. How much did this Taser cost?'

'Uh . . .'

'How much?'

He looked sheepish. 'About sixteen hundred dollars.'

'Sixteen hundred dollars! Couldn't you get me a tennis bracelet like any other man?'

SEVENTEEN

A morning at the morgue was nothing to look forward to, but Chris helped. He fixed me breakfast, fortified me with coffee, and then sent me out the door with a torrid goodbye kiss. This was a routine I could get used to. I swung by the Forest Doughnut Shop for a dozen doughnuts, plus a bag of doughnut holes.

The Chouteau Forest Medical Examiner was in the back of Sisters of Sorrow hospital. I parked away from the black funeral home pick-up vans and unlocked the keypad with my code. As soon as the morgue door swung open, I was hit by the chilled air and smell of industrial disinfectant.

Katie's office was about the size of a galley kitchen. It had just enough room for a desk, a file cabinet and a torture device masquerading as a chair. The highlight of the room was an autumn woodland scene on the wall behind Katie's desk. Hidden in the foliage was a grinning plastic skull. Katie had her tribe's mordant sense of humor.

My friend was my age – forty-one – and at first glance with her short brown hair, brown eyes, sensible shoes and a blocky suit in a drab color, seemed ordinary. But that first impression was wrong. Katie's vibrant wit and sharp mind made her exceptional. Monty Bryant, the Forest's most eligible bachelor, was crazy in love with her.

Katie didn't like spectators present when she did autopsies. She told me, 'I got sick of the detectives turning green and passing out, and I had to stop to revive the bozos. And let me tell you, the bigger they are, the harder they fall.'

The last straw was when a detective watched Katie peel back the decedent's face so her assistant could cut off the skull cap with a Stryker saw. That cop barfed all over the corpse. After that, Katie preferred to work without an audience. That was fine with Jace and me. Unlike some of the bigger cops, I was proud that I'd never fainted at autopsies, but they left me queasy. I was happy to hear Katie's autopsy reports in her cramped office.

I got to Katie's office first and claimed dibs on the edge of her desk, the only comfortable seat in the room. Jace opted to stand rather than sit in that crippling chair. We made small talk, munched doughnuts and drank coffee until Katie was ready to give her report. She sat on the other end of the desk, and used her hands to illustrate her points.

'First, the good news. For the victims, anyway. Tests showed they were drugged. We found a massive dose of sleeping pills in their wine.' She mimed drinking.

'The victims ingested about six hundred milligrams of Ambien – not enough to kill them, but if they'd survived, they might have had some brain damage, especially a small person like Lydia. It should be some comfort to their families that they didn't feel a thing while the killer chopped them into mincemeat.'

'I'll be sure to use those words when I talk to their parents,' I said.

Katie ignored me and continued. 'If you find the killer, you might want to see if they or someone close to them has a prescription for Ambien.

'Whoever killed those two hated them. Lydia's throat was slashed from ear to ear. The wound transected her carotid artery and she died instantly. But the overkill continued. She had clusters of stab wounds in the right lung, the right kidney and the small intestine, which is mostly on the right side of the body. I also found a shallow cut and abrasion on her ring finger. Angela, didn't you note that her engagement ring was missing?'

I nodded. 'That rock was so big it would have embarrassed a Kardashian.'

Jace laughed.

'The killer used the knife to pry the ring off her finger.' Katie made prying motions with her hands. 'You couldn't see those wounds because of the blood. I found thirty stab wounds on the female victim's body.' Katie showed us Lydia's autopsy report with a line drawing of a body, and pointed out the groupings of the wounds on her chest and abdomen.

'I counted twenty-seven, Katie. What did I miss?' I hated carelessness, especially my own.

'Nothing. Some of the wounds were on top of one another and you couldn't see them with all the blood. Two stab wounds were V-shaped wounds and one was L-shaped. That meant the killer twisted the knife. The female victim was small: five feet three inches tall and she weighed ninety-eight pounds. Two wounds went all the way through her body. That takes a lot of energy – and hate.

'And, if the killer hated her, he despised Trey, her fiancé.' Katie showed us the knife wound groupings on Trey's autopsy report. 'The male victim had thirty-six stab wounds in his chest and abdomen and another ten in his genital area. Those turned the family jewels into hamburger.'

Jace winced.

'This victim took longer to bleed out, since none of the wounds hit any major arteries,' Katie said. 'In some wounds, the killer plunged the knife in so hard, he left abrasions on the skin where the knife went in all the way to the hilt.'

'What about the mutilation to their mouths?' Jace asked.

'Lydia's tongue was slit almost to the root, and Trey had a fraternity pin stuck in his tongue,' Katie said. 'The pin had the words "truth," "honor," and "integrity" on it, as Angela reported. Judging by the amount of blood, I believe both victims were alive when those wounds were inflicted.'

My stomach lurched, and I put down my half-eaten doughnut.

'Despite Trey's genital mutilation, I don't believe this was a lust murder,' Katie said. 'I think the killer wanted revenge and he was making a statement with those mutilations. As you know, the two victims were involved in a nasty controversy – a rape at a fraternity party – and many people believe they both lied in court. The victim said she'd been roofied and raped by Trey at the party. Lydia said the victim was sexually promiscuous. Trey said he had sex with the victim, but it was consensual.

'I think Lydia's slit tongue was a way to say she was a liar – her tongue was forked like a snake's. The idealistic "truth," "honor," and "integrity" on Trey's frat pin mocked his behavior.

He was rich enough to get out of trouble. Trey's slick lawyer asked for a bench trial, which meant no jury. The judge agreed with the lawyer that they couldn't "ruin that poor boy's promising future."'

'And the victim was shamed and harassed until she dropped out of college,' I said. 'Nobody cared about her future.'

There was a moment of silence, while we contemplated the injustice of that ruling.

'The killer continued denigrating the corpse by urinating on Trey. Angela found a pubic hair and urine.'

'Did you get any DNA?' I asked.

'Yes, off the pubic hair. And we were very lucky to get DNA in the urine.'

'Why is that lucky?' Jace asked.

'Because urine is not a good source of DNA,' Katie said. 'Not like hair or blood. Depends on how many skin cells are in the stuff. The pubic hair was male, and so was the urine. The hair's DNA matches the urine. So when the killer unzipped to show his contempt, he gave us a good clue. Too bad he's not in the system.'

'Too bad,' Jace said. 'But you've given us lots of new information. Find anything else that could help us?'

'I gather you haven't found the weapon?' Katie asked.

'No, and we did a grid search of the crime scene and the grounds,' he said. 'Checked all the trash bins and Dumpsters. Nothing.'

'Both victims had multiple stab wounds and no defensive wounds,' she said. 'They were too drugged to fight their attacker. There appears to have been only one weapon used in the murders, so that's good news.

'The wound depth was approximately seven inches. The weapon was single edged, possibly a kitchen knife with a blade about an inch wide and six inches long.

'Most of the wounds on both victims are on the right side. If I'm left-handed' – Katie raised her left hand – 'I'm going to stab the right side of your body. Also, the blood spatter goes from right to left, another indication the killer was a lefty.

'So look for a left-handed killer. Someone strong. Most likely a man in his twenties.'

As we left the medical examiner's office, I told Jace, 'Great. We're looking for a killer who's in his twenties on a college campus overrun with men that age, and a weapon that could be found in any kitchen in the county – hell, the country.'

'Don't forget,' Jace said. 'The killer's left-handed. That narrows it down. How many people are left-handed?'

'Ten percent of the population.' I knew that statistic because my dad was a lefty.

'That's something,' Jace said.

But not much. This was going to be a tough case.

EIGHTEEN

Poor Beatrice Fynch. She had been planning a breakfast celebration for the morning when her daughter, Lydia, and future son-in-law, Trey, would triumphantly emerge from the crypt and Beatrice would take her place at the pinnacle of Forest society.

Jace dashed those hopes when he told Beatrice her daughter was dead. Now those dreams were shattered. I was glad I'd been working the death investigation of the man in the lime-green Kia, and avoided that grim chore. The news of Lydia's murder sent Beatrice to the hospital. Jace and I were going to talk to Beatrice this morning.

'All death notifications are bad,' Jace told me, as we hurried through the halls of Sisters of Sorrow Hospital, 'but this one was especially awful. I thought I was going to lose the mother.

'When I told Beatrice, she collapsed. Fell on the floor like her strings were cut. She was lying on the carpet, gasping for breath. She had chest pains. She felt dizzy.'

'Classic symptoms of a heart attack,' I said.

'Exactly,' Jace said. 'I called an ambulance, and Beatrice was taken to SOS. The ER doctor said she'd had a mild heart attack, and she was admitted. Naturally, I couldn't question her any more. I talked with her doctor this morning, and he said I could question her, as long as "she doesn't get too upset."'

We were at the nurses' station now on Beatrice's floor, where we were stopped by Judy, a sturdy nurse in blue scrubs. Her hair was an iron helmet, and she was ready for battle. 'Please don't upset Mrs Fynch.' Judy glared at us. 'That poor woman has had an awful shock.'

Judy led us to Beatrice's private room, and posted herself at the door, arms crossed. Beatrice looked like a plump version of Lydia. She seemed lost in the big hospital bed, as pale as the hospital sheets. Beatrice was connected by tubes and wires to beeping machines and a stainless-steel tree hung with plastic bags of fluids. Every surface in the room, from the windowsill to the nightstand, was covered with bouquets of hothouse flowers. The place smelled like a funeral home.

An older woman with harsh black hair sat in a chair next to Beatrice's bed, talking to her in a low, soothing voice and patting her hand.

When she saw us, Beatrice managed a fragile smile, and introduced the black-haired woman as her sister, Harriet.

'I am so sorry, Mrs Fynch,' Jace said.

Beatrice started sniffling and her sister handed her a tissue. 'It's so hard to accept,' she said. 'My daughter was so happy. She was engaged to the scion of one of the first families in the Forest.'

I looked up, startled. I'd never heard someone use 'scion' in everyday conversation. And Trey was no scion, though his family was rich.

'It's just too cruel.' She dabbed at her eyes.

'Yes, it is,' Jace agreed. 'Mrs Fynch, was your daughter wearing her engagement ring that night?'

'Yes, she'd never taken it off since Trey proposed.'

'Was it a new diamond?'

'Of course not,' Beatrice said. 'Trey comes from an excellent family. It was his grandmama's ring.'

Yes, she really said 'grandmama.' And if it was Trey's grandmother's ring, we probably wouldn't be able to trace it.

'The ring was three carats.' Beatrice smiled proudly. 'In a platinum setting.' Three carats was a big diamond by any standard. On a hand as small as Lydia's, three carats would look like a boulder.

'Your daughter was seen wearing the diamond at the auction, but it was not found with her later,' Jace said.

'Like I said, my daughter never took it off.'

Jace already knew the killer had pried the ring off Lydia's finger. He asked questions where he knew the answers because it could be a good lie detector.

'It must have been stolen!' Beatrice said. 'Whoever took my daughter's life stole her ring. How could they?'

'I don't know ma'am.' Jace looked so sad. 'I don't understand how anyone could do this.'

I prayed Beatrice would never know the exact details of how her daughter was butchered.

'After the auction, did your daughter change out of her dress at home?'

'No, there wasn't time to go home. Trey's family rented a suite at the inn and let us use it. I helped Lydia change there.'

'Did your daughter receive any threats before the auction?' Jace asked.

'No, of course not.' Beatrice managed a lopsided smile. 'Everyone loved Lydia. She was an A-student, homecoming queen, and campus fashion icon. She had her own vlog – that's video blog – on college fashion and make-up, and she made good money at it. Why, she made enough to pay for her entire senior year at college, and that's important. I'm divorced, but Lydia was a success despite her worthless father. *People* magazine declared her one of the top one hundred campus influencers. *People*! That's how good my daughter was. I'm sure you've seen the TV interviews about Lydia. No one had a harsh word to say about her. Not one single person.

'Everyone was so happy for Lydia when she got engaged to Trey in June. Ever since, it's been one party after another – first to announce her engagement, and then we were going to have a victory celebration the other morning. And now . . . now . . . we're planning a funeral instead of a wedding.'

Beatrice burst into heart-wrenching sobs. Nurse Judy cleared her throat and frowned at Jace and me. We held our breath, expecting to be banished. Fortunately, none of the machines Beatrice was hooked up to sounded an alarm. Jace waited for the tears to subside, then said, 'I know this is a painful subject, Mrs Fynch, but two years ago, your daughter was involved in a controversial court case.'

Beatrice sat straight up in bed. 'Do you mean when Cecilia Stone accused Trey of – of having unlawful intercourse with her?'

Unlawful intercourse? She couldn't say the word rape?

'Yes,' Jace said. 'The rape trial.'

Beatrice's eyes flared with anger. 'There was no rape! None. That's slander, pure and simple.'

Jace's voice was soft. 'I know this is upsetting, Mrs Fynch, but some people think that Lydia lied to protect Trey.'

'Lied! Lydia would never lie. She told the truth at great personal cost to herself. One of the girls in her sorority called her "racist" and refused to talk to her. Lydia was mortified, but she still told the truth.

'That trial was a ridiculous example of political correctness gone wrong. The young woman who accused Trey was . . . uh, colored . . .' Beatrice stopped for a moment, and then said, 'I mean, a person of color. Cecilia seduced Trey because she wanted to get pregnant. Then she'd be fixed for life – Trey would have to pay child support and she'd never have to work again. That young woman had a bad reputation, and Lydia was brave enough to say so.

'Trey would never have sex with someone like Cecilia. A nobody from Mississippi. He could have any woman he wanted. He was one of the most popular boys on campus.'

'Cecilia said she was a virgin,' Jace said. 'She claimed she'd never had sex before she was attacked at the fraternity house.'

'Hah! Of course she said that. Cecilia was twenty years old. Not even white girls are virgins at that age, much less someone like Cecilia. We had her investigated, Detective. I hired my own private eye. She was born out of wedlock in Greenwood, Mississippi, and her mother was fifteen when she had her. Fifteen! Like mother, like daughter, that's what I always say. Trey's just lucky he didn't get some snowflake judge. He was completely vindicated, and Cecilia went back to Greenwood, where she belongs.'

'Who do you think killed your daughter and Trey?' Jace asked.

Beatrice's eyes narrowed. 'I'll tell you who did it – Nathan Tucker, that's who! Trey was nothing but kind to that young man. He even got him into his fraternity when everyone else wanted to blackball him. But Nathan was an ingrate. He punched Trey in the face and said he'd kill him. He put Trey in the hospital and that poor boy had ever so many operations.

You check out that story, Detective, and you'll find I'm telling the truth. Nathan Tucker is the killer.'

Beatrice's voice had risen to a scream. Her chest was heaving, and the medical equipment alarms were blaring. As Nurse Judy ran over to the bed, she said, 'You two should leave. You've upset this poor grieving woman. Shame on you! Out! Out now!'

We left. Despite Judy's anger, I sure didn't feel guilty. Beatrice seemed to be grieving over the loss of her new social position rather than her murdered daughter.

Back in the SOS parking lot, Jace said, 'Are you up for tackling Trey's parents?'

'Might as well,' I said. 'They can't be any worse than Beatrice.'

'What do you know about the Lawson family?' Jace asked.

'Just local gossip, most of it malicious. Trey's father is a hedge funder from New York. When they moved here, his parents had bought an old Forest mansion and – to the horror of the locals – completely gutted the interior. The Lawsons said the dark woodwork and stained glass were gloomy. Then they painted the walls white and filled them with so-called modern art. In the Forest, that's any art which is not representational. The Lawsons were denounced as Philistines and thoroughly shunned.'

'I could see where you'd get tired of that dark, old stuff and want to show off your art collection,' Jace said.

'In the ancestor-worshipping Forest, you're not allowed those opinions,' I said. 'The Lawsons' sins get worse. They also had enough dough to put in central heating and new plumbing. In the Forest, it's fashionable to humble-brag about how drafty your family home is and how there's only a lukewarm trickle of water in the shower. The Lawsons broke those rules and many others, and then tried to shoehorn their son into society. The auction was the culmination of their ambition.'

I followed Jace in my car to the Lawson home, a white stone castle surrounded by sculpted shrubs. A Hispanic, black-uniformed housekeeper with a sorrowful face answered the doorbell. Jace asked to speak to Mr or Mrs Lawson and showed his credentials.

'This is a house of mourning.' The housekeeper's voice was mildly reproving.

'That's why I want to speak to the family,' Jace said.

'Mrs Lawson is not at home,' she said. 'I'll see if Mr Lawson will see you. Please have a seat in the salon.'

Jace and I sat on a cushiony white couch in a white room hung with abstract art. I thought I recognized a Picasso, a Mondrian, a Jackson Pollock and maybe a Kandinsky.

'This is an amazing collection,' I said to Jace.

He nodded. 'I like all the colors.'

The housekeeper returned and led us to the study, another white room with fabulous art. Trey's father sat behind a desk the size of Kansas, a single slab of gray marble that held only a slim laptop and a white orchid. Roger Lawson Junior was in his early sixties, a strong-jawed man with short gray hair. In his dark charcoal suit and skinny tie, he looked like a parody of a Fifties executive.

Jace introduced both of us. Roger Lawson ignored me and said, 'I remember you, Detective. You were here on the worst day of my life. Please be seated.'

Jace and I sat in what looked like vintage black Eames side chairs.

'I'm sorry for your loss,' Jace said.

Lawson nodded.

'Can you tell us if your son received any threats before the auction?' Jace asked.

'Yes,' Lawson said. 'The night before the auction, about seven o'clock.'

I sat forward. This was news.

'Trey received a phone call. The voice was obviously disguised to sound like Darth Vader. The caller said if Trey outbid the Du Pres family, he would die.'

'Did your son report the call?'

'Of course not.' Lawson looked shocked. 'We assumed it was some crank and ignored it. Neither one of us expected that Trey would be murdered. Things like that don't happen here.'

I stifled a sigh. There it was again – that line. The rich believed their money shielded them from everything unpleasant and were stunned when that belief failed.

'This was no crank,' Jace said. 'Did your son get the call on his cell phone?'

'No, our landline, I'm afraid,' Lawson said. 'That means it can't be traced, right?'

'Right,' Jace said. 'Who has your landline number?'

'Everyone, I assume.' Lawson shrugged. 'The number's listed in the directory.'

'I have to ask you an unpleasant question,' Jace began, but Lawson cut him off. 'If you're talking about the rape accusation by that young woman, the court found my son innocent.'

'Not exactly,' Jace said. 'The charges were dismissed.'

'And she went back to nowhere Mississippi. A sure sign she wouldn't fight the verdict.'

Jace changed the subject. 'Who do you think killed your son and his fiancée?'

'Lydia?' Lawson dismissed her with a wave of his hand. 'A nice girl with a social-climbing mother. But she was a nobody. Collateral damage. The real target was my son.

'It could only be two people who would do this. One is Nathan Tucker. He punched my son and threatened to kill him, and Trey had him arrested for assault. He was convicted and Tucker has been bitter ever since.

'But I think it was one of the Du Pres. They're sneaky, all of them. My son was smart and clever and they wanted him out of the way. Mark my words, Detective. Someone in that family killed him.'

NINETEEN

As we walked to our cars, Jace said, 'I'm going to talk to Nathan Tucker. He's definitely a person of interest. He was arrested for assaulting Trey, and he's violent: he has a sheet for felony assault. Nathan beat Trey so bad he went to the hospital.'

'What did Nate do that caused so much damage?'

'He popped Trey in the nose.'

I almost laughed. 'And Trey went to the hospital for a punch in the nose?'

'Nathan must have really slugged him. Trey couldn't breathe and needed a plastic surgeon to reconstruct his nose. It took two operations to restore it.

'That punch got Nathan arrested for first-degree assault, but his charges were reduced to third degree. Nathan got three years' probation and a thousand-dollar fine, plus he had to pay Trey's medical bills.'

'Sounds fair.'

'I think the judge let him off lightly. If the judge had followed the sentencing guidelines, Nathan would have faced four years in jail and a ten-thousand-dollar fine.

'I checked with Nathan's parole officer. He's at work now.'

'Where? The car wash? McDonald's? Forest Foreign Car Repair?' Those were the local companies that hired felons.

'No, he's an apprentice stonemason at the Remember Forever Monument Company.'

'He makes gravestones?'

'His family does. It's been their business since before the Civil War. Want to go with me?'

'Can I still do that?'

'Technically, you're still on loan to me to help solve this case. The national media has been piling on.'

'I saw the TV news last night. It was on all the channels.'

'The chief is under incredible pressure. If it's not solved

soon, he could lose his job. At least, that's the scuttlebutt. He can't leave the station without a mob of reporters following him. The mayor calls him hourly. Now a couple of guys are in town, talking about a Netflix miniseries. The chief is frantic to have this solved. Your boss, Evarts, said you could help me unless you get a call for a death investigation.'

'I'm still on call today,' I said. 'I'll meet you there.'

The Remember Forever Monument Company was on the same road as the Chouteau Forest Cemetery. The company's dignified black sign announced the name in gold letters, along with this phrase: 'Since 1843.' The yard was surrounded by a black wrought-iron fence topped with fleur-de-lis. Gray granite headstones and grieving angels were showcased in the yard.

Jace and I were met at the reception desk by a young, brown-skinned woman in a dark suit and white blouse. A sign on the counter said, 'Samantha Freeman, Receptionist.'

'Mr Tucker is in the back,' Samantha said. 'I'll find him.'

While she made a call on her phone, I studied the company history posted on the walls.

'A Proud History,' said the first panel. 'Our monuments adorn historic Black burial grounds, including the Father Dickson Cemetery and Greenwood Cemetery in the St. Louis area. These cemeteries are from the time when even death was separate and unequal. Before the Civil War, enslaved people were not allowed headstones or grave markers with their names. Slave owners were so frightened, they didn't want Black people gathering for any reason, not even funerals. Our stonework marks the graves of Black authors, Underground Railroad leaders, victims of lynchings, formerly enslaved people and the military heroes of five wars.'

I had just started reading 'Remember Forever Monuments in Modern Times' when a young man entered the reception area. Nathan was a striking man in his early twenties, with dark brown eyes, light brown skin and strong hands. Now I could see how he could have seriously damaged Trey's nose with a punch. Nathan was conservatively dressed in a gray shirt, darker gray tie and black pants. He wore no socks and black Wolf & Shepherd SwiftKnit shoes, an upscale athletic shoe.

'You wanted to see me?' Nathan seemed to be struggling to keep his voice neutral. Samantha peeked over the top of her desk to watch the show.

Jace showed his ID and said, 'Let's go somewhere private.' It was a command, not a request.

Nathan led us to a small dark blue office with a round table holding a thick book of gravestone photos. Headstone photos covered the walls. The place was starting to creep me out.

We sat at the round table, and declined the offer of coffee. 'I want to ask you some questions about the death of Trey Lawson,' Jace said.

Nathan quickly flared into anger. 'Why me? Trey had lots of enemies.'

'That may be, but you were convicted of assaulting him.'

'I punched him because he was a racist, constantly ragging me. He never stopped needling me.'

'What did Trey say that sent you over the edge?' Jace asked.

Nathan avoided Jace's eyes and studied his hands. 'Nothing. He just kept at me. One day I had enough and punched him.'

I wondered if Nathan was lying, or holding something back. Jace let the silence build until Nathan burst out, 'I've paid for it, too. Three years' probation, a thousand-dollar fine and I had to pay for Trey's nose jobs. That's another eight thousand dollars. I'm still working off that money.'

'Where were you October thirtieth, the night of the murder?' Jace asked.

'I was here, helping my uncle finish a special order. He can tell you.'

'Anyone else see you here?' Jace asked. 'Someone who's not related?'

'Reggie Weston. He transported the headstone. We didn't load it until two a.m.'

Jace quickly changed topics. 'What can you tell me about the tunnel leading to the Cursed Crypt?'

'I don't know what you're talking about.' Nathan kept his head down, refusing to look at either of us.

'Also, we'd like your shoes.'

Nathan looked dumbfounded. 'My shoes? Why?'

'We found a shoe print and we want to see if they'll match it.'

'What if I say no?'

'Then I'll get a court order,' Jace said.

Nathan took off his shoes and sighed. 'These shoes have been nothing but trouble,' he said. 'I bought them a month ago, and one night, after I worked out and showered at the gym, they were missing when I came into the locker room. I looked all over and couldn't find them. It must have been some kind of Halloween prank, because the same shoes showed up in the gym's Lost and Found a couple of days after.'

'When was this?' I heard suspicion in Jace's voice.

'They went missing two days before Halloween. I got a call from the gym yesterday that they'd found my shoes. And someone had covered the soles with bleach.' Nathan untied his shoes, slipped them off and showed the right shoe to Jace. 'See this mark here on the black fabric? That was caused by bleach.'

'Huh,' Jace said. 'Which gym do you use?'

'The Chouteau U gym. Students can use it for free.'

'Do you have a carry bag for these shoes?' Jace asked.

'I'll get one, and my other shoes in my locker,' Nathan said. 'I'll be right back.'

He was back five minutes later, wearing a disreputable pair of tennis shoes, with his shoes in a plastic grocery bag.

That's when my work cell phone buzzed. Jace looked at me. I showed him the display: 'Ray Greiman.' I had to leave, and Jace knew it. Nathan looked relieved when we both stood up.

'Don't look too happy, Nathan,' Jace said. 'We'll be back. And next time we'll get the truth. All of it.'

Outside, on the way to our cars, Jace said, 'He's lying.'

'He's definitely not telling us everything,' I said. 'What do you think of the story about the bleached soles on his shoes?'

'I think if he was crawling in that tunnel and tried to get

rid of the blood on the soles, he's given us a good excuse.'

'Do you think he knows about the stone memorial in the tunnel?'

'I'm sure of it.'

TWENTY

My cell phone was buzzing like an angry hornet. Jace looked concerned. 'You'd better answer, Angela, or Greiman will go ballistic.'

As soon as I answered, Greiman screamed at me. 'Where the hell have you been? You're supposed to pick up your phone immediately.'

'Good afternoon, Detective Greiman. What do you want?'

'I want you to get your sorry ass over to a Toonerville crime scene.'

Toonerville was the sneery name for the working-class side of the Forest. Greiman gave me the address. Ten minutes later, I was at a small white bungalow with green shutters, surrounded by a fleet of official vehicles. If the place had been painted and the lawn raked, it could have been as attractive as its neighbors.

I rolled my DI case up the sidewalk to the front door, and was happy to see Mike, the talky uniform. After I signed the crime scene log, Mike gave me the case number and a pair of booties. 'This is a weird one, Angela. A drowning. In the living room, of all places. Be careful. Greiman's in a bad mood.'

'So what else is new?'

'Just sayin'. You've been warned.'

The small living room held a bizarre scene: an overturned metal bucket, a dead woman sprawled face-up on the carpet in a pool of water, and a large man in blue mechanic's overalls weeping on a brown plaid couch. Greiman was standing next to the man, patting his brawny shoulder.

The wall-to-wall carpet was soaked with a clear liquid, and the east end of the coffee table had been pushed against a brown club chair.

I squished nearer to the body for a closer look. The woman was wearing a plain pink T-shirt, cutoff jeans and one flip-flop. The other sandal was broken. The woman had a ring of livid bruises around her neck and more on her biceps. Both her knees were bruised, and some of her fingernails were broken. Tossed on the floor near her body was a pale pink plastic belt.

I met Greiman in the kitchen. As usual, he was as well-dressed as a clothing store dummy – and just as smart.

'What happened?' I asked, keeping my voice low.

'That's Charlie Wheatly on the couch.'

On closer inspection, Charlie was built like a pro wrestler. His overalls were open at the neck. A gold chain nestled in a thick carpet of black chest hair. His hands sported homemade tattoos that spelled 'Love' and 'Hate.' Livid red marks crossed his hands. He had more marks on his arms, where he'd rolled up his sleeves.

'I'm guessing those are jailhouse tattoos on his hands,' I said. 'He's got a sheet, doesn't he?'

Greiman shrugged. 'If he does, he's reformed. He works for us in the motor pool, and he's the only one who can keep the chief's 1986 Mercedes running. His wife's name is Emmelina. She's a wetback.'

'A what?'

'Sorry to offend your tender sensibilities, Snowflake.' Greiman's voice was mocking. 'I meant to say she crossed the Mexican border illegally and then hit the jackpot when she married Charlie and became a citizen.'

'So how did Emmelina drown in her living room?' I asked.

'According to Charlie, he came home about an hour ago – says he forgot his lunch – and found his wife dead. He thought she must have tripped, fallen head-first in the bucket, and drowned.'

'That's convenient,' I said. 'Why did she have a scrub bucket in the living room? She has wall-to-wall carpet.'

'I don't know. I guess she'd been scrubbing the bathroom, and she wanted to empty the dirty water in the kitchen.'

That man had never done any serious cleaning. 'So why carry the heavy bucket through the house to the kitchen sink? She could have dumped the water down the toilet.'

'I don't know. I don't scrub things.' He sounded proud of that.

'And you believe the husband?'

'Like I said, he works for us.'

'So what? Have you bagged his hands? Taken his clothes for evidence? Checked his body for scratches and photographed them? Did you send the uniforms to question the neighbors and find out if the couple argued? You sure haven't called for a crime scene tech.'

'No need. I believe him. It was an accidental death.'

'Why is there a pink belt near the body?'

Now Greiman was red-faced with anger. 'I have no idea. Let me remind you, Angela Richman, I'm the detective in charge of this case. Just because you've been hanging around with Jace playing cop doesn't make you a homicide detective.'

'I never said I was. But my report will show evidence of drowning, and the medical examiner will back me up. I'm betting those bruises around Emmelina Wheatly's neck are enough to prove she was held down in that bucket until she drowned. The bruises on her arms and knees are more evidence. I'll bag her hands, and the ME will probably find DNA under her fingernails.

'And when the new Chouteau County prosecuting attorney asks for the husband's clothes, photos of his skin, and scrapings from his nails, what are you going to tell her, "I don't have anything, but Charlie sure knows how to fix the chief's car"?'

That was a threat, and Greiman knew it. Liz Freeman, our newly elected prosecuting attorney, had no patience for sloppy police work or the Forest's old boys' network.

Greiman stomped out to the kitchen and began making phone calls.

I opened the Drowning Victim Investigation form on my iPad and started with her demographic information.

Charlie, who was still crying what I considered crocodile tears, stopped long enough to give me Emmelina's information. She was thirty-two, and born in Monterrey, Mexico. Both her parents were deceased. She was eighteen when she crossed the border, and lived with her aunt in Austin, Texas. She met Charlie at a music festival and married him when she was twenty-two. According to Charlie there were no problems with the marriage, and he brought Aunt Maria to

Chouteau County 'because I loved Emmelina and didn't want her to be lonely.' I took those last two bits of information with a boulder of salt. I definitely wanted to talk to Aunt Maria Constanza Zarcos.

'Did you see your wife fall, Mr Wheatly?' I asked.

'No, when I arrived home, she'd already fallen into the bucket. I tried to revive her but it was too late.'

'How do you think she managed to fall into a scrub bucket?'

'I guess she's just clumsy,' he said.

I was furious, but didn't respond. Instead, I photographed the body – long shots, medium and close-ups – then pulled on four pairs of nitrile gloves and began the formal body inspection.

Charlie said when he saw Emmelina, he'd removed her head from the bucket and tried to revive her with chest compressions. The decedent's long black hair was wet and tangled, and spread over the carpet. She was lying face-up, her head pointed east and her feet west, with both arms neatly folded on her chest. There were contusions on both wrists.

Emmelina's face was swollen. Her eyes seemed bruised and bulging, and the eyelids were closed. She had a two-inch abrasion on her forehead and a cut-like defect on the tip of her nose, as well as a two-inch contusion (bruise) on her left cheek. Around her neck was a three-inch band of bruises, a horrible necklace. Both biceps had extensive contusions.

Emmelina's hands testified she'd fought for her life. She had abrasions and contusions on the wrists and knuckles of both hands – more than thirty. Her nails were medium length and unpolished, and she had three broken nails on her left hand and four on her right. I bagged both hands in paper bags and sealed them with evidence tape. I also photographed the belt near her body and bagged it.

'Is this your wife's belt?' I asked Charlie.

He shrugged. 'I guess so. I can't keep track of the crap she wears.'

Her T-shirt had a four-inch tear at the neck, and the shirt was soaked. The color showed the damp areas well. I photographed the bruises on both knees and a two-inch contusion on her right foot, the one missing the flip-flop.

Emmelina was a small woman. I measured her at five feet tall and guestimated her weight at a hundred pounds.

Greiman finally started doing his job. He ordered a uniform to accompany Charlie, the new widower, to the bedroom. Charlie would have to change out of his clothes under the uniform's supervision, and then his clothes would be bagged as evidence.

Nitpicker arrived shortly after Charlie retired to the bedroom, and Greiman sent her to photograph the husband's body for scratches and other marks.

I went back to my drowning victim form.

'Type of Body of Water,' the form said. 'River/lake/stream, swimming pool, bathtub/bucket.'

Apparently bucket drownings happened often enough to be listed on the form. I knew mop buckets were hazards for toddlers, but this was the first adult bucket drowning I'd encountered.

I waited for Nitpicker to come back, then spread a sterile sheet from the DI case on the damp carpet. She helped me turn the decedent. I documented the bruises on her neck, back and shoulders, as well as her arms.

'Looks like the bastard held her down in the bucket until she drowned,' Nitpicker said. 'I bet he used her belt to restrain her.'

'You think the husband killed her?' I whispered.

'I think the husband has an unusual number of scratches on his arms and hands, and someone yanked a clump of hair out of his chest.'

'I didn't find anything in the victim's hands.' Victims sometimes held valuable evidence in a death grip.

'He could have found it and flushed it,' she said. 'I'll check the toilet. If I'm lucky, I'll be able to retrieve it with a wet vac.'

If she wasn't lucky, Nitpicker might have to take out the toilet. That would definitely wilt her jaunty lavender hair.

Nitpicker went to check the bathroom, to see if it corroborated the husband's story that it had been cleaned. She came back and said, 'The bathroom is clean as a whistle. But I found this by the door.' She showed me a photo of a blue rectangular bucket. 'It's ten inches high and six inches wide.'

'Too narrow to drown someone in,' I said.

'But the perfect size for a small woman to use. The bucket's still wet. I'll process it shortly.'

The police photographer and videographer had finished working the room. I photographed the overturned five-quart galvanized bucket, then asked Nitpicker to print it.

'This bucket is brand-new,' she said. 'It still has the Forest Hardware sticker on it. I wonder when it was bought.'

She went into the kitchen to talk to Greiman. He came out, and told Nitpicker to examine Charlie's wallet, which was with his bagged clothes.

The wallet held four crisp twenties, a wrinkled ten-dollar bill and three ones, and two receipts: one was an ATM receipt for a hundred dollars, dispensed at 12:13 p.m. today, and the other was a cash receipt from Chouteau Forest Hardware for a ten-dollar galvanized bucket bought at 12:47 today. The hardware store was down the block from the bank.

'Looks like he bought the bucket and then went home to drown his wife,' Nitpicker said.

'When I want your opinion, I'll ask for it,' Greiman said.

When Nitpicker finished printing the bucket, I went to work on the details.

My DI form wanted to know the room where the victim was found and the 'liquid submerged in.' There was about a cup of liquid left in the bucket. After I photographed the overturned bucket, I carefully stood it up and photographed the remaining liquid. It was grayish white and smelled strongly of some pine-scented cleaning product, possibly Pine-Sol. I carefully poured the remaining liquid into a sterile plastic container from my DI case, then sealed and labeled it for the lab. The five-quart scrub bucket was also placed in a container and sealed.

About that time, two uniforms came back to report what they'd heard from the neighbors. Greiman met them in the kitchen, and I wandered over there to listen.

Patrick, the younger cop, said, 'According to Mrs Janelle Jamison, the lady next door, Charlie and Emmelina fought like cats and dogs. Mrs Wheatly went to the ER at least twice this year for treatment. Mrs Jamison says to check her medical records and you'll see a history of abuse. Mrs Jamison felt sorry for Emmelina and gave her the name of a women's shelter, but Emmelina never went.'

Ted, the second uniform, said, 'Same story from the house on the other side. Lettie Edelman, a retired schoolteacher, says there was a history of long-term abuse. Charlie would get a couple of six-packs in him and start knocking his wife around. She says Charlie sent the gal to the hospital two or three times last year. Three neighbors across the street—'

Ted was interrupted by a woman screaming, 'Who says I cannot go in? That worthless *pendajo* finally killed my Emmelina!'

I wasn't sure what *pendajo* meant, but from her tone, it wasn't flattering. Greiman rushed by me so fast, he almost knocked me over.

I didn't need to eavesdrop this time. We could all hear her shouting at Greiman. I caught a glimpse of a slender woman in her late fifties with short iron-gray hair and a stylish black pantsuit. She carried a heavy leather briefcase with brass corners. Maria Zarcos spoke educated English with a slight Spanish accent.

'I am Emmelina's aunt, Maria Constanza Zarcos.'

Greiman quickly sized up her clothes and demeanor, and guessed Maria might be important. He tried to soothe her, but she wasn't having it.

'I want to see my niece.'

'I'm sorry, ma'am. I can't let you do that. This is a crime scene.' Greiman was right. Emmelina had already been identified, and it could interfere with the investigation.

'However, I am going to arrest Charles Wheatly, and bring him out.' Funny, he wasn't Charlie now.

That seemed to appease Maria.

Greiman went back inside and read Charlie his rights, then arrested him. 'No, no! I'm innocent,' Charlie said.

Greiman ignored the man's pleas and asked Mike and Ted to take Charlie into custody.

Ted went to get his car and bring it up to the end of the drive, while Mike escorted the handcuffed suspect down the front walk. Maria quietly approached and slugged Charlie in the head with her briefcase. He'd soon have a sizable contusion near his ear.

'Whoa, ma'am,' Mike said. 'You can't do that.' But she managed another swing at Charlie. Now his lip was bleeding.

'I'll sue,' Charlie said. 'How are you going to explain my injuries?'

Mike pushed him in to the backseat of the police car. 'Why, I guess you're just clumsy.'

TWENTY-ONE

Emmelina's aunt agreed to talk with me at Supreme Bean, the nearest coffee shop. We both wanted black coffee. Maria Zarcos's hands were trembling so badly, she couldn't pick up the mug. I carried her coffee to the table by the window, then got her a big, sugary cinnamon bun.

'Eat up,' I said. 'You're in shock. The sugar will help.'

Maria squeezed the coffee mug so tightly her knuckles were white. 'I wish this was his neck. I have hated Charlie Wheatly from the day my niece brought him home. Hated him. I begged her not to marry him. Begged her. But she wouldn't listen. She was pregnant and she said her baby had to have a name. I said Zarcos was a perfectly fine name, but she insisted on getting married. Abortion or putting the baby up for adoption was unthinkable for her. She married Charlie.'

Where was the child? I didn't see any sign of children in that house.

'As it turned out, she miscarried the baby. Charlie beat her so badly she had to have a hysterectomy. He spent three years in prison for domestic assault, and *still* she refused to leave him. She waited for him to get out of prison. Charlie was good with cars. He got a job here in Missouri at a repair shop that specialized in foreign cars. Chief Butkus drives an old Mercedes and Charlie keeps that car running, so the chief hired him to repair the police vehicles and protects him when he's arrested for beating my niece.'

She took a long sip of coffee and a bite of cinnamon roll. We sat in silence for a moment.

'Charlie said he brought you here from Texas to be with your niece.'

Anger flared in Maria's eyes and she shouted, 'The hell he did!'

Conversation stopped in the coffee shop, and the customers

stared at us. I glared at them until they went back to their coffee.

'I moved here to be with my niece,' Maria said. 'I was worried about her. I'm a lawyer. My specialty is domestic violence. She wouldn't leave him, no matter how hard I tried to persuade her. I helped other women, but not her. Looks like I could help everyone but my own family.'

The coffee mug slid from her shaky hands and fell to the floor. I moved my chair over, and held her while she cried. Then she dried her tears and tried to clean up the spilled coffee.

'Forget that,' I said. 'Let me take you home.'

'I'm fine. My home is a block from here. I'll walk there.'

'Do you have someone to stay with you?'

'My office assistant, Leslie. I work out of my home. Leslie must be wondering where I am. I ran out of the office as soon as I heard about my niece. I should get back. Thank you for your help.'

She rose slowly, and seemed ten years older than the woman who'd run into Emmelina's house and beat up Charlie. I watched her go, then used napkins to clean up the spilled coffee while the coffee shop owner swept up the remains of the broken mug. I thanked him and left a tip that I hoped would cover the cost of the mug.

TWENTY-TWO

By the time I left Supreme Bean, it was nearly five o'clock. When my work cell phone rang, I prayed it wasn't another death investigation.

The caller was a young woman with a voice so faint and hesitant that I could barely understand her. 'Mrs . . . uh . . . Miss . . . I mean, uh, Ms Angela Richman?'

'That's me.'

Now her voice picked up speed and confidence. 'I don't know if you remember me, but I saw you today at Remember Forever. The monument company. I'm Samantha. Samantha Freeman, the receptionist.'

Her picture flashed into my mind. She was the young, brown-skinned woman dressed in the somber suit. The one who'd tried to listen in when Jace questioned Nathan Tucker.

'Nathan told me all about your visit,' she said, as if to reassure me she hadn't been eavesdropping at the door to the conference room. 'I have some information that may help you.'

'What is it?'

'Can I meet with you? I'd like to talk in person. I get off work at five o'clock. We could meet at Mel's Truck Stop off I-55.'

That sounded like a safe meeting place. And Mel's had good cornbread.

'Does five thirty work for you?'

'It does. I'll see you there.' I called Jace so he'd know where I was going.

'Has Katie called you yet?'

'No.'

'She wants to see us at eight tomorrow morning for the Kia guy's autopsy. Enjoy Mel's cornbread.' Jace hung up.

Mel's was an old-fashioned truck stop with special parking for the big rigs and a section of booths where tired truckers could park their carcasses. Inside, under the crossover country music soundtrack, I heard a comfortable hum of conversation and smelled fried food and coffee. My stomach growled.

I was met by a hostess. 'Are you waiting for the young lady in the second booth by the window?'

I was. I could see her waving at me. I sat across from Samantha. She greeted me and we both studied our menus. A waitress named Dee-Dee in a turquoise uniform appeared quickly at our table. 'What do you want, hon?' she asked Samantha.

'I'd like a cheeseburger, fries and a Coke.'

'I want the special, chicken and dumplings, and a Coke,' I said.

Dee-Dee was back with our drinks in plastic glasses big enough to hold a dozen roses.

'Thanks for meeting me.' Samantha tore the paper off her drink straw.

'How did you get my phone number?'

'I called your office and they gave me your cell phone number.'

'Why didn't you call Detective Budewitz? He left his card.'

Samantha studied her long manicured nails, with a swirling black-and-white pattern. 'He's kinda, kinda . . .' She stopped, then gathered her courage. 'He's kinda scary.'

Jace? I thought. He's a teddy bear. But the bear had growled about potential eavesdropping.

'I thought you would be easier to talk to. About Trey and Lydia. A lot of people wanted that pair dead.'

'Who?' I sounded like an owl. Before Samantha could answer my question, our waitress bustled over with our dinners. Samantha spent a long time preparing her burger: she removed the onions and put them on her butter plate, then took off the pickles, spread ketchup and mustard on her burger, replaced the pickles, added the top bun, and cut her sandwich in half.

While she fussed with her burger, I dove into my chicken and dumplings. These were the fat, puffy Southern-style dumplings, not the noodle-like strips. The dumplings were light and fluffy. My dinner came with a small skillet of warm cornbread. I slathered the cornbread with whipped honey butter. Heavenly.

Dee-Dee was back. 'How's your chicken and dumplings, hon?'

'Delicious. The dumplings are like gravy on clouds.'

Dee-Dee laughed. 'I'll tell the cook. It's her mama's special recipe.' Samantha assured the waitress her burger was good, too.

After we'd had a few more bites, I asked Samantha again, 'Who wants Trey and Lydia dead?'

'A lot of people,' she said.

'If you watch TV, you'd think those two are saints,' I said. 'But nobody says so.'

'They don't want to miss their fifteen minutes of fame.' Samantha sipped her Coke, then said, 'They look like the perfect couple.'

'Except for Trey's rape trial,' I said.

'There's more to their dark side. You probably know that Lydia was an A-student, a homecoming queen, and a campus fashion icon.'

'Her mother told me. She said Lydia made enough money as an influencer to pay for her tuition.'

Samantha laughed, and dragged a French fry through a pool of ketchup.

'As an influencer, she barely made enough to pay for her textbooks. She made real money ghostwriting term papers for twenty dollars a page. Lydia promised a "guaranteed B or higher or your money back" and she always delivered.

'Now that some of her customers have graduated and are successful, she blackmails them about their good grades. Do you know Colin Dickson?' Samantha popped a ketchup-y fry into her mouth.

'Is he the son of the trial lawyer, T.D. Dickson?'

'That's him. Colin is cute, but dumb as a barrel of hair. Lydia's term papers got him through college. Her As and A-pluses helped balance his lackluster test scores.'

'How did he get through law school?'

'His father had him tutored, and if Colin didn't pass, he threatened to disinherit him. Colin squeaked through. Now he's at his father's firm, doing well enough. Until Lydia threatened to reveal how he made it through school. She kept copies of all his term papers, and the receipts.'

'She gave Colin receipts?'

'I told you, he wasn't the sharpest knife in the dishwasher. Lydia wanted fifty thousand dollars for her silence.'

'Does Colin have that kind of money?'

'Barely. When he marries Heather Hardesty at Christmas, he'll have much, much more.'

'Unless Lydia spilled the tea.' I spread more honey butter on the last piece of cornbread.

'There's also William Garland Harris, a young lawyer now up for promotion at his firm. She's blackmailing him, too.'

'How do you know all this?'

'I go to Chouteau Forest University, too. My friend Alison is Lydia's sorority roommate, and Lydia liked to brag about how smart she was.'

'I heard she perjured herself during the rape trial and lied about Celia Stone to help Trey escape jail.'

'She did. According to Alison, Lydia told her that Trey slipped a date rape drug in Celia's drink at a frat party. After that, Celia didn't remember anything. She woke up alone in his room, and discovered that she had had sex with someone. She went home and showered repeatedly. She had no physical evidence of the rape. Lydia trashed Celia's reputation. She told Alison – and anyone else who would listen, that Celia was "generous – the frat boys would pass her around like a bottle of tequila, and she didn't care who she slept with." Lydia also said that Celia liked to drink, so she probably couldn't remember who she slept with at the frat house.'

'That's terrible,' I said.

'Yes, it was. Lydia tried hard to persuade everyone that Celia had a lot of sex partners. You probably heard that Lydia called her "Susie Spreadlegs" in court.'

'I did. Why didn't Celia fight back?'

'How do you prove a negative? Celia's a sweet, naive country girl and Lydia was a schemer. Poor Celia was so humiliated she went back home.'

'Did Celia have a boyfriend?'

Samantha painted a heart in her pool of ketchup, using a French fry. She didn't talk for a long time.

'Samantha?'

The words burst out of her. 'Her boyfriend was Nathan. My Nathan. But it wasn't a serious romance. They weren't going to get married and she really was a virgin. The trial was two years ago, and when Celia went home, Nathan kept in touch with her for a while, but long-distance romances don't always work. He started dating me a year ago. We're engaged. We're getting married after we graduate.'

She held up her left hand and showed me a rose-gold ring with a small, perfect marquis-cut diamond.

'I see.'

Samantha must have heard the doubt in those words. Her brown eyes turned to stone. 'No, I don't think you do. Lydia was willing to marry a rapist. A multiple rapist. I'm not going to marry a man like that. Nathan would never do such a thing. If I thought for one moment he would, I'd leave him. You have to believe me.'

She seemed sincere. I wanted to get her talking again.

'Why did you say Trey was a multiple rapist?'

'Lydia told Alison. She seemed to think that Trey was clever. He started in his sophomore year, when he picked up a thirteen-year-old runaway on the highway and brought her back to his frat house. He drugged her and then he and two frat brothers raped her. The girl escaped and never told the police. Trey got away with it. Lydia claimed Trey date-raped at least two more young women. One victim, Geneva, committed suicide.'

'What about her family? Would they want revenge?'

'Her parents are dead, and she lived with her grandparents. They're in their eighties.'

'Do you know the name of the other woman he raped?'

'Donatella,' she said. 'Donatella Sommers. She transferred to City University in St. Louis.'

'Why would Lydia want to marry this awful man?'

'She wanted money, and Trey had plenty of it. They were both ambitious. Lydia thought they would be social leaders in the Forest, especially after he won the auction.'

I laughed. I couldn't help it. 'No way. Even if he made it into the Chouteau Founders Club, they'd still be ostracized.'

'That's what I thought.' Samantha gave me a small smile of satisfaction and said, 'Also, I'm not quite sure Lydia really believed Trey was a rapist. She told several people, "Any woman can yell rape. It happens after she changes her mind about the guy the next morning."'

'I can't believe a woman would say that.'

'Lydia did. Did you ever hear why Nathan punched Trey and broke his nose?'

'Because Trey taunted him about being black?'

'That was pretty much it,' Samantha said. 'Nathan never told me the full story, but I know it upsets him. He said it was too personal to talk about.'

With that, Dee-Dee the waitress appeared. 'Can I get you ladies some dessert? We have homemade lemon meringue pie.'

I looked at my empty plate. Every scrap of chicken and dumplings had disappeared, along with the last crumb of cornbread. 'I'd like more cornbread, please. And decaf coffee.'

Samantha's plate was equally bare. Even her ketchup was gone.

'I'll take that homemade pie and decaf coffee,' she said.

'Be right back,' Dee-Dee said.

I waited impatiently for the waitress to return. Meanwhile, I asked Samantha, 'What's your major at Chouteau U?'

'Marketing. When Nathan takes over the family business, I want to be able to help him. His degree is in business administration.'

'Here are your desserts, ladies.' True to her promise, Dee-Dee was back quickly.

Samantha's slice of lemon meringue pie had to be at least five inches tall. Her eyes widened. 'Wow!'

'We're famous for our mile-high pies.' Dee-Dee looked proud. She set the small skillet of warm cornbread in front of me, along with a tub of honey butter, then poured us both mugs of hot decaf and left behind an insulated pot.

When she was gone, I said, 'OK, what else can you tell me about Trey and Nathan?'

'Very little.' Samantha toppled her pie and cut off a forkful. 'I know Trey made himself out to be a scion of the Old South with a "family plantation," but I thought he was showing off, so I did some research. His ancestors were nothing but dirt-poor farmers who managed to scrape together enough money to buy one enslaved woman, Elizabeth Lawson.' Samantha took a big bite of pie.

I remembered that name. 'She married Jonathan McKee.'

She nodded. 'Right. Nathan was the first person in his family to go to college. He wanted to join Trey's frat for its business connections, but most everyone wanted to blackball him. They didn't want a black man in the fraternity. Trey persuaded his frat brothers to let Nathan join. And then Trey turned on Nathan and began tormenting him.'

'How did he do that?'

'Nathan wouldn't tell me. All I know is he got a harsh sentence for hitting Trey. Nathan's lawyer tried to explain, but the judge said there was no excuse for his behavior.'

'Anyone else who wanted Trey dead?' I asked.

'Vincent Du Pres. He didn't want Trey in the Chouteau Founders Club.'

'I know about him.' I signaled Dee-Dee for the check. 'You've been a big help, Samantha. I'll pick up dinner.'

'Thank you,' she said.

I had three more names to check: Lydia's blackmailed lawyers and Trey's other rape victim.

TWENTY-THREE

That night, the temperature dropped to nineteen degrees, giving Chouteau County the first killing frost of the season. I didn't want to get out of bed the next morning. The lead-gray sky, low and threatening, didn't allow the day to warm up. I dug my winter coat out of the closet and hurried to the medical examiner's office. I shivered as I ran from the parking lot to the ME's door and unlocked it with half-frozen fingers. For once, the morgue felt warm and inviting.

Today I would find out about the mystery man in the green Kia. I gratefully clutched the cup of hot coffee Katie handed me when I reached her office. Jace, in a neat blue shirt and striped tie, had commandeered the edge of the desk. He raised his coffee cup in greeting as I passed. I leaned against the bookcase rather than sit in the contraption that passed for a chair.

Katie was in rare form this morning. She wore a lavender wool pantsuit, which was practically a tropical color for her. She was alert and bright-eyed, and sat forward in her chair, eager to talk. Her report was short and blunt.

'Whoever rear-ended this poor bastard's car killed him twice,' she said. 'The notes say the car apparently flipped and rolled before it struck the tree, and the airbags weren't deployed. Why not?'

'I didn't see them,' I said.

'The lab believes they were stolen,' Jace added. 'They were definitely missing.' He sipped his coffee.

'When I opened John Doe up and looked at his brain,' Katie said, 'I found a significant hematoma – a blood clot – that could have killed him. He definitely would have needed brain surgery. He also had a collapsed right lung, three broken ribs, and a diagonal contusion across his chest caused by his seat-belt. If he'd survived the accident and the surgery, he would have needed a substantial recovery time.

'As you know, he didn't get that chance. Someone stran-gled him with their bare hands. His hyoid bone was fractured.'

I knew a broken hyoid often happened in manual strangling. The hyoid, sometimes known as the tongue bone, is a U-shaped bone between the upper front part of the chin and the thyroid cartilage. Basically, it holds up your tongue, which sits on top of the bone.

Katie was still talking. 'The victim also had other signs of manual strangulation, including petechial hemorrhaging. That's pinpoint hemorrhaging in the eyes. It looks like the killer sat on the man's chest to kill him.'

She looked at Jace. 'You're looking for one cold-blooded killer, who could sit on a dying man's chest and strangle him.'

'What else can you tell me about this victim?' Jace asked.

'Angela's report had it down pretty well. He was in his mid-twenties, five feet seven inches tall, and weighed one hundred forty-two pounds. He may have been in several fights some time prior to his death. He had more than one boxer's fracture.'

Jace said, 'I remember those from when I was on the job in Chicago. That's a break in the bones of the hand that make up the knuckles.'

'The metacarpals,' Katie said.

'It's caused by punching something hard,' Jace said.

'Right.' Katie took control again. 'The decedent also had an old, healed fracture of the nasal bone. He was lucky. Hit someone the wrong way, and a good punch in the nose can drive that bone into the brain and kill them.'

'Do you think he was a boxer?' Jace sipped his coffee.

'I doubt it,' Katie said. 'Boxing takes training and attention to diet, and this guy rarely hit the gym. He wasn't fat, but he was out of shape. In a few years, he'd have a dad bod.'

'Hey!' Jace pretended to be hurt. 'We can't all be ripped. Some women like us softly rounded types.'

'I wasn't referring to anyone in this room.' Katie grinned at him.

'Back to our John Doe. His tox screen came back with traces of cocaine, and his nasal septum – the wall that separates the left and right sides of the nasal passages – was developing a small hole. In other words, John Doe was a frequent flier with the white lady. Any questions?'

I felt like a C-student, but I couldn't think of anything to ask Katie.

'Now tell me what you found, Jace,' she said.

Jace set down his coffee cup. Today, he was carefully dressed in a blue shirt and blue striped tie. 'The lab found two ounces of coke in his car – that's fifty-six grams. He also had a small bag of pretty pills in several colors that turned out to be MDMA, also known as ecstasy or molly. He had nearly an ounce of molly. Missouri law says those are felony amounts. If caught, he was looking at seven years in jail, and a five-thousand-dollar fine.'

'Most states are decriminalizing drugs, but not Missouri,' I said.

'Do you think he was dealing?' Katie asked.

'Yes,' Jace said. 'If he was, we hadn't caught him yet. He didn't have a sheet.

'The good news is, we may be able to identify John Doe. The killer damaged two VIN numbers on the green Kia, but the lab found a third under the hood. That let us look up the owner. He's Gavin Bronson, a student at Chouteau University. He's younger than our accident victim – twenty-one – but about the same height and weight.'

'So it could be him,' Katie said. 'I just gave you estimates, not the exact age.'

'We'll see. Let's go talk to Gavin, Angela.'

Before we went left, I told Jace and Katie about my dinner with Samantha, Nathan's fiancée. 'You realize she also gave you more reasons why Nathan could have killed Lydia and Trey,' Katie said.

'I do, but I think she was telling the truth. And if you want, Jace, I'll do the interviews with the lawyers and the other rape victim and report back.'

'Fine with me,' he said. We said goodbye to Katie and walked briskly to our cars, chased by a cold winter wind. 'I sure hope this Gavin Bronson is a good lead,' Jace said. 'The chief is going crazy. The BBC is in town now for the story.'

I noticed Jace looked more tired than usual. 'The pressure on you must be enormous.'

'I can't turn on a computer or TV without some mention of the Cursed Crypt murders, and every time the chief sees something, he's on the horn to me.' Jace's shoulders were hunched against the cold. 'Once word gets out there were three murders, it will only get worse.'

I followed Jace to the registrar's office at Chouteau Forest U, where we learned that Gavin was an engineering student. We checked his student ID photo and learned he would soon be getting out of a class called advanced trigonometry.

Jace and I waited outside the class. When the bell rang, chattering students gathered their books and backpacks and left in groups. Gavin was one of the last to leave, and he was alone.

His longish brown hair, jeans, gray T-shirt and plaid shirt needed a wash. Gavin was about average height, with a thin face, bony nose and denim-blue eyes with long lashes. He'd look distinguished as he aged.

As soon as Jace showed Gavin his credentials, the student's face lit up. 'Did you find my car already?'

'What do you drive?' Jace asked.

'A green Kia,' he said.

'Let's find a place where we can talk,' Jace said.

We followed Gavin across campus to the student union. On the walk there, I asked Gavin what his advanced trig course covered. He said, 'The inverse trigonometric functions, solving equations involving trig concepts, and additional identities, including double and half angles.'

'Interesting,' I said, as if I understood.

The student union smelled like the special of the day: cheeseburgers and onion rings. 'You want some lunch?' he said. 'The food's not bad. I work the breakfast shift in the kitchen.'

'No,' Jace said. 'I'm not interested in food. I want to hear about your stolen car.'

'I'm not sure it's stolen,' Gavin said. 'I lent it to my friend Eli, Elijah Coffey, last Friday.'

'October thirtieth?'

'Yes, that's it. Eli was supposed to bring it back Monday, but he didn't. I was worried about my car. Eli, too, of course. I haven't seen him since he drove off with the car Friday afternoon.'

'Does Eli go to school here?' Jace looked Gavin in the eye.

Gavin shifted in his seat, suddenly uncomfortable. 'He used to, but he dropped out. Said he made more money doing deliveries.'

'Who did he deliver for: Amazon, Instacart, FedEx, Grubhub?'

The tips of Gavin's ears were bright red. 'None of them. He was a freelancer. If you wanted a pizza or something, you'd call Eli, and he'd pick it up and bring it to your dorm room.'

'Along with the drugs,' Jace added. 'Which did you use – molly or coke?'

'Me? Nothing! I'm too broke to afford that stuff. Please. Don't say that. I could lose my scholarship – and my job.'

'So why lend a drug dealer your car?'

'Because he paid me,' Gavin said. 'I got twenty-five or thirty bucks for giving him my car.'

'You realize that makes you an accessory,' Jace said.

'All I knew was he delivered pizza and beer.' Gavin studied the tabletop. 'He didn't use me all the time. He borrowed other kids' cars. He thought – I don't know what he thought.'

'That he'd be harder for the police to trace if he didn't use the same car?'

Gavin shrugged. 'I guess so.' He spoke so softly we could hardly hear him.

'Where does Eli live?' Jace asked.

'He rents a house in Toonerville. A whole house. I've never been there.' He gave Jace the address.

'What time did Eli contact you about borrowing your car last Friday?'

'Late afternoon – about four. He said he had a pick-up and delivery and he was getting five hundred dollars cash upfront and another five hundred after the delivery. He said he'd pay me fifty bucks if he could have the car until Monday morning. He took my Kia about six that night, and never returned it.'

'And you didn't call the police,' Jace said.

'No, I didn't know if he had . . .' Gavin suddenly stopped.

'Done something illegal?' Jace finished the sentence.

Gavin looked trapped. 'No, I thought he might have been stopped by the police, even though he told me this job was totally legit.'

'A thousand dollars to make a delivery sounds legitimate to you?'

Gavin shrugged again.

'Did Eli say anything else about this job?'

'No. Eli told me he was paid the extra money so he wouldn't say who hired him, but it was a name I'd know.'

'What does Eli look like?' Jace asked.

'He's about my height but he has dark hair dyed blond on the edges. He spends major money on his hair. It's a trendy style – I think he said it was short tight curls with faded sides and blond highlights, but I'm not sure.'

Gavin looked frightened now. 'Why do you want to know this? Is Eli in trouble?'

'Not any more,' Jace said. 'Eli's dead.'

'Dead? Who shot him?'

'Why would you say that?' Jace asked.

'Well, if you're dealing drugs, you must know some bad people.'

'I thought you said Eli wasn't doing anything illegal.'

'You're getting me all tangled up.' Gavin looked frightened – and very young.

Jace leaned forward. 'That happens when you lie. It's a very bad idea to lie to the police. Now tell me the truth. Why did you think Eli was shot?'

'Maybe he crossed some bad people. Other drug dealers.'

'Do you have any reason to believe that?' Jace asked.

'No.' Gavin shook his head. 'What about my car?'

'It's totaled.' Before Gavin could react, Jace said, 'Does Eli have any family here?'

'He never talked about his family. I'm not even sure he has a steady girlfriend.'

'Then you'll have to come along with us,' Jace said. 'To identify the body.'

'No! This is terrible.'

'Yes, it is. But it's even worse for Eli.'

TWENTY-FOUR

Outside again, the sun was shining, and it was gloriously warm. Missouri's changeable weather had flipped in the right direction. Jace drove Gavin to the medical examiner's office to ID the man in the green Kia, and I followed them. Jace told me Gavin never said a word the whole trip. Jace wondered if the kid was too frightened to talk.

Identifying a body is not like you see in the movies. You know the scene: the friend or family member goes to the morgue, and enters a bleak room that looks like a cross between a surgical suite and a butcher shop. A morgue attendant, a hugely fat man with bad hair, puts down his ham sandwich on an autopsy table, and escorts the person to a row of stainless-steel coolers. There the attendant rolls out a cold steel drawer and whips back the white sheet on the body, revealing just the face. The dead person is eerily beautiful.

If a man is identifying the body, he gives the morgue attendant a stoic nod. The women always collapse. Wash, rinse and repeat if the person IDs the body through a viewing window at the morgue.

The reality is nothing like that. At the medical examiner's office, Gavin was escorted to a soothing beige room that looked like a comfortable living room, where Betty, a grandmotherly social worker, talked to him. I sat on a beige couch in the corner.

Gavin looked young and frightened. He sat at an oak kitchen table, drinking coffee and eating oatmeal cookies. Finally, when he seemed calmer, Betty said, 'I'll show you the photographs of the person, but only when you're ready. There's nothing scary about the photos.'

Except that Eli was dead, I thought. And murdered.

Half a dozen cookies and two cups of heavily sugared coffee later, Gavin said, 'I think I can do it.' He signed the permission papers, and Betty brought out four photos. 'Turn them over when you're ready,' she said. 'Take as long as you want.'

Gavin gulped, and turned over the first photo. It showed only Eli's face and hair. In death, Eli had a sculpted face, with high cheekbones. His stylish hair was a straggling mop. His skin had a slight green tinge and his eyes were closed and sunken. His neck was covered, to hide the brutal strangling.

Gavin turned white as coffee cream and his voice was shaky. 'That's him. That's Eli. I mean, Elijah Coffey. He's really dead. Oh, gawd, I'm gonna barf.'

Gavin ran for the restroom. Several minutes later, I heard a toilet flush, and Gavin emerged. He still looked shaken, and his face was damp. He must have washed it.

'Would you like some water?' Betty asked.

'Yes, please.' Gavin's voice was a croak.

Betty handed him a bottle of water, and he drank nearly half. 'Would you like to talk to me or someone else, dear? To help you process what you've seen?'

Gavin rose. 'No, thanks,' he said. 'I've processed it. Eli's dead. For real. I'd like to go home, please.'

'Just sign this paperwork for me,' Betty said.

While Gavin signed the papers, Jace made a call.

'All finished, Detective,' Betty said.

'Can I go home now?' Gavin asked.

'Certainly,' Jace said. Gavin's face brightened for the first time since he'd entered the building.

'I'll call a uniform to drive you back to campus.'

'In a police car? I have to ride in a cop car?' Now Gavin looked scared and queasy.

Jace looked at him. 'Yes. Unless you want to walk. I'm not charging you as an accessory, even though you knew Eli was borrowing your car to deliver illegal substances.'

'But—' Gavin said.

Jace held up his hand. 'Don't lie. And don't tell me you didn't know he was delivering drugs, or beer to underage students. As for Eli's last job, getting a thousand dollars to deliver a package was too good to be true. You're smart, Gavin. And if you're as smart as I think you are, you won't lend your car for shady deals again. Got it?'

Gavin nodded.

'Here's a copy of the accident report,' Jace said. 'I hope you have insurance.'

Gavin nodded again.

'The police car will be waiting by the entrance,' Jace said.

Betty gave Gavin a Ziploc bag of oatmeal cookies and patted his shoulder. 'Go down the hall and turn right, dear. You'll see the exit.'

TWENTY-FIVE

After Gavin left, I asked, 'Are you trying to scare Gavin straight, Jace?'

'You're darn right.' Jace checked his watch. 'It's twelve thirty. I have reports to write.'

'I want to go talk to Donatella Sommers, Trey's date-rape victim.'

'Good idea. She'll probably be more comfortable talking to a woman. I'll get her address and cell phone number for you.'

Ten minutes later, Donatella had agreed to see me at the City University campus in St. Louis. We were meeting at the Sweet Shoppe, a nostalgic take on a 1950s malt shop.

The retro shop should have been packed with bobbysoxers and guys in flattops and saddle shoes. The college students in modern dress looked oddly out of place amid the chrome, black-and-white tile, and red leatherette booths.

Donatella was sitting in a booth in the back, away from the other students, sipping a chocolate malt from a tall glass.

I introduced myself. 'The malts here are amazing,' she said.

'Thanks. I'll have a Coke. I haven't had a real fountain Coke in a while.'

The soda jerk, who was about eighteen and wore the traditional paper hat and apron, poured soda syrup into the glass, added seltzer and asked, 'Would you like a scoop of vanilla ice cream?'

'Sure.'

While I waited for my ice-cream float, I studied Donatella. She was a pretty, rather prosaic young woman with enviable ivory skin and long brown hair, parted on the right side. She had the thin, wiry body of a runner. Donatella wore a gold crucifix on her neck and a modest pink cotton blouse with the sleeves rolled up. On the inside of her right arm was a tattoo.

Odd. She didn't seem like the tattoo type.

As I returned to the booth, I saw the tattoo was a Bible verse. The words were written in cursive: 'I can do all things through Christ, who strengthens me. Philippians 4:13.' The verse was surrounded by lilies.

'You have the right skin for a tattoo,' I said.

She blushed. 'I had the tattoo after the . . . after Trey . . .' She stopped.

'It's OK, Donatella. This must be hard to talk about.'

She took a deep breath. 'It is. But Pastor Dave says I won't heal until I can talk about what happened. He said talking to you might help other young women. I'm not supposed to rejoice that Trey is dead, but I do.'

'When did this happen?'

'Springtime, nearly three years ago. A warm, beautiful day, with flowers blooming everywhere. I went to Chouteau Forest University then. I met Trey in the student union. I was alone, eating my lunch. He asked if he could sit at my table. Trey was very handsome and I was flattered. Boys like him didn't pay attention to girls like me. We talked and laughed and I had a good time.

'After lunch, we went for a walk. After about half an hour, I said I had to go to class, and told him goodbye. I didn't expect to see him again. But Trey invited me to a party at his fraternity house the next night.

'I was so excited. The party was all I could think about. My roommate, Nina, went with me to shop for a new dress. I found the perfect one: powder blue, with lace on it. I bought new shoes, too. Black patent high heels.'

My heart hurt for the naive young woman as she described her innocent preparations for the party.

'When I got there about nine thirty, the party was in full swing. I could hear the music all the way down the block. There were so many people, they couldn't fit inside the frat house. Some were on the porch, where there was a keg of beer. Others were on the lawn or hanging out on the upstairs balcony. Everyone was drinking. I told Trey I didn't drink alcohol, and he said that was OK – they had punch for nondrinkers.

'We went inside, and everyone was dancing. He told me to

wait by the stairs to the second floor. He came back with a red cup of fruit punch. It was hot and crowded and I was thirsty. I drank it all and we danced for a while, but then I felt dizzy.'

She stopped and her face started to crumple. She quickly sipped more of her chocolate malt. After a while, she gathered the strength to continue her story.

'And I woke up the next morning. I was in a bed. Trey's bed, and I wasn't wearing any clothes. There was blood on the sheet.'

'It was your first time?' I asked.

'Yes. And I don't remember anything. I threw on my clothes and went home and showered and showered and scrubbed myself until my skin was raw, and then I threw away everything I'd been wearing, even my new dress and shoes.

'I went to see Pastor Dave. He wanted me to call the police, but I couldn't. I refused, and he didn't force me. Later on, when I saw how Celia Stone was treated when she told the police about Trey, I was glad I didn't.'

'That poor young woman was slut-shamed,' I said.

'What people did to her was terrible. I don't think I could have survived it. I stayed at Chouteau U until the end of the semester and then I transferred here to City University. I still see Pastor Dave for spiritual counseling. He's been a big help.

'At first, I wanted revenge. I would lie awake at night and think about ways to kill Trey. I was filled with hate and rage. Pastor Dave helped me get past that. He told me that revenge wasn't free. It came at a very high cost, and if I didn't learn to let go of my hate and forgive Trey, I would hurt myself. I knew he was right. I couldn't sleep, and my grades were starting to slip.

'Pastor Dave suggested that I take up running, along with daily prayer. Both of those helped me.

'I never saw Trey again. I still haven't forgiven him, but I'm working on it. And I'm glad he's dead. The Lord gave me justice.'

Or the Devil, I thought, but didn't interrupt.

'God took away Trey's life at the moment of Trey's greatest triumph. He never got to join the Chouteau Founders Club.'

'How are you doing now?' I asked.

'I'm getting my life back. I'm dating Bill, a good Christian man I met at church. He's going to divinity school. And I was lucky I didn't get pregnant from my encounter with Trey.'

Donatella still couldn't say the word 'rape.'

Maybe she really had started to move on, but I still needed to check. 'What were you doing Halloween weekend?'

Her face lit with delight. 'I was chaperoning the younger church children the whole weekend. It was such fun. I love working with little kids. I want to teach kindergarten. Our church has special programs for them and a sleep-over in the church basement. I was with the children from after-school Friday through Sunday morning service. Pastor Dave didn't want the little ones to participate in the pagan celebrations of Halloween.'

That alibi should be easy for Jace to check, I thought.

Donatella glanced at the clock on the wall. 'I have to meet Bill at two o'clock.'

I thanked her and she stood up and waved goodbye. When I finished my float, I called Jace and told him about my interview.

'Good work,' he said. 'I'll take it from there. Go enjoy this beautiful day, Angela. Take the afternoon off.'

'Are you sure there's nothing I can do?'

'Go enjoy yourself,' he said. 'You've seen too much blood, death and mutilated bodies. I'm worried you're too wrapped up in this case.'

I hesitated and he said, 'That's an order.'

TWENTY-SIX

C hris sounded pleasantly surprised when I called him. 'Angela! What are you doing?'

'Jace is sending me home early. Are you free?'

'As a matter of fact, I am. Let's spend this afternoon at Forest Park in St. Louis. We're supposed to get more cold weather later this week. This could be our last nice day until spring. How about if I pick you up at your home?'

That sounded perfect. I hurried home and changed into jeans, a white shirt and tennis shoes, then added a jacket. Missouri weather could be treacherous.

Chris knocked on my front door. He kissed me and held up a picnic basket. Our drive to St. Louis was a preview of the fall foliage show. It was almost three thirty when we got to the park, and Chris drove through the winding streets, many designed for walking and carriage rides. Forest Park was old by Midwestern standards – almost a hundred and fifty years – and way bigger than Central Park in New York City. (St. Louis' Forest Park has 1,300 acres versus New York's 843 acres, if you keep track of that stuff, and St. Louisans do.)

We passed oaks, maples and sweetgum trees. The sweetgums, with their star-shaped leaves, were the most colorful – fiery red, yellow and plum.

Chris found a parking spot under the flame-red trees, and we walked hand in hand through a section carpeted with red leaves. I enjoyed crunching the leaves. Every few feet we would stop and kiss. The air smelled fresh and clean.

'What was your day like?' Chris asked.

'The last few days have been nothing but death, blood, dust and cobwebs. I don't want to talk about it now.'

'Fair enough. Let's walk to Round Lake for our picnic.' Chris grabbed the picnic basket out of the car trunk, and we walked to the lake, which was shaped just like its name. Round Lake had a lovely old fountain with a tall, fanlike spray that the sun turned in to diamonds. A pair of young lovers were sitting on a bench by the lake. The girl had her head on the man's shoulder, and he was wrapping her long brown curls around his fingers.

Chris spread a plaid blanket on the ground, and opened the picnic basket. He brought out china, silver – real silver – and linen napkins.

'Classy,' I said.

'I've just started.' He opened a container. 'First, the sandwiches: crostini with prosciutto and extra sharp white cheddar.'

'Yum.'

'And the salad. Strawberry and spinach with poppy seed dressing.'

'I can't wait to try this.' I must have sounded impatient because he said, 'But wait, there's more.' With a flourish, he produced a wicker bowl. 'These are figs, grapes and Honeycrisp apples – the state fruit of Minnesota.'

'Nothing beats a good northern apple.'

'And for dessert, a loaf of pumpkin chocolate chip bread.'

'This is a meal to remember,' I said.

'Oh, and last but not least, I also have a bottle of Malbec.'

'I've died and gone to heaven.'

'Not till you try my sandwiches,' he said. 'One bite, and you'll know what heaven is.'

He fixed me a plate with salad and the prosciutto and white cheddar sandwich.

'Oh.' I moaned. I couldn't help it. 'What is that sauce on the sandwich?'

'Honey and orange zest.' He poured me a glass of Malbec. We sat side by side, enjoying our sumptuous meal and the perfect day. The scene was idyllic: the flaming fall trees, the china blue sky, couples walking their dogs, young mothers with babies in strollers, kids on bicycles.

'This is amazing.' I sighed happily.

'You're amazing.' He kissed me again, and soon I was snuggled safely in his arms. The sun was setting and the wind was picking up. 'Shall we go back to your place?' I asked.

'We could. But why don't we ever go to yours?'

'Uh . . .' I had no answer. What could I say, 'My house is full of happy memories of my time with Donegan, and there's no room for you?' Or, 'I'd feel like I was cheating on my dead husband if I brought you into his bed. I mean, my bed. The bed he used to sleep in.'

The silence stretched endlessly, and finally Chris said, 'Angela, you can still love your late husband. I'm not trying to replace Donegan.'

'You're right,' I said. 'Let me think about it.'

He sighed, but he wasn't happy.

A gust of cold wind hit us, knocking over the wineglasses and blowing dead leaves on our picnic. We quickly packed up and ran for the car.

Our perfect day was over.

TWENTY-SEVEN

On the drive home, Chris asked, 'What's wrong?'
'Nothing. Nothing at all.' My arms were folded tightly across my chest.

Chris tried to cajole me out of my mood. 'Come on, Angela. I know what that means. When a woman says, "Nothing's wrong," it means everything is wrong.'

'No, I meant what I said.' Why did my voice sound so snippy? 'Nothing. Is. Wrong.' I repeated the words slowly. 'I just want to spend some time alone. To think. Please take me home.' I gave him a tentative smile.

When Chris pulled into my driveway, I said, 'Thanks for the lovely picnic,' and walked slowly up to my door. I wanted him to run after me and sweep me into his arms, saying, 'Angela, I didn't mean it. I don't care if I ever spend a night in your house. I want to be with you, on your terms.'

My romantic vision vanished as I heard his car back out of my drive. I unlocked my door, and knew I was facing a long, troubled night.

Once inside, I was saved by the bell. My cell phone rang. It was Katie.

'Hey, Angela, are you free tonight?' she said. 'Monty's working a case and barely comes up for air.'

'I just happen to be home.'

Katie sounded suspicious. 'How come?'

'No reason. I wanted to do some laundry.' My voice broke.

'I'll be right over,' Katie said.

'But—'

'Don't argue. I'll bring wine and garlic hummus.'

Fifteen minutes later, Katie was at my door with two bottles of wine. She handed me a plastic bag. 'The pita bread is in here. Nuke it.'

I did, while she opened the Merlot and poured a healthy swig into two glasses. She carried the wine and the glasses

into the living room and set them on my coffee table, so
we could sit on my comfortable leather couch. I followed
with the hummus and warm pita, leaving a fragrant trail of
garlic.

'Lot of garlic in that hummus. Good thing I'm sleeping
alone tonight.' Then I burst into treacherous tears. I hated
them, and tried to wipe them away.

'Stop it!' Katie pulled my hand away. 'Quit clawing your
face. You'll hurt yourself.' She handed me a wineglass. 'Take
a long drink, and then tell me what happened.'

Katie, in jeans and a long-sleeved turtleneck, was curled up
on the couch. I told her what happened at our picnic, ending
with Chris saying he'd never spent a night in my home.

'Is that true?' Katie asked.

'Yes.'

'Why not?'

I shrugged. 'I don't know.'

Katie's laser gaze bored into me. 'You're lying, Angela.'

'OK, I'm not telling the whole truth. I have too many happy
memories of Donegan in this house.'

'Like here, on this couch?'

'Yes.' I felt my face grow hot. We'd made love on the
couch when we were too impatient to run upstairs, tossing
our clothes all over the living room.

'Does my sitting here harm those memories?'

'No.' My voice was tentative.

'Then why can't Chris sit here?'

'Because we might start that way – just sitting – but it could
end with . . .' I skidded to a stop.

'Sex,' Katie finished. 'You and Chris might have wild sex
on this couch.'

I burst out with, 'There's not room on this couch for three
people.'

'There is if one's dead.'

I winced.

'You love Donegan. I know you do, and he loved you.
Would he want you to follow him to the grave?'

'Why do people always try to speak for the dead, saying
what they would and wouldn't want?'

'Answer me, Angela.' Katie was remorseless. 'Would Donegan want you to live like a walking dead woman?'

'No.'

'Exactly. He was too good a man to demand that. But you feel like you're cheating on him.' Katie was right.

'Not at Chris's house, but I would here. I can still see Donegan here.'

'You *imagine* you can see Donegan here,' Katie said. 'Just like you can still see your parents sitting at that kitchen table.'

I glanced over at the table. I couldn't help it. Sure enough, I saw them drinking their breakfast coffee together. Mom was in her housekeeper's uniform. She kissed my father goodbye on the top of his head, and vanished. So did Dad.

Katie pulled me back into the present. 'Donegan is gone, and you know it. You'll always have his love, Angela, but that doesn't mean you can't love someone else. You're not Queen Victoria, forever grieving for her prince, and even she took up with a Scots ghillie. How far they went is Victoria's real secret.'

I managed a smile and took another sip of wine.

'What I'm trying to say is that grief will twist you in strange ways.'

'So what should I do?' I took a big scoop of hummus.

'Invite Chris over for dinner. Let things take their course. If you wind up on the couch, so what?'

'And if we go upstairs?'

'Then you do.'

'But what about . . .?' Again, I stopped.

'What about the bed?' Katie finished.

I nodded.

'Get rid of it. And while you're at it, you might want to take off your wedding ring. No wonder you feel like you're cheating on Donegan.'

'I can't take off my ring. As for getting a new bed, that seems so calculating.'

'It's not calculating. It's facing facts. You love Chris, and you know where that leads. Look, Angela, I know this is hard for you. But we both spend too much time with dead people. If we've learned anything, it's that life is short, and happiness can disappear in an instant. You have another chance at love. Grab it while you can.'

I sat silently on the couch, sipping my wine.

'Enough with the lecture.' Katie topped off my wineglass, and we spent the rest of the evening drinking wine, eating hummus, and talking like the old friends we were. By eleven o'clock, we'd demolished both bottles of wine and all the hummus. I stood up, rather unsteadily.

'Come on,' Katie said. 'It's time for you to go to bed.' She helped me up the stairs to my bedroom.

'Are you on call tomorrow?' she asked.

'Yes. At midnight, actually. I hope everyone stays alive.' I pulled off my shoes, socks and pants and fell into bed, while Katie plugged in my cell phone. I fell asleep in a haze of wine and garlic fumes. Blessedly, it was a dreamless sleep.

Until my phone rang at eight thirty the next morning and woke me up. I scrabbled around on my nightstand and finally answered the phone. My hello was a raven's croak.

'Angela?' Jace said. 'Is that you? Are you feeling OK?'

'I'm fine,' I lied. 'I must have a touch of something.' The wine flu.

My head cleared enough to ask, 'Is there a murder, Jace? I'm on call today.'

'I'm next up, too,' he said. 'Greiman's working an early morning murder at the convenience store by the highway. His DI sister is working that one. That means I'll probably work the next murder with you.

'The good news is there are no other murders so far. But I may have a killer. The tech got a hit on someone going into the Cursed Crypt tunnel in the basement last night. I can show you the video. Have you had breakfast yet?'

'No.' My stomach roiled at the thought of food.

'Can you meet me at Mandy's Café at nine thirty?'

'Of course.' I hung up the phone and stood, very carefully, as if I was made of porcelain. The room spun, and I sat back down. My mouth was stuffed with gravel and cotton. Garlic-flavored cotton.

My second attempt was more successful. I stood, made it to the bathroom, and took a cold shower. It must have been freezing outside, because the water felt like ice needles. Once I was awake, I quickly flipped the water to hot, then showered and dressed.

By nine thirty I was at Mandy's Café, an institution in downtown Chouteau Forest. The blue-checked curtains were cheerful and the breakfast special was chocolate chip pancakes with two sausage links. The perfect balanced diet, with all the major food groups: sugar, grease, carbs and cholesterol. Mandy's was homey and comforting. It smelled like pancakes and coffee.

Jace, sitting in a blue leatherette booth in a far corner, waved me over to his table. Velma, a venerable waitress in a pink smocked uniform, poured us both coffee. We ordered the special. As soon as the waitress bustled off, Jace said, 'I got a hit. Let me show you.'

He called up a video on his iPad. It was poorly lit and set in a sub-sub-basement. 'Whoa, all I see are fifty shades of gray, and not the fun ones.'

Our pancakes arrived, and we were busily applying butter and maple syrup while the video played. I cut myself a generous bite and tasted it. Perfection.

'Keep watching that corner there.' Jace pointed at it with his fork. 'See that shadow moving toward the janitor's closet door?'

His fork followed the shadow until it separated from the darkest part of the basement and began moving, silently, slowly. Now I could see it was a man – probably a young man by the graceful way he moved.

'What's he got strapped to his belly?'

'Some kind of carrier bag,' Jace said. 'If he's going into the tunnel, he can't carry it on his back. There's no room.'

Jace and I silently ate our pancakes while we watched the figure reach the closet door and open it. The closet light was on. Jace and the tech had left it on deliberately. Now I could see the man's face. I was so shocked my fork stopped in midair.

'Nathan. That's Nathan Tucker.' I felt oddly disappointed. I liked Nathan and thought the judge gave him a raw deal. 'Is he the killer?'

Jace used his fork like a professor's pointer, leaving little drops of syrup on the iPad. 'Don't let the fact that Nathan seems likeable influence you, Angela. He certainly had a good reason to hate Trey. Lydia was collateral damage.'

'Why would he slice her tongue and humiliate her?' I asked.

'Didn't she insult the woman he was dating, and lie about her?'

I couldn't argue with that. Instead I said, 'Then why kill Eli, the guy in the green Kia?'

Jace looked at me. 'That's what we're going to find out.'

TWENTY-EIGHT

E xcept we didn't. I was itching to learn why Nathan was caught on camera crawling into that tunnel, but before we could find out, Jace and I were called out on the same case.

We both threw down money to pay for breakfast, and declined offers of coffee to go. Jace paused at the door and looked both ways.

'What's wrong?'

'I'm looking for reporters,' he said in a low voice. 'Some have given up on getting the chief to talk and they're following us. They know I'm the detective on the case. They camped outside my house last night and I couldn't go to the grocery store.'

I laughed.

'It's not funny. I'm out of beer.'

Now I really laughed. Jace glared at me and then said, 'All clear. Let's go.'

As we sprinted for our cars, Jace said, 'Another woman is dead – possibly more domestic violence.'

'Not again. Not after that creep drowned his poor wife in a mop bucket.'

'Yep. And this one's in the rich part of town, on Du Barry Circle.'

I whistled. 'Prime real estate. What do you know?'

'The death is on the Toussaint estate. The victim is the daughter, Vivian. Do you know her?'

'Sort of,' I said. 'She's ten years younger than me. I've been to a few parties at her parents' home. Viv had a big society wedding, but her husband turned out to be a hound. Chased anything in a skirt. After the marriage fell apart, Viv divorced her husband and went home to Mother. She's been living in a guesthouse on the estate.'

'What's she like?' Jace asked.

'Typical Forest rich girl.'

'Long blonde hair, good skin, straight teeth,' Jace said.

'Empty head,' I added, then wished I could call back my words.

'She went to Chouteau Forest U and majored in domestic science,' I added, 'which at that school means learning how to run a mansion. I think she minored in flower arranging.'

Jace stared at me. 'Seriously?'

'Yes. I'm not being snarky, Jace. Students learn both western and eastern styles of flower arrangement, including the Japanese art of ikebana, which is difficult to learn.

'Viv didn't want a career outside the home. My mother would have said Viv went to college for her MRS.'

'So she caught a rich husband, did some charity work, but never held a job,' Jace finished.

'That's it.' In my mind, I could see how she looked at her father's funeral a year ago: pretty, pale, and impeccably dressed in a black suit and a small hat.

'Last I heard, she was dating Royce Somebody, another rich guy, and he'd moved in with her.'

'That's about what I know,' Jace said. 'The boyfriend called nine-one-one at eight fifty-seven this morning and said, "Something's wrong with Viv. Somebody beat her up. I found her wandering in a daze in the back garden. She's totally out of it."

'The nine-one-one operator dispatched an ambulance and a patrol car. Good thing Mike, who's been around, caught the call. Mike got there at nine fourteen this morning. By then, the wandering girlfriend had been raped and beaten.'

'By the boyfriend?'

'He claims she was attacked by an intruder.'

'On the Toussaint estate?' I tried to laugh, except it came out as a snort. 'That place has a ten-foot-tall stone fence topped with iron spikes, and it's patrolled by private security. Professional armed security, not a bunch of retirees. An intruder would have to work hard to get in there.'

'Are there cameras?' Jace sounded hopeful.

I shrugged. 'Not sure.'

We hopped in our cars and drove to the estate. My head

was still pounding from last night's wine, although not so much. It had been soothed by lifesaving doses of caffeine, carbs, sugar and syrup.

All the way there, I tried to think of an innocent reason why Nathan Tucker would go into the tunnel for the Cursed Crypt, but couldn't. My gut said he didn't kill Trey and Lydia, but in its current roiling state, my gut wasn't reliable. I *wanted* Nathan to be innocent, which wasn't the same thing.

Focus on this job, I told myself.

Ten minutes later, Jace and I were at the Toussaint estate. We stopped at the guardhouse, a miniature version of the white stone main house, down to the gray slate roof. Only the mullioned windows were missing.

A trim guard in a spotless khaki uniform came out of the guardhouse. From his shined shoes to his buzzed hair, he looked ex-military. I followed behind Jace's car, and showed my identification. The guard pointed the way. 'Follow that blacktop road to the right. Miss Vivian's house is the first one you'll see. Sergeant Walters, our commander, is there, and so are the police and the ambulance.' The guard showed no trace of emotion.

I followed the curving road past velvety green lawns and the stone main house, framed by oaks and maples ablaze with fall color. About a quarter of a mile later, I was at a white stone guesthouse that looked a lot like my own home, down to the gingerbread woodwork on the porch. Fat yellow 'mums bloomed in terracotta pots.

The cheerful scene was spoiled by the cluster of official vehicles, including a tan golf cart with 'Kentan Security' on the hood.

I hauled out my DI case and rolled it up to the door. This time Pete, the muscular newbie, was on duty.

'Hi, Pete. I see you survived your night in the Cursed Crypt.' I smiled.

Pete grunted. He gave me the case number, had me sign the log, and handed me a pair of booties, all without saying a word. Either his night inside the crypt was a sore subject or he was the strong, silent type. Maybe both.

Jace and Mike were waiting for me inside the front door.

Mike's normally smiling face was somber, and his voice was low, almost a whisper. While I slipped on the booties, Mike said, 'That poor girl is upstairs in the bedroom. I put the boyfriend, Royce Edwards, in the sun porch out back. He's talking out of both sides of his mouth.

'First, Royce tells nine-one-one that the victim was beaten and wandering in a daze in the back garden. So nine-one-one dispatched the ambulance and I was the first responder. Royce runs out to my car, all wild-eyed with his hair messed up. Now he tells me he came home after jogging and found Vivian on their bed – without a stitch on. Royce said she'd been raped and beaten by an intruder.'

'What happened to wandering in the garden?' Jace asked.

'I guess he forgot that nine-one-one calls are taped. He sure changed his story fast.'

'How was Royce dressed when you saw him?' Jace asked.

'He wore a yellow T-shirt, jeans and bare feet. If he went jogging, he must have showered and changed clothes.

'After I escorted him to the sun porch, I checked the bathroom. The shower was wet, and the bathmat had big wet footprints on it. The washing machine was running. I turned it off. The load of clothes stinks of bleach, and a pair of men's running shoes are inside it along with some clothes and towels.'

'Good work, Mike. Any CCTV cameras?' I heard the hope in Jace's voice.

'The place has topnotch security. Cameras are everywhere – and they all work.'

'We caught a break.' Jace sounded relieved. 'Half the time the systems are out of order.'

'Or the cameras are dummies,' Mike said. 'Sergeant Bruno Walters just left to check the video. He'll get us copies.'

'Where are the victim's parents?' Jace asked.

'The father is deceased, and the mother is flying back from Paris,' Mike said. 'Security notified her.'

'Let's talk to Royce and see how many lies he'll tell us,' Jace said.

As I headed upstairs to the death scene, Mike patted me on the shoulder and said, 'Brace yourself, Angela. It's a bad one.'

Right, I thought. What could be worse than the blood-spattered Cursed Crypt?

I found out in the bedroom at the top of the stairs. The scene inside the crypt had been surreal, and that gave me some distance from the horror. Vivian's bedroom was terrible in its ordinariness.

The room was pale blue with gauzy white curtains – the same paint color and curtains as my bedroom in the same style house. The dark four-poster bed faced the door. Vivian's bloody body was in the bed, her legs spread wide to show her genitals. Her face was bloody, bruised and swollen and her long blonde hair was matted with blood.

Viv was past feeling pain or embarrassment, but I was outraged. Her killer had treated her with contempt.

Once I was past the initial shock, I could take in more details. The coppery smell of blood mixed with a floral perfume hit me in the nose. There were signs of a struggle. The spindly vanity table had been overturned, and its delicate gold chair was smashed. Lipstick and make-up were scattered across the floor. A broken pink bottle of Gucci's Gorgeous Gardenia perfume was seeping into the blue and white rug. The white eyelet duvet had been torn off the bed and tossed on the floor. It was spattered with blood.

Vivian's head was on a bloodstained pillow. There was more blood on the right side of the bed and drag marks through the blood to the center of the bed, where her body had been placed.

I took my photos, then pulled on four pairs of nitrile gloves and began the body inspection. The ambient temperature was seventy-two degrees, and the hall thermostat said seventy-one.

The body was in the middle of the bed, with the head pointing north and feet pointing south. The victim was completely nude, and wore no jewelry, not even a ring.

'I'm so sorry, Viv. We'll find who did this.' I felt foolish blurting that out, and hoped no one heard me.

I measured the body. Viv was five feet one. I guessed her weight at about a hundred pounds. Another small woman. Were they easier to brutalize?

I started examining her head and worked my way down her battered body. The head showed major blunt-force trauma. In other words, she'd been badly beaten.

Her face was swollen, and she was bleeding from her mouth, nose and ears. She had two black eyes and multiple contusions and cut-like defects on her face. I counted at least six major areas of bruising and twelve different cuts, though it was hard to tell on her bloody face. Her lower lip was split and swollen. From the way her head was caved in, I suspected at least one of her skull bones was broken.

She had more contusions on her arms, including both biceps, where the killer might have grabbed her, and a bloody shoe print on her chest. The shoe sole had a diagonal slash across the toes. The killer had kicked her in the ribs and the chest, but that disrespectful stomp might prove his undoing.

I spent a lot of time with the shoe print. The image was made by blood and some dirt. An infrared camera was better at showing contrast. I photographed the print from several angles, using an L-shaped ruler to show the scale. The shoe prints would be easier to photograph at the morgue, but I had to capture the image now, in case any evidence was lost in transit.

I used tweezers to carefully pluck two long hairs from the print. If the hairs belonged to Royce, they wouldn't make any difference because he lived with the victim. But if I didn't collect them, the defense could claim someone else killed her. I was taking no chances.

I flipped on my UV flashlight and put on my orange goggles. They showed a zillion tiny fibers. I picked up the biggest ones with the clumsy plastic disposable tweezers, a tedious task that took almost half an hour. Then I used forensic tape to pick up the rest of the material, the way people use tape to get pet hair off their pants.

Most of the damage was to Vivian's upper body – her head, arms and chest. She'd fought hard for her life. Her French manicure was destroyed. Two fingernails were broken on her left and four on her right. Her right index finger's nail was nearly torn off. I bagged her hands and sealed the bags with evidence tape.

Next, I checked for semen stains with a UV light. Nothing. If she had been raped, the killer could have used a condom or an object, such as a bottle. The ME would do a more thorough examination.

There were no contusions or cuts on her legs. Her bare feet were clean – so much for Viv 'wandering in a daze in the back garden.' There were no clothes on the floor – men's or women's.

The killer had hidden that vital evidence.

Unless it was covered with bleach in the washing machine.

TWENTY-NINE

Nitpicker appeared in the bedroom doorway, saw the bloody scene, and shook her head. 'Jeez. That poor woman.'

'She's a brave woman,' I said. 'She only weighs about a hundred pounds, but she fought her killer hard. Her nails are broken and torn. I hope she ripped his face off.'

'I'd like to do it for her,' Nitpicker said. 'I've been downstairs, going through the laundry after Mike turned off the washing machine.'

'Find anything good?'

'One woman's blue nightgown, size two. It would probably fit her. One pair of men's large navy running shorts, along with an extra-large gray sweatshirt, athletic socks, and four light blue towels. All appear to have blood on them. Someone poured in about half a bottle of bleach to get rid of the blood.'

'I'll use BlueStar on it,' Nitpicker said. 'That works on old or altered bloodstains. The true crime shows are mostly sticking with Luminol, which doesn't work as well. Back at the lab, I'll hang the laundry in the drying locker, and then use the BlueStar. I think BlueStar will let us pick up the blood, despite the bleach.

'Look what else I found in the washer.' Nitpicker sounded triumphant. She held up two cardboard evidence boxes, each containing a wet red high-top shoe. 'These are Converse Chuck Taylor All Stars, size thirteen wide.'

She examined the shoe print on the victim's chest. 'And that looks like the print of a big ol' Chuck Taylor on her chest. See this distinctive pattern with the big diamonds on the sole?'

'And the word "Converse,"' I said.

'Athletic shoe sole patterns change constantly, but not classic Chucks. They've been the same for nearly eighty years. And look at this diagonal slash across the toes on the right shoe.' She held the shoe with gloved fingers close enough to compare the slash on the body to the distinctive shoe print stomped on the victim's chest.

'I'd say that's a preliminary match,' she said. 'We'll confirm it at the lab.'

Nitpicker switched the subject. 'I hear the boyfriend's in the sun porch. Have you seen Royce Edwards? Do you know him?'

'No to both. What about you?'

Nitpicker lowered her voice, a signal this was Grade-A gossip. 'He's been away from the Forest about five years. Just came back. He's rich – at least he was born that way. I heard Royce went through at least two fortunes: the money his mother left him and his grandmother's legacy. He's a gambler with a serious problem.'

'And St. Louis has enough casinos he can indulge it.'

No gambler would mistake the city for Las Vegas, but it had five major casinos. Thanks to a weird state law, all casinos had to be on or near a body of water – and St. Louis was right on the Mississippi River. It's hard to escape the casinos' gaudy glamor.

'What's this guy look like?' I asked.

Nitpicker shrugged. 'Handsome enough if you like curly black hair and a nice body. But he has mean eyes and a weak mouth. Looks like trouble to me.'

'Any idea where Viv met him?'

'I heard it was some kind of charity benefit at the River City Casino. About three months ago. He moved in with her two weeks later, so he's a fast worker. Do you think he killed Viv?'

'That's my guess. Jace is trying to find out.'

I had to finish my body inspection. 'Will you help me turn the decedent so I can examine her back?'

'Of course.' Nitpicker was good about that. Though the decedent was a small woman, she was still heavy and unwieldy. Dead weight in the truest sense.

I spread a sterile sheet on the bed, and we turned the body. The cruel bruises showed all around her arms – someone with big hands had gripped her entire arm. She had significant patches of blood on the back of her head, neck and back. She had more contusions on her back and shoulders. I measured and photographed them.

Purple patches of livor mortis – where the blood settles after death – were also on her shoulders, buttocks and the backs of her legs. Apparently, Viv had been dragged to the center of the bed either during or shortly after death. Was she raped there – or did someone pose the body to make it look that way?

I photographed and measured everything, and my sad duty was finished. It was time to put Vivian in a body bag and call the morgue van to take her to the ME's office.

I zipped the black bag and suppressed a shudder. That sound had an awful finality.

Nitpicker had been photographing and printing the bedroom. In addition to the overturned vanity and smashed chair, a heavy chest of drawers was knocked sideways, and the wicker stand for a potted philodendron was upended. The plant's blue Chinese pot had shattered, and black soil was scattered on the carpet.

'You know what's weird about this room?' Nitpicker said. 'There's no sign of the boyfriend. Nothing. No photos, no guy stuff lying around. He only had two drawers in the chest over there for his things, and about ten hangers in the closet. Everything else is hers.'

'Did she refuse to let him into her life?' I asked.

'Sure looks like it,' Nitpicker said.

I checked the bathroom. It was as fluffy and feminine as the bedroom. I noted that it smelled steamy. I photographed the powder blue bathmat with the big wet shoe prints. It took some doing, but I finally got the shoe prints to show in the photos. The L-shaped ruler revealed that foot was big – way too big to be Vivian's. Nitpicker would take the bathmat to the drying room and test it for blood and fibers. There were no towels on the floor or the towel rack.

I photographed the water on the shower doors. The sink was dry – wiped clean. The white bar soap in the shower was bloody. I photographed it, and hoped it had a fingerprint in the blood. Nitpicker would process it.

The medicine cabinet had the bare minimum: aspirin,

Tylenol, rubbing alcohol, tampons, stick deodorant, mouth-wash, Old Spice aftershave, and a man's electric razor. No scissors, safety razors or blades.

I photographed the medicine cabinet and packed the contents in a container to go to the ME.

Back in the bedroom, Nitpicker was on her knees, printing the leg of the overturned vanity.

I gave her my report. 'I found a bloody soap bar in the shower and an electric razor in the medicine cabinet, but no other razors. If Royce is the killer, he'll have a hard time claiming he got blood on the soap when he cut himself shaving.

'And you've got your work cut out for you in the bathroom, Nitpicker.'

Nitpicker shrugged. She stayed cheerful during the worst jobs. 'I knew that as soon as I saw someone had showered in there. I'm going to have to really work that room. Use BlueStar to look for blood, then take apart the shower and sink drains, not to mention the toilet. If I ever get fired, I'll have a new trade as a plumber.'

'Plumbers probably make more,' I said.

Nitpicker stood up, her knees popping. 'I'm going outside for my tool kit. I'll tell Jace about the shoes and the print on the victim's chest.'

'I'm finished here. Just waiting for the van to arrive. I'll show Jace the photos of the victim's hands, and see if Royce has any scratches on him.'

As we made our way down the stairs, we heard screaming from the sun porch. A man was shouting, 'I'm telling you, I never touched her.'

Jace sounded almost bored. 'Where did you get those scratches on your face?'

'I chased a rabbit into a rose bush.'

'What are you, a dog?' Mike taunted the suspect.

I didn't dare laugh or look at Nitpicker.

Nitpicker knocked on the door. Jace came out, looking rumpled. He'd loosened his tie and his hair stood up in spikes from running his fingers through it.

He kept his voice low. 'Royce is going to lawyer up any moment now. What do you have?'

Nitpicker showed him the shoes and said the soles were a probable match for the print on the victim's chest, and I showed him the photos of the victim's hands.

'Good,' he said. 'I'll get a warrant for his nail clippings and DNA.'

He left the door open just far enough so Nitpicker and I could listen. I heard Jace say, 'Royce, what size shoe do you wear?'

'Thirteen wide. Why?' Royce sounded relieved to answer this easy question.

Jace let the silence stretch, then said, 'Let me play part of this nine-one-one call recorded at eight fifty-seven this morning.'

'You already did.' Royce's voice was a whine.

'Let's hear it again.' Jace's voice was patient, a teacher with a reluctant student. 'Ready?'

A man's voice, sounding frantic, shouted, 'Help! You gotta help me! Something's wrong with Viv. Somebody beat her up. I found her wandering in a daze in the back garden. She's totally out of it.'

Now Jace spoke. 'By the time Patrol Officer Michael Reynolds got here at nine fourteen, you told him a different story. This time, you said Vivian had been raped and beaten by an intruder.'

'She was! It's true.' Royce sounded desperate.

'When did this assault happen?' Jace asked.

'I went for a run this morning on the estate,' Royce said. 'When I came back, I found her in the bedroom. Someone had attacked her.'

'Before or after the nine-one-one call?'

'I didn't make that call. I was set up.'

'Who did that?' Jace asked.

'Someone who hates me. Her mother. It was her mother. Julia doesn't like me.'

'Mrs Toussaint killed her daughter because she hates you?'

'No. I don't know who did it. But I'm innocent. I want a lawyer. Do you hear me? I want a lawyer right now.'

'Good idea, Royce. You're going to need one. I'm arresting you for the rape and murder of Vivian Toussaint. You have the right to remain silent . . .'

By the time Jace got to the last line of the Miranda warning, 'If you cannot afford a lawyer, one will be provided for you at government expense,' the morgue van had arrived.

Vivian's killer was arrested before her body left her home.

THIRTY

It was too late to see Nathan Tucker that day. Jace and I agreed to meet at Remember Forever, the gravestone company, at eight the next morning.

'I'm finally going to find out why Nathan was crawling into the Cursed Crypt,' I said.

Jace was skeptical. 'If he'll tell the truth.'

'How can he lie when we've got him on video?'

'You'd be surprised. I'll see you tomorrow morning.'

So much for work.

My love life was not so simple. Chris had called and texted my personal cell phone sixteen times since our disagreement. I was afraid to talk to him on the phone. I didn't want my already weak resolve to disappear. In the car, I mustered the courage to text him back. 'You gave me a lot to think about, Chris. I'd like to be alone, just for a night or two. I'll call tomorrow. I love you – Angela.'

Everything I'd texted Chris was true. He and Katie both had given me plenty to ponder – and so had Vivian's death investigation. He texted back, 'I love you, Angela, whatever you decide.' But he didn't come running to me. I respected his strength, but still wished he'd rescue me from the decisions I had to make.

I drove home, prepared for a battle with myself. The last rays of the setting sun gilded my white stone house, the one that resembled Vivian's doomed home. I thought of the good times Donegan and I had there. I missed them. I missed him.

Inside, my living room looked comfortable and cozy, from the big leather couch to the fireplace. Framed photos of my family and friends, as well as Donegan, brightened the walls. The room was a little dusty, but otherwise fine. I'd keep it the way it was.

Upstairs was another matter. I took a long, hard look at my bedroom, painted the same blue color as the murdered Vivian's room. I hadn't noticed before, but the paint was dingy. The once white sheers were dishwater gray. The flat pillows slouched and the mattress sagged. In my memory, they were perfect, fresh and vibrant.

And that's where they belonged – in my memory, I decided. Time to make new memories – good ones.

I fired up my iPad and went online, where I ordered a new mattress and a new bedstead, a wrought-iron one. Then I bought new curtains. I'd keep the Persian Bijar rug. I loved the vibrant ruby red color and elegant center medallion.

Next, I called Rick DeMun, the Forest's hippie handyman. He answered on the first ring, and I could almost smell the pot smoke through the phone. 'What can I do for you, Angela?'

'Can you paint my bedroom?'

'Yeah, sure. Did you choose a color? Do you have the paint?'

'Not yet. What brand do you suggest?'

He gave me the brand name and the estimated number of cans, along with his advice. 'Go to the hardware store in person, Angela, and pick several sample cards in the same color family. Then tape them on your wall and look at them – at night, in the morning, in bright sunshine and on a cloudy, gloomy day. Especially on a gloomy day. Call me back when you're ready.'

It was good advice. Chouteau Forest Hardware was open until seven that night. After a long search through the yellows, blues, greens and oranges, I decided on a white-on-white room. White walls and white molding. I loved the color names and took home five sample cards for white paint: 'frost,' 'painter's white,' 'polar bear,' 'cotton sheets,' and 'Swiss coffee,' which was actually a warm white that looked like whipped cream.

Back at home, I taped the samples to my bedroom wall, plugged in my personal and work cell phones and set my alarm. Then I got ready for bed, snuggling under the covers, and waiting for sleep. It didn't happen. I missed sleeping with Chris's arms wrapped around me. The memory of Chris's kisses made my face feel hot and my body restless. I missed Donegan, too, although Donegan was a distant, unattainable dream.

I turned on my light and reached for a mystery on my nightstand. An Agatha Christie, my comfort read. I slipped into *Death on the Nile*, like it was a warm soothing bath, and soon fell into a dreamless sleep.

The next morning was cold, gray and grim. I checked my paint samples on the wall. I didn't like what the light did to the samples called 'frost' and 'polar bear,' and eliminated them. I dressed, ate a quick breakfast, and poured myself coffee to go. I was still sleepy.

Once outside, the cold slapped me in the face. Now I was awake for sure. I wasn't looking forward to visiting the monument company on a gloomy day, but I definitely wanted to know what Nathan Tucker had to say.

The morning traffic was light, and ten minutes later, I was parked outside Remember Forever, right behind Jace's car. Jace texted me that he was powering up his iPad with the video of Nathan, so it would be ready to show. We went in together. This time, Nathan was sitting behind the reception desk, drinking a mug of coffee and working in a sudoku puzzle book.

'Nathan Tucker,' Jace said.

Nathan looked up and smiled. 'How may I help you, Detective?' He stood up, put his pencil in the sudoku book to mark his place, and closed it.

'You can tell me what you were doing in a sub-basement of the Main Building at Chouteau Forest University two nights ago.'

The smile slid off Nathan's face and his voice grew cold. 'I have no idea what you're talking about.'

'How about if I show you a video?' Jace put his iPad on the counter and said, 'See, that's you, down in the sub-basement at the old Main Building.'

'So?' Nathan shrugged, but I saw fear in his brown eyes.

'And here, you're opening a door,' Jace said.

'And I can't go into a janitor's closet?' Nathan said.

'How did you know that was a janitor's closet?' Jace looked triumphant.

Nathan took a long drink of coffee, stalling for time. 'Maybe because I'm black, and black people have a special affinity for janitorial work.'

Jace stared at him. 'I'll give you one more chance before I take you into custody, Nathan. What were you doing in that closet?'

The silence stretched on. The air in the room seemed to vibrate with tension. Finally Nathan said, 'I wasn't doing anything. Just checking it out.'

Jace rounded the corner of the counter and said, 'That's it. Nathan Tucker, hold out your hands. I'm cuffing you, and—'

Before Jace could finish, Nathan said, 'OK, OK, I'll tell you.' He sat down.

Jace stood over him, looking intimidating.

'Have you been through the tunnel?' Nathan asked.

Jace nodded.

'Then you know it's the last resting place of Elizabeth McKee and Jonathan McKee. I'm the keeper of the tombs. It's my job to make sure they are clean and fresh flowers are in the vases.'

'Who are Elizabeth and Jonathan McKee?' Jace asked.

'My great-great-whatever grandparents. What do you know about the history of black people in St. Louis?'

'Not very much,' Jace said. I nodded my agreement.

'Before the Civil War, Missouri was a slave state, and St. Louis was a stop on the Underground Railroad. Enslaved people were spirited through the city and across the river to Illinois, a free state. Jonathan McKee, the founder of this monument business, was a free person of color, and also what they called a "conductor" on the railroad. He helped bring enslaved people to freedom, and the tunnel in the tomb was part of the railroad. Jonathan dug the tunnel, and made a small room to hide people.

'McKee was in charge of remodeling the marble tomb for Eugene Cortini. He sculpted the divan, added the angels and more.

'He would bring in wagonloads of brick, marble and supplies. Hidden in some of those wagons were enslaved people. Jonathan would keep the fugitives in the small room, and then take them away to safety when he could.

'One of those people was Elizabeth Lawson, a young woman who had been raped and impregnated by her so-called owner,

Jamison Beauregard Lawson, who lived in Kentucky. When her child was two years old, Elizabeth fled North with her boy by way of the Underground Railroad. By the time she got to St. Louis in 1857, she was sick with tuberculosis.

'Jonathan fell in love with Elizabeth. He married her and adopted her son, Nathan, as his own. He tried to nurse Elizabeth back to health, but it was too late. She'd suffered too much. Elizabeth died during the winter of 1857.

'Jonathan was heartbroken.'

I believed that. The tomb sculpture was an expression of pure grief.

'Elizabeth's husband sculpted that tomb for her. He called it his masterpiece.'

It was. I remembered the heartbreaking details of that sculpture. The exquisite woman with the high cheekbones and full lips, her waves of long hair, the marble lace at her throat and the bouquet of roses.

'Why did he keep the tomb in the tunnel instead of putting it in a cemetery?' Jace asked.

'He couldn't. It wasn't safe. Back then, enslaved people couldn't have tombstones or funerals, much less a marble monument like Elizabeth's. White people were too afraid of blacks congregating.

'This took place about the time of the Dred Scott decision. You do know about that, don't you?' Nathan sounded like an impatient teacher dealing with slow students.

'Yes,' I said. 'The Dred Scott decision was one of the worst decisions ever made by the US Supreme Court. An enslaved couple, Dred and Harriet Scott, sued to be free because they'd lived for a time in places where slavery was forbidden.'

Nathan nodded and smiled. 'Right. The Supreme Court decided that people of African ancestry could not be citizens of the United States. The Supremes also said that freeing Dred Scott would deprive his owner of their legal property – that property was the Scott family.'

'That decision took place right in downtown St. Louis,' I said. 'At the Old Courthouse.'

'You got it,' Nathan said. 'The Dred Scott decision stirred up a lot of anti-black feeling. Life got worse for black people in Missouri. Two years later, the state legislature approved a bill that said free people of color could be removed from the state – and if they didn't leave, they could be enslaved. The bill was never signed into law, but Jonathan McKee kept a low profile. You can see why he was afraid to put Elizabeth's tomb on display in a cemetery.

'Jonathan never remarried. He visited his wife's tomb often and kept the vases filled with fresh flowers. Elizabeth's son, Nathan McKee, inherited the family monument business and promised his adopted father that he would maintain her burial place. When Jonathan died, Nathan kept his promise, and so have his heirs. I'm the latest person in that tradition.'

'Nice story.' Angela heard the sarcasm in Jace's voice. 'That closet leads to the Cursed Crypt. You crawled through the tunnel and killed Trey and Lydia, didn't you?'

'What? Me? Of course not!'

'I have a warrant here for your DNA.'

'Me? Why?'

'Because we found blood and a bloody shoe print at the scene.'

Nathan examined the warrant, and then submitted without protest while Jace swabbed the inside of Nathan's cheek for DNA.

'Don't leave town,' Jace said.

'You've got to be kidding,' Nathan said.

'No, I'm dead serious.'

Jace stood up, and we left Remember Forever, walking toward our cars.

Outside, I asked, 'Did you really say, "Don't leave town"? Like a TV cop?'

'I did. It sounds impressive, but Nathan doesn't know it's more of a suggestion than an order. Only a court could issue that order. Or a bail bondsman if it's part of the bond agreement.

'If Nathan gets a good lawyer, they may enlighten him.'

'I don't think he's going to run.' I still believed Nathan was innocent.

'I hope you're right,' Jace said. 'For his sake.'

THIRTY-ONE

' I heard that bastard Charlie Wheatly confessed.' Katie, the assistant ME, was riled up. Her voice was flat with fury as she paced behind her desk, too upset to drink her coffee or eat the lunch I'd brought.

I'd stopped by her office for news about the autopsy of Emmelina Wheatly, the woman who was drowned in her own living room. Detective Greiman was supposed to be there with me, but he couldn't be bothered.

'No thanks to Greiman, though he got credit for the confession.' I sipped my coffee and took a bite of Mediterranean flatbread.

'That guy's Teflon,' Katie said. 'If the Forest is nuked, Greiman will crawl out of the ashes with the other cockroaches. I hope they hang Charlie.'

'I doubt it,' I said. 'His public defender got him a plea bargain. He'll be doing ten years.'

Katie's eyes widened in outrage. 'Ten years? First-degree murder is a death penalty offense in Missouri. Who did Charlie know?'

'More like what,' I said. 'He worked on Chief Buttkiss's Mercedes.'

Katie threw herself into her desk chair. It creaked. 'I know Emmelina's aunt, Maria Zarcos. She does a lot of pro-bono work for battered women. Monty consults her often. I bet she's furious. Ten years! That's just wrong.'

Katie's eyes narrowed. 'With a sentence that light, word could get out that Wheatly was a narc. The other inmates wouldn't like that.'

Katie was quiet after that, munching her flatbread. We ate in thoughtful silence. The black olives and salty feta cheese were so good, I didn't mind that they were healthy. I wondered what was going through Katie's mind.

I waited a bit and then asked, 'How did Emmelina die?'

'Badly,' Katie said. 'Painfully. Her no-good husband drowned her in a bucket of Pine-Sol. She only weighed ninety-eight pounds, but he used her own belt to bind her hands. Emmelina fought hard and had a good chunk of his skin under her nails, so we've got his DNA. That may be why he confessed.

'He stuck her face in the scrub water, and she hyperventilated. She breathed in the water, and that caused agonizing pain. It must have felt like her lungs were being seared. She also suffered terrible panic and who knows what else. She was betrayed and murdered by the man she'd married.'

I shuddered. 'That's horrible.'

'It's worse than horrible.' Katie glared at me, but I knew her hatred was for the killer.

'It was inhuman. It can take more than ten minutes to drown. It happens in stages, you know. First, Emmelina fought the douche bag and scratched him while he bound her hands behind her with her own belt. Her arms were bruised where he held her down in that bucket, and so were her knees. Well, you saw the bruises, Angela.'

I nodded.

'As Emmelina's lungs started to fill with water, she may have tried to hold her breath,' Katie said. 'Most people can hold theirs for about thirty seconds. A few make it to two minutes.

'Next, Emmelina lost consciousness. If someone had walked in then, she might have had a chance to survive. But that didn't happen. Instead, she probably had what's called "hypoxic convulsion," which looks like a seizure. She died soon after that.

'The only good thing is that once her brain was starved of oxygen and she passed out, Emmelina didn't feel much.'

'That's cold comfort for her poor aunt.' I shook my head. 'I talked with Maria the day of the murder. She told me Charlie had a long history of abuse, but Emmelina wouldn't leave him.'

'You know the stats on abuse, Angela. One in four American women has experienced some kind of abuse during their lifetime. It's hard for even the smartest women to leave their abuser.

'Some women think they're to blame. Controlled and hurt, they're not only beaten, they're beaten down. There's no escape.'

'But Emmelina could have gone to her aunt for help.'

'She might have been too afraid to leave Charlie. Emmelina's husband could have threatened to kill her aunt. The poor woman must have felt trapped.

'And while we're talking about relationships, how are you and Chris?'

Every part of me was suddenly alert. I had to get out of Katie's office. Quick.

'Oops, that's my phone.' I grabbed my purse and started for the door. I didn't want to talk about Chris.

'You left most of your lunch,' Katie said.

'I'm not hungry.' I was almost to the door.

'Your phone's not ringing.'

'It's on vibrate.'

'Liar! And you're always hungry, Angela.'

'See you, Katie,' I called over my shoulder as I fled her office.

Out in the hall, I breathed a sigh of relief. That was a narrow escape. I didn't want another lecture on my love life from Katie. I'd work out my problems with Chris my way.

Back in my car, I called the office of Colin Dickson, the lawyer who was supposed to be cute, 'but dumb as a barrel of hair.' The one who was being blackmailed by the late, unlamented Lydia because he used her 'term-paper' service.

'Mr Dickson is in his office,' a dulcet-toned secretary said. 'Would you like to speak with him?'

'I'll call him later.' I hung up and drove toward the law office of Dickson, Warner and Patterson in downtown Chouteau Forest. I didn't make an appointment with Dickson because I didn't have any police authority. I knew he wouldn't willingly talk about being blackmailed. I'd have to bluff my way in.

The office was in what passed for a skyscraper in the Forest, a six-story mirrored-glass building that reflected the buildings nearby. It reminded me of a cop's sunglasses. Inside, the law office was on the top floor.

The elevator was paneled in blond wood with brass rails. I

know it was supposed to look classy, but it reminded me of an expensive coffin. I could almost see the pallbearers grabbing those brass rails. I shook my head to clear it. I'd been hanging around the morgue too much.

The elevator opened into an office decorated in Standard Successful Lawyer: dark green walls, mahogany woodwork, and brown leather wing chairs. A sleek blonde receptionist asked, 'How may I help you?'

'I'd like to speak with Mr Colin Dickson,' I said.

The receptionist frowned. 'Do you have an appointment?'

'No, but I'm sure Mr Dickson will want to talk to me. Tell him it's about his college term papers.'

Now the receptionist looked puzzled – and curious. She hesitated, index finger hovering over the phone.

'Just make the call,' I said.

She did, and tried unsuccessfully to hide her surprise when Colin Dickson agreed to see me. I followed her past a cube farm, where anonymous men and women labored over computers, to the executive row. And there was Colin, sitting behind a massive desk in an office the size of my living room. He'd done well for himself, this member of the Lucky Sperm Club.

He stood up to greet me. Colin was undeniably good-looking: he was about six feet four with pale blond hair that curled over one eye. His shoulders were broad and his face was perfectly proportioned, from the high brow to the noble chin. Until I noticed those deep blue eyes. They were lavishly fringed with dark lashes, but missing the bright spark of intelligence.

The receptionist lingered near the door. 'Thank you. You can go now, Miss Hall,' Colin said, and she left.

'What can I do for you, Miss Richards?' The lawyer shot his cuffs on his blue Egyptian cotton shirt. It went perfectly with his hand-tailored suit.

'It's Richman. And you can tell me about your college term papers.'

'I have no idea what you're talking about.' But he did. His empty blue eyes were wide with fear.

'Yes, you do, or you wouldn't have agreed to see me. I

know that Lydia Fynch ran a term-paper writing service and she got you high grades – high enough so you could graduate.'

'No, she didn't!'

'She most certainly did. She was blackmailing you for fifty thousand dollars.'

'You can't say that. You can't. Or I'll tell—' He reached for his desk phone.

I interrupted him. 'Or what? You'll tell Daddy? Go ahead. Be my guest. I bet he'd like to hear this story. Especially now that Lydia is dead. Murdered, actually. Right before your wedding to Miss Hardesty.

'Lydia's death must be awfully convenient, Counselor.'

Colin sounded defiant, like a kid on a playground. 'So what? Lydia's dead and I'm glad. But I didn't kill her.'

'Really? Where were you on the night of October thirtieth?'

'I was at a house party to celebrate my engagement to Heather Hardesty. At her family's cottage in Newport.' Heather's family was descended from robber barons, and their Rhode Island 'cottage' would have twenty or thirty rooms. A Newport cottage was an outrageous humble-brag.

'You flew there?'

'Of course.'

Jace could check that one. I left, and Colin looked relieved. Two potential killers down, two to go.

My next stop was William Garland Harris. Despite his posh-sounding name, I knew William was a working-class kid, and he must have been smart. He'd been hired after graduation at Brenner, Thomas, the third-largest law firm in the area. I called him through the company switchboard and William answered his phone. 'I need to talk to you as soon as possible, Mr Harris.'

'What's this in reference to?' he asked.

'The term paper that Lydia Fynch wrote for you. And don't tell me you don't know about it.'

'I . . . uh . . .' He was too frightened to continue.

'Talk to me, William, or I'll have the police show up at your office.' I felt like a rat making that threat, but it had to be done.

Now I heard panic in William's voice. He lowered it to a near whisper and pleaded, 'No, no! Please. That would ruin me.' He gulped. 'I can take a break in half an hour. I'll talk to you then. Come up to the second floor and ask for me. Is that OK?'

William's office was three blocks away from Colin Dickson's firm. The interior was ultramodern. The walls were painted warm, bright colors and the furniture was minimalist.

Unlike the genetically lucky Colin Dickson, William Garland Harris toiled in the windowless cube farm at his firm, and even the brightest paint didn't disguise its dreariness.

A colleague directed me to William's cube. 'On the right. He's wearing a gray suit.'

The suit was neatly pressed but definitely off-the-rack. William saw me and turned whiter than his shirt. He managed a weak smile. 'Ms Richman? Let's go to the break room.'

I followed him to a small, stark white room that smelled of microwave popcorn and burnt coffee. He poured himself a cup of inky liquid.

'Would you like some coffee?' he asked.

I gave him points for playing host. 'No, thanks. Tell me about Lydia Fynch.'

'She did a term paper for me two years ago. Just the once. It was a mistake. I knew it, but my mom was dying of cancer and I couldn't concentrate. I was living at the hospital.'

'Come on, William, you can give me a better story than that.'

He looked at me with earnest eyes. 'It's not a sob story, Ms Richman. She died on June sixteenth, 2021. Her name was Rosalie June Harris and her obituary was in the newspaper.'

I nodded. I could check that.

'I graduated in the top ten in my class and got hired here. I was starting to do well, until I got a call from Lydia. She wanted to meet at a coffee shop near here. At first, she seemed nice. She congratulated me on my success. Then she said I owed her for that success and she wanted ten thousand dollars or she'd tell Mr Brenner, a managing partner. I said I didn't have the money, but she said I did. She knew I'd inherited my mother's house and I could sell it. I was living there, but she said that didn't make any difference. She wanted her money by November fifteenth.'

'Did you put your mother's house up for sale?' I asked.

'No. I was sure I'd find a way out of this mess.'

'You did. She was murdered.'

'I didn't kill her.'

'Where were you the night of October thirtieth?' I felt like someone in a bad movie.

'I was at a company retreat at the Camelback Inn at Scottsdale, Arizona. The big dogs all play golf there and they like the course.' William was about fifteen hundred miles from the Forest – at least two and a half hours by plane.

'See? I have photos.' He showed me pictures of corporate wonks in khakis and polo shirts, standing in front of a pumpkin-studded buffet under an orange 'Happy Halloween' sign.

It was four o'clock when I left. Time to head home. On the drive there, I decided I didn't like who I was, working this case.

I was turning into a bully – and starting to enjoy it.

THIRTY-TWO

At home, I studied the paint samples pinned on my bedroom wall. This was going to be my last check. I wanted to see how the remaining shades of white looked in the setting sun. My choices were down to 'painter's white,' 'cotton sheets' and 'Swiss coffee.' I liked the creamy white of 'Swiss coffee' best. Time to paint my bedroom.

I called the handyman, Rick DeMun and told him I'd made my decision. 'When can you start?'

'Tomorrow,' he said. 'Should I buy the paint? I get a contractor's discount – ten percent off retail. The painting should take two days, and I'll need another day to clean up, set up your new bed and mattress, and hang the curtains.'

Despite Rick's easy-going drawl, he was a hard worker. He never seemed bothered that his socially ambitious parents, who wanted him to climb the corporate ladder, thought he was a disappointment. Rick liked his freedom too much to be trapped behind a desk. He was ambitious in a different way. He'd struggled through two semesters of college, then dropped out to start his own business. Rick was successful, but his parents wanted a conventional son who wore a suit and didn't smoke pot.

'Sounds good. I'll have coffee and pound cake for you.'

Rick was a sucker for homemade pound cake. I bought them at the church bake sales and stashed them in the freezer.

'Good. I'll see you about eight thirty tomorrow. Oh, and Angela, your bedroom is going to stink of paint. You may want to sleep at someone else's home tomorrow night, or downstairs on your couch.'

My choices were either Katie's guest room, or Chris's place, and right now I wanted to avoid them both. My couch would work fine.

I called Jace and told him about my interviews with the two lawyers today. He sounded rushed. 'I'll check their alibis. We should have a busy day tomorrow. I expect word back on that shoe print from the crypt, and Katie should have finished the autopsy on the other domestic violence victim.'

Before bed, I packed away the books, pictures and knick-knacks in my room, then took down the dusty, drab curtains and tossed them, along with the ratty bedspread.

I slept well that last night in my old bedroom. I had one dream, just before I woke up. I dreamed that Donegan came to see me, with a big bouquet of red roses. He always brought me roses, and I was happy to see him. I set the roses on the kitchen table when the doorbell rang. It was Chris, and he had a bouquet of fall flowers. I put both bouquets in the same crystal vase, and admired them.

And then I woke up at seven thirty. I sighed and stretched, feeling good. I thought the dream was telling me that I loved Donegan, and always would, but there was room in my heart for Chris Ferretti.

My work cell phone rang. It was Jace.

'Angela, Katie wants to see us ASAP – at eight thirty – for the autopsy report on Vivian Toussaint. Your turn to bring the bakery goods. I'll bring the coffee.'

I took two cinnamon swirl pound cakes out of the freezer and defrosted them in the microwave, then made coffee and set the butter on the kitchen table to soften. I texted Rick: *Leaving for work. Front door open. Pound cake and butter on the kitchen table, fresh coffee in the Thermos on the sink. Enjoy.*

He texted back: *Cool!*

The homey smell of warm cinnamon coffee cake filled my car, distracting me from my dreary duty. At the morgue, I parked my car away from the black funeral home pick-up vans, and punched in the code. Much as I liked Katie, I was dreading another visit on this grim subject.

Jace was already in Katie's office with the coffee. The office had a new addition on the wall over the file cabinet: A Mexican Day of the Dead sugar skull clock. The grinning skull wore a crown of roses and ticked loudly.

Jace spotted it the same time I did. 'What's that?' he asked.

'A clock,' Katie said. She was primed and ready to go. By that, I mean determined to deliver a lecture.

Before she started, I said, 'This is the second domestic violence death in a week. What the hell is going on here in the Forest?'

'Nothing.' Katie shrugged. 'We're just a normal, all-American community. Let me give you the sad statistics.'

She counted them off on her fingers. 'One, domestic violence is the leading cause of injuries to women. It kills more women than car accidents, muggings and rapes combined.'

She stopped and told us to watch the second hand on her new skull clock. The hand had just barely cleared the crown of roses when she said, 'That was nine seconds. Every nine seconds a woman is assaulted or beaten in the US. By the time that hand reaches twelve, another five women will suffer.'

Now she counted on her third finger. 'In most homicides involving sexual partners – and that's what Vivian Toussaint and her killer were – the man physically abused the woman before the murder.

'It was definitely true in this victim's case. Viv had old bruises and healed breaks before her scumbag boyfriend Royce beat her to death. When he killed her, he pounded the sh—' Katie stopped and selected a more polite word. 'He pounded the stuffing out of that poor woman, mostly around her head and shoulders. He broke or cracked at least four bones in her skull.

'Those were bad enough, but then the worthless mother-scratcher—'

'Mother-scratcher?' I didn't realize I'd said it out loud.

Katie glared at me. 'I promised Monty I'd tone down my language. He clocked me at six eff-words per minute.'

I bit my lip to keep from laughing and didn't dare look at Jace.

'As I was saying, that worthless mother-scratcher stomped on the victim's chest, broke the first three ribs at the top of her ribcage, and punctured her aorta.'

'The largest artery in the body.' Jace sounded like a kid hoping for a gold star.

Katie paused for a deep breath, then continued, 'Right. Viv went into shock, bled out, and died.'

'Was the victim raped?' I asked.

'No. He just made it look like she was raped. Left her with her legs spread. To humiliate her one last time. There was no semen in her mouth, throat or vaginal vault.'

Katie stopped to glare at Jace. 'Did that dingleberry confess?'

'No, he lawyered up,' he said. 'But that was definitely his shoe print on Vivian's chest, and he can't say someone borrowed his Chuck Taylors – only his DNA was found in the shoes. That was also Royce's skin – and no one else's – under her nails.'

'So there was no mythical attacker roaming through the house,' Katie said.

'And a dazed and confused Vivian wasn't wandering in the back garden, as Royce claimed. Her bare feet were clean. So much for the mystery killer.' Jace took a big bite of pound cake and we waited while he chewed and swallowed.

'Also, that was his blood and DNA on the clothes in the washing machine that he doused in bleach,' Jace said. 'Along with Viv's, of course.

'He had a heck of a motive. He'd gambled away two fortunes: the money he inherited from his mother and his grandmother. He was pressuring Vivian to marry him. He even bought her an engagement ring. With her own money.'

We all sipped coffee and pondered that statement. Finally, Jace said, 'Royce was outraged when she returned the ring. We have video of him following Vivian into the jewelry store, screaming at her. Store security ushered him out.'

'So he wasn't just a mooch, he was a controlling mooch,' I said.

'Yep, her mother told me that story,' Jace said.

'Why was he still living with Vivian after the break-up?' I asked.

'He asked for a month to find a new apartment, according to her mother,' Jace said. 'She also said Royce spent most of the time trying to win Viv back, wining and dining her.'

'With her own money?' I asked.

'Of course. He didn't have any of his own,' Jace said. 'He also brought her flowers – which he cut in the estate gardens. Vivian's mother says she wishes she'd insisted that Royce leave the property, but she played bridge with his aunt, and she didn't want to make a fuss.'

'I wonder what will happen to the bridge games after Vivian's funeral,' I said.

Katie snorted. 'Typical Forest. Jace, is that enough to get a conviction?'

'Almost. I forgot the best part. Royce made two calls to nine-one-one and gave them two different stories about the attack. The first time, he claimed Viv was wandering dazed and confused in the garden and he wanted an ambulance.

'The second time he called nine-one-one, he said he came home from a run on the estate and found her raped and murdered. Royce didn't realize that nine-one-one calls are recorded, and he told all sorts of outlandish lies. Mike and I watched him squirm.'

Jace grinned, and I saw the canary feathers.

'He talked himself right into a jail cell.'

THIRTY-THREE

Before Jace and I left Katie's office, he made sure the press wasn't lurking outside the morgue doors. As we walked toward our cars, he checked his voice messages. 'I've got one call. The lab. And that print in the crypt was made by Nathan Tucker's shoe. It's time for a talk with that young man.'

'Are you going to arrest him?'

'Yes, unless he has a good explanation,' Jace said.

'Can you hold off?'

Jace stopped walking. 'Why?'

'In case he's innocent.'

'Why do you think he may be innocent?'

Why did I? Because I liked Nathan? Because I believed he'd been given a raw deal by the Forest?

'Uh . . .' I was stalling for time and we both knew it. Jace moved in closer to me. He was way bigger, and suddenly my friend seemed intimidating. He never had before.

'Let me guess.' Jace's voice sounded sharp, almost angry. 'Because you like him.'

'I do like Nathan,' I said. 'And he let you take his shoe for comparison, Jace. Someone who's innocent does that.'

'Or someone who's a brazen liar and doesn't know that we have a shoe print.'

'What if someone stole Nathan's shoe, the way he told us?' I asked.

'You believe that cockamamie story?' The scorn in Jace's voice was withering.

'It might be true.'

'And I might be head of the FBI some day, but it's highly unlikely.'

'Can we at least go to the gym first, and ask about the shoe? Please?' I was groveling now.

Jace gave me a condescending chuckle, and all but patted me on the head. I was furious, but tried not to let it show.

What was going on with my friend and sorta partner? I hoped he just needed to show he was in charge.

'OK, Angela. Let's swing by the Chouteau University Gym on the way to the gravestone place.'

Jace and I were at the university's gym in ten minutes. It was a modern, light brick building with a swooping S-curve front. Through the tall windows I could see gray ranks of exercise bikes, rowing machines, treadmills and other devices of self-torture. Inside, we heard the whirr of bikes and the slam-thunk of weight machines. An upbeat Eighties tune played on the soundtrack.

Marcy, a bouncy, pony-tailed blonde, greeted us at the reception desk. Jace showed his credentials and said, 'I'd like to ask you about an incident involving a pair of shoes lost by Nathan Tucker.'

The good humor faded from Marcy's pretty face. 'Oh, no. He didn't go to the police with that, did he? He got the blasted shoes back, but he won't shut up about them.'

'Can you tell me what happened?'

'Sure. I took the report. He works out here about three days a week. He came in on Wednesday, October twenty-eighth, and did his usual hour-long routine. Then he went to the men's locker room for a shower. Next thing I know, he's out here pounding on the desk and shouting that someone stole his new shoes. I sent one of the guys who works here to help Nathan search for the shoes, but they didn't find them. I looked out here for them myself. The whole staff was half-crazy looking for them. I did everything I could to find the shoes – even posted signs on the bulletin board. Then, two days after Halloween, they suddenly appeared in our Lost and Found, smelling of bleach.

'Nathan didn't come back here until yesterday. This time, he was wearing his old gym shoes. He did his usual workout, then collected his missing shoes on the way out. "I don't know how this happened," he told me. "But my shoes turned up in front of my locker. They're fine, except the soles smell like bleach."

'"I'm glad you have your shoes back," I told him. "I think a patron accidentally stuck them in his own gym bag and then had to sneak them back in here. The locker room floors are mopped with a bleach-based cleaner. Maybe that's how it got on your shoe soles."

'"Maybe," he said. "But it sure is odd."

'I was just glad the problem was over, and now you're back. Has he filed a complaint?'

'No, no, nothing like that.' Jace sounded so reassuring that Marcy relaxed.

'Can only Chouteau U students and teachers join this gym?' I asked.

'Oh, no.' She flashed me a saleswoman's smile. 'Anyone can join. We have a special low price for alumni, but we have a good deal for Chouteau County residents. We have the best gym in Chouteau County. In fact, people from the Forest Country Club are joining our gym, because our equipment is newer and better.

'Are you interested in joining?'

'Just checking for now.'

'Well, here's my card. Call me if you'd like a tour. I can also give you a free pass if you'd like to try out our facility.'

I took the card and thanked her.

I didn't say anything to Jace as we walked to our cars. I didn't want to push my luck.

'Let's park in the cemetery and walk over, Angela,' Jace said. 'I want the element of surprise when I talk to Nathan.'

I agreed and followed him to the cemetery.

It was a warm, sunny afternoon and a short walk to the gravestone place. Samantha Freeman was behind the reception counter. She looked alarmed when Jace said he wanted to talk to Nathan.

'Is everything OK?' she asked.

'I'll ask the questions,' Jace said. 'You find Mr Tucker.'

She looked to me for reassurance, but I looked at the floor.

Nathan came out from the back. 'You wished to speak with me, Detective?' I heard barely disguised hostility in his voice.

'Yes, in the same conference room as before.'

'As you wish.'

We followed Nathan to the room with the photos of gravestones on the walls. This time, there was no offer of refreshments.

'Tell us about why you hit Trey Lawson.' Jace's voice was flat.

'I told you, he kept ragging me about being black.'

'I want the truth!' Jace slapped the table.

Nathan and I both jumped. Samantha appeared in the doorway. 'Is everything OK?'

'Yes,' Jace said. 'Now go. And shut the door behind you.'

She did. Samantha's interruption gave Nathan time to recover. 'I want a lawyer,' he said.

'That's your right,' Jace said. 'But if you talk to a lawyer, you won't get a deal and your parole will be revoked.'

Nathan didn't ask, 'What deal?'

I wondered if Jace was bluffing.

Jace pulled out an envelope with photos of Elizabeth McKee's serene marble sculpture and said, 'If you don't talk, I'll have this monument taken apart, piece by piece.'

Could Jace do that? I didn't know, but I did know I'd better keep quiet.

I watched the emotions play across Nathan's face. First, he looked startled, then sad and finally resigned. 'Please leave my ancestor alone. She suffered enough in this life.'

'Then tell me what happened,' Jace said. 'I know that Trey Lawson got you admitted into his business fraternity.'

'I thought he was doing me a favor,' Nathan said. 'I knew the fraternity didn't want any black men. I heard Bradford Du Pres was campaigning against me behind the scenes. Trey said that Bradford belonged to the old Forest and he was part of the new, and I shouldn't pay any attention to him. It was time for a new day in the Forest. Bradford and his family belonged to the past. Trey said he had enough power to overrule Bradford's wishes.

'I was grateful. I thought I'd be OK with Trey sponsoring me. Man, I was stupid.

'Once I was in and accepted, Trey told everyone that I had Lawson blood. He bragged – actually bragged – that Elizabeth was enslaved by Trey's ancestor, Jamison Beauregard Lawson, and impregnated with his child.'

'So rape ran in the family,' I said.

'Yes, it did,' Nathan said. 'And so did getting away with it. Trey found a copy of the runaway slave notice that his ancestor placed in the newspapers when Elizabeth ran away. Here, let me show you.' Nathan stood up, and opened a drawer in a corner cabinet. He rummaged through some papers and pulled out a photocopied ad from an 1857 Kentucky newspaper.

'Read it,' he said.

Jace read the ad out loud: '"Ten Dollars Reward! Runaway on the seventh inst. (March) a Negro woman named Elizabeth, about twenty years of age, slender, middle size, yellowish complexion, sullen attitude. She had on a green coat and jacket, and took a good hat and shawl with her, also a pair of black shoes. She carried with her a male child, two years old last Christmas. Whoever delivers her to me in Clay County, shall receive the above reward. Jamison B. Lawson, Esq."'

Jace showed me the photocopied ad. At the top of it was a racist caricature of a black woman with exaggerated features. She had none of Elizabeth's delicate beauty. The ad seemed to radiate evil. I handed it back to Jace, who started to give it to Nathan.

'You can keep it,' Nathan said.

I stopped myself from saying it was hard to believe slavery was legal not so long ago. That would sound fatuous. Jace folded the ad and stuck it in with the tomb photos.

'Trey continued to taunt me about Elizabeth. He left copies of that runaway slave notice all over the frat house. He called me "Ten-Dollar Tucker" until that was my nickname. Trey showed the notice around at frat parties and told everyone, "Nathan Tucker is my cousin, but not by marriage," and then he'd laugh.'

'Horrible,' I said.

'Trey kept it up and kept it up until one day I snapped and punched him. I shouted, "I'll kill you, Trey, if you don't stop."' He looked defiantly at Jace. 'Well, you know the rest.'

'Two questions,' Jace said. 'Could anyone else find out about the tunnel in the crypt?'

'My family doesn't talk about it. We're worried about vandalism. But my mother is proud to be a descendant of a conductor on the Underground Railroad. The crypt is mentioned in our family Bible and my mother keeps it on the Bible table in our living room. Before things went sour for me when I was in the fraternity, I had everyone over for a barbecue. They all came, even the people who were opposed to me joining. That's another reason why I thought things would work out for me at the fraternity.'

'One other question,' Jace said. 'Did you date Celia Stone?'

'Yes. I stayed in touch with her for a while after she went home.'

'After the rape, you mean,' Jace corrected.

'Yes, after that terrible tragedy. But our romance fell apart. She needed to recover and I met Samantha, and we're engaged.'

He smiled, and looked happy.

'That's all for now.' Jace stood up.

THIRTY-FOUR

After the talk with Nathan, Jace and I held a conference in the cemetery. I sat on a sun-warmed gravestone that was 'Sacred to the Memory of Frances Vierling.' Since Frances was 'Safe in the Arms of Jesus,' I hoped she wouldn't mind.

Jace sat on a tombstone across from me. A warm breeze stirred the dead leaves in the cemetery. I felt chilled, surrounded by the permanent reminders of lives ended.

In the distance, a minister stood on a hill, conducting a graveside service for a group in black. The words of his prayer drifted our way. 'I am the resurrection and the life. He that believes in me, though he were dead, yet shall he live . . .'

I've got to get away from cemeteries, crypts and graves, I thought. I'm spending too much time with death.

Jace loosened his blue-and-yellow tie, which matched his blue sports jacket and yellow shirt. His wife dressed him, right down to his blue-and-yellow checked socks, and he didn't care who knew it.

'You didn't arrest Nathan. Why not?' I asked.

'Some detectives might have, but I wouldn't. The case was weak. Very weak. Professionals know that.'

Ouch. I'd been put in my place. Jace had just told me I didn't know enough about being a homicide detective.

'So what's next?'

'I'm going to continue to investigate Nathan Tucker,' he said. 'He has the big three – motive, means and opportunity.'

'Any word about the DNA on his shoes?'

'Still waiting for the lab to finish.'

'What about the third lawyer, Bradford Du Pres?' I asked. 'He should be back from his trip. We can interview him.' The warm breeze carried a hint of rotting vegetation. The flowers in the stone vases flanking a nearby headstone were as dead as the woman they were supposed to honor.

Jace paused before responding. 'You think that Bradford killed those two people.' His voice was a flat statement, not a question.

'I do.'

'You now believe some rich kid sneaked into a cobweb-infested crypt and butchered two people because an outsider wanted to join an exclusive club.'

I sat up straight. I had to make my case. 'It's more than that, Jace, and talking to Nathan helped convince me. Trey had been challenging the Du Pres's power before that auction. That auction was a test of who would rule the Forest. It was about old money and power, about the haves and the have-nots.'

'A hedge funder's son is hardly a have-not,' Jace said. 'And his fiancée Lydia was trying to be one of the first ladies of the Forest.'

'Trying. That's the key word, Jace. Let's make it the old rich versus the new rich. The old rich have a stranglehold on Chouteau County. Nothing gets started – or finished – without their approval. Trey wanted to challenge that. Heck, he'd already challenged it successfully, when he got Nathan Tucker into his lily-white frat house.

'Granted, when Trey overrode Bradford Du Pres's wishes so Nathan could join, he didn't do it for the noblest reasons. The point is, Trey did it. Trey had the power, the clout and the money to break the Du Pres's stranglehold on the Forest. He was flexing his muscles when he got Nathan in that frater-nity. Trey almost succeeded in breaking their death grip.

'So, yes, I think Bradford Du Pres would do anything to preserve his family's power.'

'And you think old Reggie would approve of that plan – taking a kitchen knife to two people?'

I suspected Jace was laughing at me, and that made me angry. 'Of course not. Reggie's not the Godfather. He won't order a hit. He's more like King Henry II, who asked, "Will no one rid me of this meddlesome priest?" and guess what? That bothersome Thomas Becket, the Archbishop of Canterbury, wound up dead.'

'I thought it was "turbulent priest."' Now Jace really was laughing at me.

'I was awake in history class that day, Angela.' He grinned. 'And I know that's how bosses get what they want without issuing a direct order. They hint around until someone does their dirty work.'

Jace leaned forward, elbows on his knees, and looked me in the eye. 'You're a smart woman, Angela, but don't make the mistake of believing everyone else is stupid. I'm not some dumb flatfoot. I don't know all the ins and outs of how the Forest works, but I've been around enough so I have a pretty good idea. I treat you as an equal – hell, you're my informal partner. I expect the same courtesy from you.'

The distant buzz of a lawn mower drifted toward us while I thought about what Jace had said. Maybe he was right. I had been arrogant. And I didn't know everything about his job. 'I'm glad you cleared the air,' I said. 'And I apologize.'

'That's OK.' Jace was quick to forgive. That's one of the things I liked about him. 'Now, let's talk more about why you like Bradford Du Pres for the murders.'

'He's rich and sheltered, and that makes him afraid. Bradford doesn't know how to make money. He got his job at his father's firm because of who he is, not because of how good he is. He'll do anything to keep his position at the top of the heap.'

'Even commit two messy murders?' Jace asked.

'He goes hunting with his father and uncle in Canada every year. It's covered in the Forest society pages. I've seen the photos. Bradford has killed, skinned and probably field-dressed large animals. He bragged about shooting a bear. So, yes, he could see this as a hunting trip. I don't think he'd balk at the blood.'

'How did he find out about the crypt tunnel?' Jace asked.

'He could have seen the family Bible in Nathan's home.'

'According to Nathan.'

'It's easy enough to check,' I said.

'Why would Bradford slit Lydia's tongue and stick a frat pin in Trent's mouth?'

'To make it look like Nathan committed the crime. That's also why he stole Nathan's shoes, left a bloody print in the tunnel, and then brought the shoes back to the gym. He wanted to set him up.'

'Don't you think that's a little elaborate?' Jace asked.

'No. And if we can get Bradford's DNA, we can prove he killed them.'

'That won't be easy. He's going to lawyer up, Angela. We'll have to get a court order and find a judge who'll go against the Du Pres family.'

'That's OK. We can do that.'

'I hope so, because if we bring down a Du Pres, it has to be by the book. You say this Bradford did the murders, but made it look like Nathan was the killer. That's too complicated, Angela. Most murders are straightforward. Look at the last two we worked on: two men killed the women in their lives. No fancy motives. They wanted them dead, and they were.

'Now back to the crypt murders. I think Nathan was angry enough to kill both Lydia and Trey. Lydia had called his innocent girlfriend a slut and lied to the court to get Trey out of a rape charge. Trey was a rapist and a racist. He provoked Nathan into punching him. Now Nathan's on probation and owes a huge fine.'

I folded my arms in front of me. 'I still don't believe Nathan is a killer.'

'Why?' Jace asked. 'Because you hate rich kids?'

'I don't hate them. But I do think too many of them get by with things because of their family names. And I dislike their smug, sneery faces.'

'Whoa!' Jace said. 'That sounds pretty angry to me.'

I guess it did. Maybe I did hate Bradford because he was a Du Pres. No, wait! It wasn't just prejudice on my part. At the auction Bradford's father threatened to kill Trey. And he was only half-joking. When the Du Pres men and their pal laughed, was that their 'turbulent priest' moment?

I changed the subject. 'What are you going to do to build a stronger case against Nathan?'

'I'm going to interview his associates, and make sure he was working late the night of the murder. I'll check his cell phone records to try and place him near the scene. I'll check his social media.'

'So you think he did a TikTok video of himself stabbing Trey and Lydia?'

Now Jace was annoyed. 'Wake up, Angela. Killers post on social media all the time – before, during and after the murders. One guy shot his wife and posted a photo of her dead body on Facebook.'

I'd sounded like a jerk. Again. What was wrong with me? 'I'm sorry, Jace. That was a stupid question. What else are you going to do?'

He shrugged it off. 'No big deal. I'm also going to check the store cams, traffic cams, and other sources to see if the exterior cameras picked up Nathan on his way to the scene.

'And I'll definitely present the case to the county prosecuting attorney to see if she has enough to file charges and to see what she would demand in order to file charges against Nathan.'

'Fair enough. Would you mind if I talked to Bradford Du Pres at his law office tomorrow? Without you?'

Jace laughed. 'I don't think you can get in trouble interviewing Bradford at his office. Just make sure you let me know when you go in for the interview and when you come out. And keep me posted on what you learn.'

'Deal,' I said.

Black cars like a line of ants crested the distant hill. The funeral procession was leaving the cemetery. I followed them out.

THIRTY-FIVE

When I got home, Rick's battered pick-up truck was still in the driveway. I couldn't wait to see how the painting was going in my bedroom. I dropped my things in the kitchen and ran upstairs, calling 'Rick!'

Rick emerged in a cloud of pot smoke and paint fumes, wearing old jeans and a tattered Grateful Dead T-shirt featuring a skull crowned with red roses. His long brown hair was held back with a bandana.

'Hey, Angela, I'm about finished with your bedroom. Come take a look. The color is sweet.'

The soft white made my room look like it was wrapped in a cloud. It also looked fresh.

A new beginning. 'I like it,' I told him. 'That color is terrific.'

'Yeah, I like it, too. I've recommended the color to some of my customers and I think they're going to use it. I should be finished here in about two days.'

'Right on schedule. I'll keep supplying the pound cake.'

Rick looked at the floor, like an embarrassed little kid. 'Uh, I hope you don't mind, but I ate all the cake you left out today. I kinda got the munchies.'

'That's what the cake is for. Anything you don't finish you can take home.'

Now he looked relieved. 'Oh, good. Maybe I should extend this job another day.'

'If you finish on time, I'll make you a bonus coffee cake.' If by 'make' you mean 'defrost,' I thought.

Rick was finished for the day. He gathered his things and left.

I sneezed when he shut the front door. My home was covered with a fine layer of dust – painting always did that. I'd need another day to clean after he finished, but I'd worry about that later. Ever since I'd started the Cursed Crypt death investigation, I'd been in a walking nightmare. It was time to return to life – and fun.

I called Chris – actually called him on my cell. No texting. He sounded happy to hear from me.

'I miss you,' I said. 'How about dinner in four days?'

'That sounds awfully far away.' I heard the disappointment in his voice.

'It is, but I want everything at my house perfect for you.' I hope he got my subtext: I want you to spend the night in my bed.

'Should I bring dinner?' he asked.

'No, thanks, I'm cooking.' Microwaving, to be precise.

'What can I bring?'

'Yourself.'

We talked for a while. I told him I was talking to Bradford Du Pres tomorrow, and he ended the conversation by saying, 'Please be careful, Angela. I'm worried about you.'

'How dangerous can it be at a lawyer's office?'

'If he's the killer, it's dangerous. He's killed three people, and he won't hesitate to murder a fourth. Don't forget what I told you about self-defense. And bring your Taser. Make sure it's charged and ready.'

'Yes, Mom.'

'Angela, please listen. Promise me you'll bring your Taser.'

'I promise.'

'Put it in your bag right now.'

I got up and took the Taser off the charger, checked that it was ready to go, and put it in my purse.

'Just did it, Chris, though I think you're overreacting.'

'No such thing. I'll see you soon. I love you.'

'And I love you.'

When we finally ended our call, I felt so lonely. Maybe this break wasn't such a bad idea. Abstinence did make my heart grow fonder. Even though I thought Chris was fussing, it was nice to have someone care.

I smiled as I scrambled two eggs and fixed toast for dinner. Then I cleaned up the kitchen, checked the pound cake supply in the freezer (six left, assorted flavors), dusted the leather sofa in the living room, and added sheets and pillows.

I got ready for bed and set my alarm for seven thirty tomorrow morning. I'd drop in on Bradford Du Pres first thing tomorrow.

I slept well on the sofa – too well. The alarm dragged me out of a deep sleep. I shook my head, then ran upstairs to shower and get dressed. I wore my best black DI suit (the one where the knees weren't shiny from crawling around crime scenes) and a pale blue blouse. Downstairs, I made coffee and fixed myself toast. I was too nervous to eat anything heavier.

By the time I'd set out the butter to soften, defrosted a chocolate chip pound cake, and filled a Thermos with coffee, Rick had arrived. He made a beeline for the kitchen and the warm pound cake.

'Awesome!' he said.

I laughed, and left for Bradford Du Pres's office. The day was perfect, cool and sunny, with a china blue sky that showed off the fall leaves. I hit what passed for a traffic jam in the Forest, which meant I had to wait two light cycles to turn onto Gravois, the main drag.

I reached the Georgian-style headquarters of Du Pres, Dunworthy and Damon by nine o'clock, and parked in a client spot. A big black Mercedes had pulled in behind me. Bradford Du Pres. He parked in a reserved spot near the brick wall.

I slid down in my seat so I could watch him. He was tall and slender, almost wraithlike, and pale as a boiled egg. His thick blond hair was in a classic Ivy League cut – short on the sides and a smidge long (but not too long) on top. And his mouth, well, I recognized that entitled rich-kid sneer from across the parking lot.

Whoa, I reminded myself. Don't let your prejudices interfere with your investigation.

Bradford walked very carefully, as if he'd been injured. What was going on there?

I waited ten minutes after he reached the building, then went inside.

Hayley, the receptionist, was at the front desk, dressed like a corporate nun in yet another gray suit. This one was dark charcoal.

'I'd like to speak to Bradford Du Pres.'

'Do you have an appointment?' Her voice was crisp and professional.

'No, but I'm sure he'll want to see me.'

'Not without an appointment.' Now she sounded firm.

'Yes, he will.' I marched past her desk and into the main office.

'Stop!' Hayley swiveled around in her chair and tried to block my way.

I whispered, 'Make a scene, Hayley, and I'll call the police. That could be embarrassing.'

Hayley backed off and picked up the phone, no doubt warning Bradford of my visit. I hurried past the cubicle farm and spotted Bradford in his office. A corner office. With a window.

'Why are you barging into my office?' he asked.

'I'm not barging, Bradford. I'm saving you from major embarrassment.'

'I don't need to be saved. I haven't done anything embarrassing.'

'You will be embarrassed if I ask Detective Jace Budewitz to join us. He'll march through this office showing his badge. And he's not from the Forest, so he doesn't care who your daddy is.'

I was bluffing, but Bradford didn't know that. He looked around nervously, checking to see if anyone had seen the small drama in his office. No one was watching us.

'Why don't you sit down and offer me a cup of coffee,' I said. 'I take it black. I'm Angela Richman.'

I said my name as if only a moron wouldn't know who I was. Bradford never asked for my credentials, which was good for me. I gathered he wasn't the brightest member of the law firm, but thanks to dear old dad, he had a walnut-paneled office and a tufted leather chair.

Bradford made a call on his phone and asked, 'Opal, could you bring two coffees to my office?'

He didn't say 'please.'

Opal, another mouselike creature in brown, soon scurried in with a serving cart. It had a pot of coffee, two china cups, a cream and sugar bowl, and a plate of thin sugar cookies. She poured two cups of coffee, and then asked me, 'Cream or sugar?'

'Black, please.'

She fixed Bradford's cup and added two sugars and a splash of thick cream.

I thanked her, and she left, narrow shoulders hunched, as if she expected to be beaten.

Bradford sipped his coffee and crunched a cookie. We sat in silence for a minute. I watched him scratch his left hand. It had an ugly red rash with a seeping yellow crust. He reached for another cookie, and I saw his right hand had the same suppurating rash. I decided I didn't want any cookies.

'Did you hurt your hand?' I asked.

'Our dumb housekeeper bought cheap laundry soap, charged us for Tide, and pocketed the difference. I broke out in a rash all over my body. She's history.'

'Looks painful.'

'It is.' He was scratching his right knee now, and I started feeling itchy.

'Well?' Bradford looked at me and raised one eyebrow. That was a demand. The entitled sneer had returned to his face.

'I want to ask you about the deaths of Trey Lawson and Lydia Fynch in the so-called Cursed Crypt.'

Like a good liar, Bradford looked me right in the eye. 'Don't know. Don't care.'

His manicured nails were digging into his left hand until he drew blood. That's when it dawned on me: Bradford had killed Eli, the delivery guy in the green Kia. The car had rammed through a patch of poison sumac. And if he'd killed Eli, he'd also killed Lydia and Trey.

I needed Bradford's DNA. Could I steal something from his office? If I was a law enforcement officer, I'd have to get the DNA legally. I wasn't sure what I was. Jace had called me his 'almost partner.'

Better play it safe and make it legal.

I poured myself more coffee to buy time and asked, 'A warm-up for you?'

He shook his head no and reached for another cookie on

the plate. The plate. And the cups. Where had I seen that china before? Then I knew.

'Your china. It's the PBS pattern,' I said.

'The what?'

'Those cups and saucers. I've seen them on a lot of PBS shows.' The old-fashioned pattern was red roses and blue leaves, trimmed in gold. 'Do you know what it's called?'

I could have turned over my saucer and checked, but I didn't. Neither did Bradford.

'Let me ask the legal administrative assistant. Opal keeps track of all that stuff.' He picked up his phone and said, 'Opal! Get in here!'

Once again, Opal materialized in the room. 'How may I help you?'

'This lady wants to know the name of this china pattern.'

'Blue Mandalay,' she said. 'It's hand-painted.'

'I've seen it on PBS shows.' I smiled at her.

Opal smiled back, and her face was quite pretty. 'Me, too. It was featured on *Downton Abbey*, one of my favorite shows. I've seen the series and the movie.'

Here goes nothing, I thought. 'My mother is crazy about *Downton Abbey*, and her birthday is next week. Could I buy my coffee cup from you?' My cheeks burned with embarrassment. I couldn't believe I'd made such a tacky request, but I wanted Bradford's DNA.

Bradford waved at my cup. 'Yeah, sure, take it. It's no big deal. Opal, you'd better get back to work.'

Once again, Opal disappeared as quietly as morning fog. Now I had a witness who could say I didn't swipe the coffee cup.

'Can we get this over with, Ms Richman?' Bradford sounded like a petulant child. 'I have work to do.'

'I was asking you about the murders of Lydia and Trent.'

'And I told you I couldn't care less.'

'Really?' I smiled at him. 'I'm not sure I believe that. At the auction, Jefferson R. Morgan said, "Trey Lawson will join the Founders Club over my dead body." And your father said, "Why not make it *his* dead body?"'

'Who claimed my father said that? I want their names.'

Now Bradford the bully was speaking. But I wasn't one of the browbeaten women in his office.

'Two credible witnesses.' The police chief's wife and me.

'So what? It's just a figure of speech. My father also said he'd kill for another dessert.'

Bradford used the same argument as his father and I borrowed Jace's answer. 'But the waiter is still alive and Trey Lawson is dead.'

Bradford stood up. 'It's time for you to go, Ms Richman. And if you come back, bring that detective with you, and I'll have six lawyers with me.'

We heard a tentative knock on the door and a small voice quavered, 'Mr Du Pres?'

'What now, Opal?' Bradford sounded put-upon.

'I brought a bag for the lady. For her cup.'

'Thank you, Opal,' I said. 'That was so thoughtful.'

And helpful. Opal gave me a tentative smile. She wasn't used to people being polite in this office.

'It's just a plastic grocery bag,' she said, 'but I thought—'

'Opal!' Bradford shouted. 'No one cares what you think.'

'Yes, sir.' Opal hung her head.

I grabbed Bradford's cup, the one that had the remains of his coffee with cream and sugar, and carefully placed it in the bag. Then I moved my cup over to his side of the desk.

Meanwhile, Bradford was still berating the young woman. 'Listen, if I want anything from you, Opal, I'll call you. Don't volunteer. Got it?'

'Yes, sir.' She was trying not to cry.

I slid past them, feeling terrible that Opal had to endure his wrath. Hang in there, Opal, I thought. He's going to get his.

I sprinted out the front door, clicked open my car and dialed Jace's cell phone. He didn't pick up right away. 'Come on, Jace,' I said out loud. I had the cup cradled in my lap.

He answered after six rings. 'Angela! What's going on?'

Since we were on cell phones, I spoke in code. 'I think the person I saw this morning is someone we want. I got DNA. How do I get it to you?'

'I'm driving back from St. Louis,' he said. 'Don't go to the station.'

Good advice. If Greiman or one of the other Du Pres toadies was there, that cup could disappear.

'Take the item straight to Katie's office. I'll meet you there in ten minutes.'

I hung up and saw Bradford running for my car.

'Hey, you! Stop! You took the wrong cup,' he shouted.

I knew I'd taken the right one. I peeled out of the parking lot and roared toward SOS.

THIRTY-SIX

I heard Jace yelling, 'Angela! Talk to me! What's going on?' I'd stuck my phone in my jacket pocket, so he could hear what was happening.

'That person. The one whose DNA I have. He's chasing me through downtown in a big black Mercedes.'

'Oh, jeez. Are you OK?'

'So far. I'm staying ahead of him.' I checked my rear-view mirror. Bradford was gaining on me. I quickly recited his license plate for Jace.

Jace said, 'I'll radio Mike and Chris and see if they can get to SOS quicker than I can.' That was a relief. Jace would call two cops we both trusted. 'Keep your phone on, Angela.'

I hoped my Dodge Charger was a match for the Mercedes. I raced through the crowded downtown streets, flipped off by frightened drivers and dodging pedestrians. For once, I prayed a police car would pull me over, but no such luck.

I ran a red light to a chorus of horns and a screech of brakes. Finally, mercifully, I was past downtown Chouteau Forest. Now the road was a rollercoaster – a hilly, two-lane blacktop ribbon bordered by shade trees and exclusive subdivisions. The trick was to avoid hitting a tree or an SUV.

I crested a hill and saw the black Mercedes only two hills behind me. I poured on the gas just as a lawn service trailer swung out ahead of me. To keep from rear-ending it, I swung into the oncoming lane – in front of a monster trash truck. The only way to avoid hitting the trash truck was to duck into the Oak Hollow subdivision on the left. My car shot into Oak Hollow Lane, and the irate trash truck driver blasted me with his horn. A quick right turn, and I was on Oak Hollow Trace, a calm street lined by handsome homes and shaded by stately trees.

The trace paralleled Gravois, in a winding sort of way. I hoped the Mercedes didn't see me turn left into the subdivision, but the trash truck had made so much noise, Bradford figured it out. Now I could see him behind me, roaring through the peaceful street.

Jace had heard the honking and shouted, 'Angela! What's going on?'

'Nearly hit a trash truck. I had to duck into a subdivision. I'm on Oak Hollow Trace.'

'Follow it for a quarter-mile, and you'll come out in the SOS parking lot,' Jace said. 'Mike, Chris and I are all on our way, but that Mercedes caused an accident in downtown and didn't stop – so we can add "leaving the scene" to the other charges. We're caught in the traffic.'

I didn't ask if anyone was hurt. I was too busy trying to steer past a brown UPS delivery truck stopped in the middle of the street. The driver was unloading boxes. I swerved around the UPS truck and took the side mirror off a post office van in the other lane. I kept going. I'd report it later.

The post office van's brakes screeched and the driver blew its horn at me. Bradford's Mercedes tried to squeeze between the post office van and the UPS truck. The UPS driver had unwisely decided to wheel a dolly loaded with boxes across the street. He saw the approaching Mercedes, abandoned his load and ran. The Mercedes knocked the dolly sideways into the truck and crunched over the boxes.

The new accident didn't slow Bradford down.

I said into my phone, 'Jace, I can see the back parking lot for SOS. It's two blocks away. I still have the item. The person is gaining on me.'

'Park in front of the ME's office door and go inside. Mike called Katie's office. Chris is two minutes out.'

Two minutes out was still too far away. The Mercedes was only a block behind me. I was going nearly seventy miles an hour in a twenty-mile zone and I prayed I wouldn't hurt anyone. Up ahead, I saw a car backing out of a driveway, and hit my horn. The driver ignored my warning and kept going.

I swerved to avoid it and wiped out a black residential mailbox on a wrought-iron post, but the car was safe. The black mailbox came loose from its post and spun in the street. The Mercedes hit it and sent it flying into the car I'd just avoided.

Was someone injured? I couldn't stop. The Mercedes was three car lengths behind me.

Where were the cops? I needed help.

My heart was pounding so hard it felt like it would break my ribs. Once I got to SOS I'd be safe, but Bradford was close. I glanced in the rear-view mirror again. Too close.

Ah, there it was. A sign. The sign I needed. 'Sisters of Sorrow Hospital, South Entrance. Chouteau County Medical Examiner.' The beige sign had never looked more beautiful.

I was in luck: this SOS parking lot was nearly empty, and it didn't have those concrete parking bumpers to block my way.

I roared across the vast blacktopped lot, the Mercedes right behind me, and the china cup with the DNA protected in my lap.

'Talk to me, Angela.' Jace's voice pleaded from my cell phone.

'I'm at SOS, Jace, with the car right on my tail. I can see the ME's office. Where's Katie? Where's Chris?'

'He's at the north entrance, Angela. It's crowded with valet parkers and he's slowed down. Mike didn't actually reach Katie. He left a message.'

So she could be in a meeting or conducting an autopsy. I was on my own. Totally alone. Just my luck there were no smokers out by the Dumpsters. Not even a funeral van to pick up a body from the medical examiner.

I swung my car in front of the ME's office, leaving about ten feet so I could open the wide office door. My plan disintegrated when Bradford's Mercedes roared into that empty space next to the door, blocking the passenger side of my car.

Up close, I could see his car was dented, the hood was crumpled and the sides were scraped. He popped the trunk, and wriggled out on his passenger side. He had to be a contortionist to get out of that tiny opening.

'Angela, what's going on?' Jace again.

I was talking so fast, I wasn't sure Jace could understand me. 'Bradford's car is blocking the entrance. He's out of his car, and looking for something in his trunk. He pulled out a long metal thing.'

'A tire iron?'

'Yes, a tire iron – and he's swinging it. He looks crazy.'

'He is crazy, Angela, and hopped up on adrenaline. Stay in the car and hit your horn.'

First, I had to save the DNA. I opened my glove compartment, tossed the windshield scrapers, car maintenance manuals and old tissues on the floor, then shoved the cup inside and locked it.

'Jace, if anything happens to me, the cup is in my glove compartment.'

'Nothing bad is going to happen, Angela. Lean on your horn. And Chris says to remember your training.'

My training. Right.

I grabbed my Taser out of my purse and pounded on my horn. Was I going to have to roll down the window to Tase Bradford?

Crack!

A wild-eyed Bradford was hammering my window with the tire iron. His face was contorted by rage and he was drooling. He swung the tire iron like a baseball bat and the safety glass spidered into a million cracks on the first swing.

Crack!

On the second swing the safety glass bent inward. I knew it was going to break soon. I readied my Taser to fire. I could hear Chris's directions in my head:

'First, make sure the safety is flipped up and the power switch is "off." Now, aim the Taser at the center of the target mass.'

Crack!

The glass held together for the third swing, but just barely. I pulled my jacket over my head to protect my face and eyes from flying glass. The window should break into pebbles, but I was taking no chances.

Crack!

This time, glass pebbles rained inside my car, covering the seat and my clothes.

Bradford was screaming. 'Give me my cup. You took the wrong cup!'

'Why do you care?' I shouted back.

He didn't answer, just readied the tire iron for another swing. This time, he'd hit me and hurt me.

I had to nail him with the Taser. He was only wearing a white shirt, and no jacket. I aimed the laser sight. I was tempted to move it below his belt. Instead I pressed the trigger, and the electricity arced. Two Taser darts shot right into Bradford's gut, easily cutting through his shirt.

He screamed, an unearthly, high-pitched squeal, as if someone was attacking a pig. I pressed the button for the full five seconds.

Bradford fell backward, his head hitting the blacktop. I jumped out of my car, glass flying everywhere, and ran over to Bradford's convulsing body.

I kicked him in the crotch and shouted, 'You miserable, worthless, piece of—'

Suddenly, I felt two strong arms around me. I fought against them until a familiar voice said, 'Angela, it's over. You got him. You can stop now.'

'Chris?'

I turned and faced the man I love.

'I missed you.' I kissed him, hard, and he kissed me right back.

'Are you hurt?' He picked glass pebbles from my hair.

'I don't think so.' I shook my head and more glass rained down.

I heard someone clear his throat. Jace. 'Good work, Angela. Chris, you can conduct a more thorough examination later. Right now, let's get this dirtbag back to the station.'

Bradford had stopped twitching. He scooted across the blacktop and leaned against my car.

Jace grabbed him and made him stand up. Bradford's legs were still wobbly, so Chris helped keep the suspect upright while Jace read him his rights. 'Bradford Du Pres, you have the right to remain silent. Anything you say can and will be used against you in a court of law. You have the right to an attorney. If you cannot afford an attorney, one will be appointed for you. Do you understand your rights?'

'Yes,' Bradford said. 'Are you arresting me?'

'You're damn right. I'm arresting you for the first-degree

murder of Trey Lawson, Lydia Fynch, Elijah Coffey, and the death of Paul Goulden.'

'Who's Paul Goulden?' Bradford asked.

'He's the man whose car you rammed when you ran a red light in downtown Chouteau Forest. He's thirty-two years old. Paul Goulden died of his injuries in the emergency room. You left the scene of that accident, Mr Du Pres. In Missouri, if a hit-and-run results in death, it's a Class D felony.

'And you gave me the wrong answer when I Mirandized you. An innocent man would have said, "I didn't kill anyone."'

'I didn't,' Bradford said. 'But I couldn't think straight. She kicked me.'

'She kicked you in the nuts,' Jace said. 'That might hurt, but I don't think your brains are there.'

'I'm filing a report for police brutality.'

'Go ahead,' Jace said. 'She's not an LEO.' That meant law enforcement officer.

Chris interrupted. 'Detective Budewitz, you were too far away to see clearly. I was on the scene. Ms Richman was checking the suspect for damage after he tried to kill her with a tire iron.'

'Thank you for that clarification, Officer Ferretti. Be sure to include that in your report.'

'I want a lawyer,' Bradford said.

'You'll get one at the station, after we book you.'

By this time, Mike had arrived. Jace asked him, 'Will you take this man to the station in your patrol car?'

'My pleasure,' Mike said. 'That young man he ran down was a plumber with three little girls. They're going to grow up without their daddy. A useful citizen was killed by this scumbag.'

'Here come the TV vans, Jace,' Chris said.

'Good. I'll alert them to go to the station so they can see the first Du Pres to ever make the perp walk.'

Mike cuffed Bradford, making sure the cuffs were behind his back in the most uncomfortable position, and escorted him to the back of his patrol car.

Jace was back. He addressed Chris and me. 'OK, you two.

I want you both to write full reports. Angela, how much damage did you do, besides Tasering Bradford Du Pres?'

'I took the side mirror off a post office truck and hit a mailbox. A residential box, not an official government one.'

'I'll make sure to report you couldn't stop because of exigent circumstances,' he said, 'but you're going to have to fill out a pile of paperwork. Chris, I'll need your report. Then you both can go home.'

Jace turned to leave, and I said, 'Wait! The DNA.' I crawled into my car, unlocked the glove compartment, and brought out the cup.

I removed the bag and presented it to Jace.

'Bradford drank from this coffee cup this morning,' I said.

'Pretty,' Jace said.

'Pretty deadly, I hope. This is a death penalty state.'

THIRTY-SEVEN

By the time Jace's car was out of sight, I was back in Chris's arms. 'Come home with me,' he said.

'Yes.' My head was on his muscular shoulder. I could smell his citrus aftershave. 'I've missed you so much.'

'Let's go.'

Duty held me back, but just barely. 'We have to finish that blasted paperwork. I want Bradford in prison.'

'Let's work on it in my car.'

Chris was right. If we went to his place, we'd forget about the paperwork.

So we sat in the front seat of his patrol car, and called up the forms we needed on our iPads. It was difficult to concentrate with Chris next to me, but I managed. I also called a tow truck to take my car to the repair shop. While we worked, the air around us seemed to crackle with tension. Chris finished his report first, and ran inside the hospital to get me a hot chocolate. Hospital coffee was like dishwater, right down to the thin film of grease on the surface.

The hot chocolate gave me the sugar rush I needed to finish my reports. I signed them electronically and sent them off.

'All finished.' Chris and I exchanged one more lingering kiss. Then he turned on his lights and sirens and headed for his condo. Never mind what the rules said. This was an emergency.

At his place, Chris parked and locked his car and we ran for his door. Inside, he didn't even ask what we were going to do. We ran up the stairs, shedding our clothes along the way, and fell into bed.

'At last,' I said. Then neither one of us said anything for a long time. We made love once, then twice, and finally three times, before we fell asleep in each other's arms.

When we woke up, it was growing dark. We made love again, and then Chris said, 'Are you hungry?'

'Not any more.' I giggled. 'Not for a while.'

'I meant for food.'

'How about pizza?'

'Fine with me. Pepperoni and mushroom for you?'

Chris got dressed, went downstairs, ordered the pizzas and opened a bottle of wine. The pizzas arrived within thirty minutes. I slipped into a robe and joined him in the living room. While we ate on the couch, Chris turned on the TV.

We watched as Bradford Du Pres made his national television debut doing the perp walk into the Chouteau Forest police station. Bradford wasn't wearing a suit jacket, and evidently Mike wouldn't lend him a blanket, so Bradford couldn't hide his face. We switched channels several times. The entitled lawyer – minus his rich kid sneer – was on CBS, PBS, CNN, MSNBC, and the local stations. I'd devoured my first slice as I watched, savoring the salty pepperoni.

The perp walk was followed by Chief Butkus's press conference. He'd scheduled it to make the six o'clock news. The chief had become media savvy.

The press conference's lead-in on CNN was perfect. The anchor said, 'Bradford Du Pres, the scion of one of the oldest families in Chouteau Forest, Missouri, has been arrested and charged with four counts of murder.'

Another slice of pizza disappeared while the anchor listed the names of the dead. The story showed footage inside the blood-drenched Cursed Crypt, as well as the body bags containing the mutilated remains of Trey, Lydia and Eli, and the wreckage of Paul Goulden's car.

The chief in a freshly pressed uniform announced the arrest of this 'prominent citizen' and read the charges. He was peppered with questions, and answered them well.

'No, the suspect has not confessed, but we have DNA and other evidence,' the chief said. 'The Chouteau County prosecuting attorney is confident we have enough to convict. Because of the heinous nature of these murders – three young people and a father with three small daughters – she is demanding the death penalty. I'll have more updates for you later.'

Chris switched off the TV, and we concentrated on finishing our pizza.

'Would you like dessert?' Chris asked.

'Just you.' We kissed and ran upstairs to bed for more lovemaking. That night, we couldn't get enough of each other. It was as if we'd been apart for years instead of days. Some time in the middle of a very athletic night, Chris asked, 'Do you have to work tomorrow?'

'Nope, I can sleep in late.'

'Me, too.'

I'm not sure when we fell asleep, but it was after ten in the morning when I woke up – and remembered Rick was supposed to be at my house. I called him and apologized.

'It's OK, Angela. I knew you weren't coming home.'

'How did you know that?'

'The whole Forest is talking about how you escaped that crazy lawyer and then zapped him with a Taser. I hope they throw the book at him, after he killed a good man like Paul Goulden.'

'That wasn't on TV.'

'It didn't have to be. You know how news spreads here. I figured you wouldn't be home, so I worked late yesterday. I'm on track to finish. I'll see you tomorrow. Nine o'clock OK?'

'Make it ten.'

As soon as I hung up, my work cell phone rang. It was Jace. 'Angela, are you with Chris? I know it's your day off, but can I come by and talk to both of you? I have major news. I'll bring doughnuts.'

'Let me ask Chris.'

I knew the answer, but I ran downstairs. Chris was in the kitchen, grinding beans for coffee. He gave the answer I expected: 'Good. Tell Jace the coffee will be ready.'

'See you in thirty minutes.' Jace clicked off his phone.

That gave me time to run upstairs, take a quick shower, dress, and then go back downstairs and pick up the couch pillows, pizza boxes and wineglasses. By the time the doorbell rang, Chris and I were the picture of domesticity, sipping coffee at the kitchen counter. I poured Jace a mug of coffee while Chris answered the door.

Jace steamed into the kitchen, all smiles, carrying a

cardboard box of Strange Donuts. That's the name of the shop. 'I got a mix of favorites.' Jace pointed them out. 'These are gooey butter.' Yum. My favorite. The four buttery doughnuts were crowned with the golden, powder-sugar top of a gooey butter cake, promising a heart attack in every bite. 'And these are maple bacon.' I could see flecks of bacon in the icing. 'Last but not least, French apple pie. Those doughnuts have an apple filling!'

I enjoyed the glee Jace took in these oddball doughnuts. This morning he wore a light blue outfit. For the first time since the start of the Cursed Crypt case, he looked relaxed. I reached for a gooey butter cake doughnut, Chris took a maple bacon, and Jace bit into a French apple pie and squirted filling on his tie. He laughed. Chris got up, found some club soda in the fridge, and dabbed at Jace's tie until the spot disappeared.

For a while we ate in respectful silence. Once our doughnut lust was sated, Jace said, 'First of all, were you hurt, Angela?'

'Not a scratch. Just my car window bashed in.'

Jace looked relieved. 'That's good. I was worried. I saw broken glass all over.'

'So what's your news?' I asked.

'DNA confirmed that Bradford Du Pres is the crypt killer. At least, he urinated on the bodies. His DNA matched the DNA found in the crypt.'

I reached for a French apple pie doughnut and said, 'You got DNA off his cup that quickly? I thought the test took at least twenty-four hours.'

'It does, but we used a fairly new technique, a Rapid DNA test. It takes less than two hours. We needed a buccal swab.' Jace helped himself to a gooey butter doughnut, and Chris had another maple bacon.

'You swabbed his cheek? My car chase through the Forest was for nothing?'

'Don't sound so disappointed, Angela.' Jace now had powdered sugar down the front of his shirt. 'We got that swab thanks to you. We didn't have enough to take him into custody before – not with a firm full of rabid lawyers. But after he chased you through the Forest—'

'And killed an innocent plumber,' Chris added.

'And assaulted Angela,' Jace said. 'There was no question we could arrest and charge him. Once he was in custody, we could take a swab for Rapid DNA without a warrant. It's a simple "swab in and profile out" process. Bradford's lawyers can't claim someone in the lab messed up, because the process is automated. No people involved, so no human error.'

Jace stopped for a moment to sip more coffee and eat his powdery doughnut. When he finished, he said, 'We also had to call a doctor. Bradford was scratching himself bloody. The doc confirmed Bradford has a severe case of poison sumac. Nasty looking stuff. Hope it hurts like hell.'

I got up to serve everyone more coffee. 'Not bad,' Chris said.

I couldn't tell if he was talking about his third doughnut or the case.

'There's more.' Jace had a smear of powdered sugar on his cheek. I wiped it off with a napkin and sat back down.

'We've also got Bradford on camera driving a beat-up Ford Fiesta registered to his father's housekeeper. According to the housekeeper, "Mr Bradford bought my old blue car for a thousand dollars. I told him it wasn't worth that, but he bought it anyway. Such a nice man."'

'Right,' I said. 'That nice man used that car to send Eli into the next world.' I was quiet while I managed the tricky part of an apple doughnut.

'And we've got it on video,' Jace said. 'Bradford didn't realize there were cameras all along that section of Gravois. Big homes have their own security, and a couple of service station videos filled in most of the blank spots.

'As Bradford got closer to the accident scene, he's on video ramming Eli's green Kia,' Jace said.

'What was Eli doing there in the first place?' I asked. 'He doesn't live anywhere near that part of the Forest.'

'We think Bradford met up with Eli to give him his five hundred bucks for the delivery. Except Eli got greedy and may have demanded more money.'

'So Bradford killed him,' I said.

'No proof, but that's my guess,' Jace said. 'Eli drove away, and sometime after that, his car went over the edge into the woods. Bradford walked down to make sure Eli was dead.'

'And take back his five hundred dollars,' Chris said.

'Four hundred bucks of it,' Jace said. 'Eli slipped two fifties through the vent in the dashboard – a drug dealer's quick hiding spot. I don't know if Eli didn't have time to hide the rest before Bradford rammed his Kia, but those two fifties were safely stashed when the lab took the car apart. Bradford must have gotten the cash from the bank and it was fairly new. The two fifties had Eli's prints, Bradford's and two or three other people who weren't in the database.

'We don't have Bradford actually killing Eli on video, but the lawyer is covered with the poison sumac rash and he walked through that to get to Eli. Also, the lab found traces of blue paint on the Kia.'

'Do you have enough to charge him with Eli's murder?' Chris asked through a mouthful of yet another maple bacon doughnut.

'It's weak,' Jace said. 'But we're going to try.'

'What happened to the housekeeper's car?' I asked.

'Haven't found it yet, but we're looking for it.'

I wanted to know more. 'How do you explain Nathan's shoe print in the crypt tunnel? And how did Bradford even get in the tunnel? And what about the disappearing pumpkin?'

'We don't know,' Jace said. 'But now that Bradford's in custody for the hit-and-run homicide of Paul Goulden, we'll have time to figure it out. You heard we're going for the death penalty.'

'That will be a first,' I said. 'The first Du Pres on Death Row.'

'I'm betting that never happens,' Chris said.

'I say it will,' Jace said. 'How much do you want to bet?'

'A box of Strange Donuts.'

'Deal.'

They shook on it with sticky, powder-sugared hands.

THIRTY-EIGHT

J ace finished his report – and the last of his doughnut. Before he left, Chris and I made sure the detective had all the powdered sugar dusted off. Then Chris and I took the box of doughnuts, the coffee, and another bottle of wine back to bed and spent the rest of the day there. Discussions of work and murder were forgotten as we indulged ourselves. After a much-needed nap, we woke up about six o'clock. Chris stood up, stretched, and said, 'How do chicken sandwiches sound for dinner?'

'Perfect.'

I knew better than to ask if I could help. I was hopeless in the kitchen. Instead, I brushed the doughnut crumbs out of the sheets, then pulled the covers up so we could mess up the bed again. I carried the doughnut box and dishes downstairs, as well as the empty wine bottle.

Chris was cooking chicken breasts wrapped in bacon in a cast-iron skillet.

I sniffed the air. 'Smells wonderful.'

'I hope so. I'm making hunter's chicken. Pub grub. Got the recipe off the internet.'

'So tell me what you're doing.'

Even though I didn't cook, I liked to hear Chris talk about cooking. 'Well, I seasoned the chicken with paprika, garlic powder, salt and pepper, then wrapped it in bacon.'

I cleaned off the counter while he talked. 'While the chicken is cooking, I cut the ciabatta rolls in half, then buttered them.'

He placed the rolls in the oven to toast. 'Tomato and red onion for you?'

'Yes, please.'

When the rolls were toasted, Chris added a juicy tomato slice and a round of onion on top of both rolls, then checked the skillet.

'Looks like the chicken is cooked. I'll let it rest while I get out the barbecue sauce.' He pulled out a bottle of Maull's

BBQ sauce. The sweet tomato-based sauce was a St. Louis favorite, with an odd ingredient for barbecue sauce – anchovies. Chris poured a big glop into a bowl. Like many St. Louisans, he 'doctored' the sauce by adding a dash of mustard and a splash of beer.

'That's how my dad used to fix his barbecue sauce, except he drank the rest of the beer.'

'I plan to do that, too.'

Chris sliced the chicken, put it on the buns, slathered on the barbecue sauce, and then piled the sandwiches with shredded cheddar cheese. 'Now, under the broiler to melt the cheese, and we're ready.'

I carried the sandwiches upstairs and Chris brought the wine and beer. Soon every last crumb was gone, and so was that lovely day.

Morning came all too soon, ending my mini-vacation. Chris and I kissed goodbye. 'I'm so glad you didn't buy me a tennis bracelet,' I said.

Chris laughed and promised to show up at seven tomorrow night. I hurried home, barely defrosting a blueberry pound cake and making the coffee before Rick arrived. We both worked all day – I cleaned and polished downstairs while Rick cleaned the bedroom, hung the new curtains, put the rug back down, added the new headboard and put the bed together.

Rick finished first. 'Come on up, Angela, and take a look.'

It was a different room. The sad blue walls were gone, along with the dingy curtains and the bedraggled bedspread. The warm white walls were sophisticated, and showed off the new headboard. The silk Bijar rug glowed.

'It's just what I wanted, Rick.'

'It's very cool, Angela.'

Back downstairs, Rick and I finished off the blueberry pound cake. He gave me a bill, and then went upstairs to pack up. I defrosted two pound cakes for him to take home, and sent his money via Zelle.

That night I slept on the couch. I didn't want to sleep alone in my new bedroom.

*   *   *

I woke up slowly, savoring the day, and was at the Chouteau Forest Meat Market when the doors opened at nine. The market didn't have any poached salmon, but the butcher talked me into roasting a duck.

'It's easy,' he said. 'Roast duck is nice and fat and doesn't dry out like chicken.' He sold me a six-pound Long Island duck, handed me a sheet of directions, then suggested potatoes roasted in duck fat and an orange and almond salad from the deli section. I threw in a loaf of crusty French bread, two bottles of Malbec and mandarin orange sorbet. While I was at it, I bought candles for the table and for my bedroom.

There. I was ready for tonight.

All afternoon, I worked on that duck. The directions said I had to remove the giblets, clean the bird, season it, and then score the skin so it would be crispy. I couldn't bring myself to truss the legs. That reminded me too much of a bad murder I'd worked a couple of years ago, where the woman was . . . never mind. I didn't truss the legs.

I did quarter an orange and put it in the cavity.

I rummaged in the cabinets for my mother's roasting pan, and hoped it had retained the memories of all the good meals she'd made. Then I put the duck in the preheated oven and let it roast for an hour.

Meanwhile, I fussed around the house, fluffing the couch pillows which were already fine, making sure both bathrooms had fresh soap, tissues and toilet paper. The timer went off at the end of the hour. I carefully pulled the duck out of the oven, pricked the skin again, and turned the duck so it was breast-side down, and set the timer.

Again, I found more things to fuss about, this time upstairs. I added more throw pillows to the bed, then took them off, then added them again. I made sure the bedspread was smooth. Inside, I was terrified. How would Chris and I get upstairs? Would it be awkward? Would I have to take him upstairs by the hand?

Would Donegan suddenly appear in my bedroom? No, I told myself. That's ridiculous. Donegan lives in my heart and he will stay there. Always and forever.

Thankfully, the oven timer went off again. The directions said I was supposed to peel the potatoes and cut them into chunks. Potato skins were healthy, weren't they? Full of vitamins and minerals? Why lose all that goodness? I just washed the potatoes and cut them up. I hated peeling potatoes.

Anyway, the healthy potato chunks went into the duck fat. The duck was looking browner and crispier. It would be ready in another hour.

I set the table carefully, with my grandmother's lace tablecloth and my mother's best china and silver. I was glad the women in my family were with me. The candles were in silver holders, with matches nearby to light them.

Upstairs, I showered, washed my hair and put on light make-up. The timer dinged again and I ran back downstairs. This was the crucial part. The duck was a beautiful golden brown, as if it had been on a Caribbean vacation.

I turned the oven up to four hundred degrees, and set the roasted potatoes aside. When the oven reached the correct temperature, I put the duck back in. It was 6:40 p.m. At 6:50, the timer dinged.

My crispy duck was ready, but I wasn't. I took the duck out, left it on the stove and ran upstairs, where I changed into a glamorous gold hostess gown. I was brushing my hair when the doorbell rang. I checked my lipstick in the mirror, threw the hairbrush in a drawer, and ran downstairs.

Chris was at the door, holding a fragrant bouquet of stargazer lilies. We kissed in the doorway. I set the flowers on the kitchen table.

'You look like a Forties movie star in that gown,' he said.

My arms were around him again. 'You're wearing my favorite blue shirt. And you smell wonderful.'

I began unbuttoning his shirt. He pulled the tie on my gown, and it pooled at my feet. Chris picked me up as if I weighed nothing, and carried me upstairs.

There was none of the awkwardness that I'd feared. The ghosts of old loves stayed away. It was just Chris and me in this small world we'd created.

Nearly an hour later, the spell was broken. My head was resting on Chris's shoulder. We sat up in my new bed, and I noticed the throw pillows had lived up to their name – they were thrown about the room.

'That was wonderful,' I said. 'I have roast duck for dinner. Do you want to eat downstairs or bring it up here?'

'Let's bring it up here.'

Chris carved the duck, while I reheated the potatoes, set out the bread and the orange-almond salad. Chris poured us big glasses of wine. We piled the food on our plates and ran upstairs back to bed.

Chris tried the duck. 'This is good.'

'I'm glad you like it. It's the first time I've ever made duck.'

'Oh, you're talking about the duck. That's good too, but this evening is good. It's perfect. Being here with you, in your home, eating a delicious dinner that you fixed. It helps me forget what's waiting out there for us.'

Our jobs were part of our bond. We both knew life could end in an instant, and take everything with it – our security, our sanity and our happiness.

But we had this moment right now.

I thought of Andrew Marvell, the English poet and seventeenth-century politician – and in my mind, the patron saint of death investigators. The man who proclaimed 'To His Coy Mistress' these wise words:

'The grave's a fine and private place,
'But none, I think, do there embrace.'

It was another verse of Andrew's that haunted me:

'But at my back I always hear
'Time's wingèd chariot hurrying near;
'And yonder all before us lie
'Deserts of vast eternity.'

I reached for my lover again, and together we drowned out the sound of that fatal chariot.

EPILOGUE

Bradford Du Pres's colossal arrogance was his undoing. Bradford had urinated on Trey's corpse and left behind a pubic hair and DNA in the Cursed Crypt. After Bradford was arrested, Jace got a warrant to search Bradford's quarters in Vincent's mansion.

In the old days, a judge friendly to (or impressed by) the Du Pres family might have denied the search warrant. But now, with all the press in town for the Cursed Crypt murders, the eyes of the world were watching. Jace got his warrant.

Jace and Nitpicker found more evidence in Bradford's rooms. Bradford had taken Lydia's engagement ring and carelessly tossed it in his cufflink box, along with old invitations and collar stays. Bradford had swiped his father's Ambien to drug the couple, and kept the bottle in his sock drawer. Most telling of all, Bradford's clothes, stained with Trey and Lydia's blood, and the murder weapon, a butcher knife from his father's kitchen, were hidden in the back of his closet, under his summer clothes.

Missouri is a death penalty state. Vincent Du Pres's law firm labored night and day to save Bradford from the needle. Even the poor souls in the cubicle farm had to help. But all those unbillable hours were for nothing.

The best deal the firm could get for Bradford Du Pres was life without parole. Bradford confessed to the murders of Trey and Lydia. Jace recorded his confession, and let me sit behind the two-way mirror to watch.

When the confession started at 8:09 that morning, Bradford looked fresh and cocky as ever. He declined to have counsel with him, over his father's objections. I figured Bradford wanted to boast of his 'accomplishments,' and couldn't do that with Vincent in the room.

Bradford condescended to treat Jace as an equal, and talked to him freely, using the unbridled speech that Forest dwellers save for their living rooms.

Jace brought him a cup of hot coffee. I watched the confession with horrified fascination as Bradford explained himself.

'I was appalled that one of Those People – a hedge funder's son – would join the Chouteau Founders Club and take the position that was rightfully mine.' Bradford said 'hedge funder's son' as if it was a disgusting term.

'Father, Jefferson Morgan and Uncle Reggie were sure they could isolate Trey so he couldn't do any damage, but I didn't trust them. They're getting older and they're not quite as sharp as they used to be. They don't understand the new rich. Those People are not part of our circle.

'But I know them. I've seen them in action, you see.'

Bradford stopped for a long drink of coffee and then continued. 'I knew Trey had enough money to buy himself out of any predicament. I saw how he turned my fraternity against me and convinced them to let in Nathan Tucker. Trey made a donation to the party fund so large it was embarrassing, but no one cared. They voted his way and that undesirable got in.'

Bradford gave a sad sigh. 'If only my father would have let me outbid Trey. We only needed another couple hundred thousand. But I knew Father would hang on to his money, so I had a plan B in place. And they knew about it – old Reggie, Jefferson and Father.'

'What's "it"?' Jace asked.

Bradford looked surprised. 'Why, my plan to kill Trey. Otherwise, why did everyone laugh so hard when Father said, "Why not make it *his* dead body?"'

The 'turbulent priest,' I thought. 'You laughed along with them,' I said.

'I had to. They underestimated me. They thought I didn't have the nerve to do it. But I did. I shot a seven-hundred-pound bear. A hedge funder was no big deal.'

'What about the death threat on the pumpkin and the threatening phone call?' Jace asked.

Bradford looked pleased. 'Oh, you noticed. I wasn't sure anyone knew about those. I thought my work had gone in vain. They were never mentioned in the press, you know.' He paused for more coffee.

'I carved that pumpkin myself. I'm quite good at it, and won the carving contest one year at the university. Anyway, I hid my pumpkin in the bushes, then nipped out after the auction and put it in the pumpkin display. Later, when I finished with Trey and Lydia, I went back, switched out the pumpkins and tossed my work of art on Gravois, where I ran over it. No one notices a smashed pumpkin on Halloween.' Bradford actually giggled.

'Why didn't you throw away the murder weapon and the bloody clothes?' Jace sounded tired.

'Oh, that. I was going to get around to it. You police were too busy going after that n—'

'We don't use the N-word here.' Jace was stern.

'OK, if you insist.'

'I do. And keep talking.' Jace sounded fed up.

'Well, that man, that Nathan Tucker, didn't belong in my fraternity. Trey had to answer for that, too.'

Bradford was proud of his elaborate plot to frame Nathan, and enjoyed giving all the details. 'I belong to the Chouteau U gym for free. My father's on the board. I nearly drove that silly n—'

'Don't you dare say that word,' Jace interrupted.

'Sorry,' Bradford said. 'May I continue?'

'If you speak properly, you can. Otherwise, the deal is off and you'll be sitting on Death Row.'

'OK, Nathan, that silly little man, went crazy when I stole his shoes while he was in the shower at the gym. I took one with me to the crypt, and dipped that shoe in the blood. Then I took the shoe back, cleaned both up with bleach and returned them.' Bradford thought that was quite funny.

'How did you know about the tunnel in the Cursed Crypt?' Jace asked.

'Oh, that was thanks to Father. He was the only one who'd ever managed to stay the full night in that creepy place, way back in the 1980s. Father stumbled over the secret – and I mean literally stumbled – after three bottles of wine. He fell on the stone angel wing and the door to the tunnel opened.

'He spent the night exploring the tunnel. Father also bragged about desecrating the tomb. The most socially acceptable thing he did was put out a cigarette on the marble lady's face.'

'And your father didn't tell anyone about the tunnel?' Jace asked.

'Of course not,' Bradford said. 'It was our secret. He knew it might come in handy one day. And it did. That's how I got in and out without being seen. May I have more coffee, please?'

Jace suspended the interview and called for more coffee. A uniform brought two cups, one for Jace and one for Bradford, and the interview resumed at 9:40 a.m.

'What about Elijah Coffey?'

'Who?' Bradford looked puzzled.

'The man who delivered the basket to the crypt.' Jace sounded impatient.

'Surely you aren't going to charge me for killing him. He was a drug dealer. I did the world a favor.' He tried his best smile on Jace, who remained stone-faced.

'Why kill him?' Jace asked.

Bradford seemed surprised. 'Everyone knows you can't trust a drug dealer. When I met him to give him his money for the delivery, he said, "Thanks, Brad. Let's make this a regular thing. Next month I want two thousand." He could identify me. He had to go.'

'So far, you've admitted you killed three people,' Jace said. 'Let's talk about the death of Paul Goulden.'

'Who?'

Jace sounded angry now. 'The plumber with three children. The man you killed when you ran a red light.'

'Oh, him. Right. He was collateral damage. I was trying to get away from that crazy Angela woman who stole my coffee cup.'

That's me, I thought.

'Angela didn't steal the cup,' Jace said. 'You gave it to her. Opal, your legal administrative assistant, backs up Angela's story.'

Should have been nicer to Opal, Bradford, I thought.

'You also damaged Angela's car and tried to kill her with a tire iron,' Jace said.

'Wait a minute. *She* assaulted me with a Taser.'

'Which is legal in Missouri. She was defending herself and you were threatening great bodily harm.'

There was more, much more. Jace spent the day meticulously tying up the loose ends. When the interrogation was over, and the paperwork finished, Bradford Du Pres wound up in the penitentiary for the rest of his life.

The case of the Cursed Crypt caused a seismic shift in Chouteau Forest. Vincent Du Pres was asked to resign from the board of Chouteau Forest University. He sent a sizable check to the alumni association hoping to change their minds, and it was returned. Even money wouldn't let him back on to the board.

The family of plumber Paul Goulden sued Bradford in the civil court, along with his father Vincent, his great-uncle Reggie and their friend Jefferson R. Morgan. Katie's lover, Montgomery Bryant, the sharpest lawyer in the Forest, represented the family.

Monty said, 'The murders in the Cursed Crypt were the crime that spawned four murders, including the death of Paul Goulden.'

The burden of proof was much lower in a civil suit. Also, rich members of the Forest do not sit on juries. The despised working people of 'Toonerville' do that, and Paul Goulden was one of their own. The Goulden family won a judgement of ten million dollars against Vincent, Bradford, Reggie and Jefferson.

Trey's family, and Lydia's, also filed suits and, when the dust settled, the Du Pres family and Jefferson Morgan were considerably poorer. I don't mean they'll be out by the highway with a handwritten cardboard sign begging, 'Will take anything. God Bless.'

But they're rich-people poor, which is a special circle of hell. Every one of those dollars was stripped from their hide, and they felt the pain in ways you and I never could.

So you could say in some ways, Trey won. He'd challenged the power of the old guard and inflicted a grievous wound in their wallets. How much power does the Du Pres family have?

That depends on how much the Forest will give them. Too bad Trey wasn't around to see his triumph.

The Howl-o-ween Benefit Auction for Chouteau Forest University was historic for many reasons. Most notably, it was the last auction ever. The university discontinued that fundraiser. Now they have a new fundraiser, that lasts all year long.

The university was thrilled when they learned their old Main Building was a stop on the Underground Railroad. Chouteau U used its sizeable endowment to have Remember Forever Monuments to clean the Cursed Crypt. When it was restored to its Victorian glory, Nathan Tucker was hired to lead the tours of the crypt and the tunnel. The money he was paid covered what he owed Trey Lawson, and then some.

Those who make the complete tour with Nathan marvel at the beauty of Elizabeth's tomb. The sub-sub-basement of the old Main Building is now a museum honoring the enslaved people who risked their lives for freedom. On display is the infamous runaway slave poster for Elizabeth McKee.

As soon as his parole was up, Nathan married Samantha Freeman. She is now a docent at the museum.

Charles Wheatly, the man who drowned his wife, Emmelina, in a scrub bucket, died in prison after serving less than a year. Someone mentioned to Emmelina's aunt, Maria Constanza Zarcos, that Charles might be a narc. When I asked Katie if she told Maria that Charles was a police informant, she said, 'Don't be ridiculous,' which I took as a yes. Charles was drowned in a prison toilet.

Chief Butkus was forced to sell his Mercedes because it needed constant repairs.

The public defender for Royce Edwards, the gambler who abused and murdered Vivian Toussaint, tried to make a deal for her client. She wanted him to confess and get life without parole. Royce refused to deal, and demanded a jury trial. He gambled and lost. Now he's sitting on Death Row.

*   *   *

One Saturday morning, Jace Budewitz showed up at my house. Chris was there with me.

Jace said, 'I've come to pay off my bet about Bradford Du Pres. I've brought a box of Strange Donuts.'

We invited him inside. The three of us ate the bet and drank coffee.

'Bradford may not be the first Du Pres on Death Row,' Jace said. 'But I bet he'll be the first member of that family to have "Love" and "Hate" tattooed on his hands.'

Before he left, Jace said, 'I have a gift for you, Angela.'

He ran back outside to his car and returned with a square box wrapped in gold paper with a big white bow.

'How pretty,' I said.

'My wife wrapped it. I'm no good at that stuff.'

I unwrapped the box and found the Mandalay Blue coffee cup from Bradford Du Pres's office.

'Now that the case of the Cursed Crypt is closed, it's yours,' he said.

My breakfast coffee tastes especially good when I drink it from that cup.

THE INSIDER'S GUIDE TO CHOUTEAU COUNTY PRONUNCIATION

Missourians have their own way of pronouncing words and names. We're called the Show Me State, and you don't tell us how to say something. The French were among the first settlers, but we resist Frenchifying words.

Chouteau is *SHOW-toe*.

Du Pres is *Duh-PRAY*.

Gravois is *GRAH-voy*.

Detective Ray Greiman is *GRI-mun*. His name is mispronounced German.

So is my name. It's pronounced VEETS, and rhymes with *Beets*.

Missouri can't even decide how to pronounce its own name. The eastern part, which includes St. Louis, calls itself Missour-ee. That's how Angela pronounces the state's name. In the west, which has Kansas City, it's called Missour-uh. Politicians have mastered the fine art of adjusting their pronunciation to please whichever part of the state they're in.

Elaine Viets

THE REAL CURSED CRYPT

Chouteau County and Chouteau University are fiction. However, a genuine cursed crypt gave me the bones for this novel. The crypt is at Transylvania University. Yes, Transylvania is a real university, and an old one at that. It was founded back in 1780. The name has nothing to do with vampires. Transylvania is Latin for 'through the woods,' and according to the school, it was in a forested area that later became Kentucky. The university is now located in Lexington, Kentucky, and it's known by staff and students as 'Transy.'

To find out more about the school and its cursed crypt, visit the Transylvania University website: www.transy.edu